FRANKY FURBO

Also by William Wharton

TIDINGS

BIRDY

DAD

A MIDNIGHT CLEAR

SCUMBLER

PRIDE

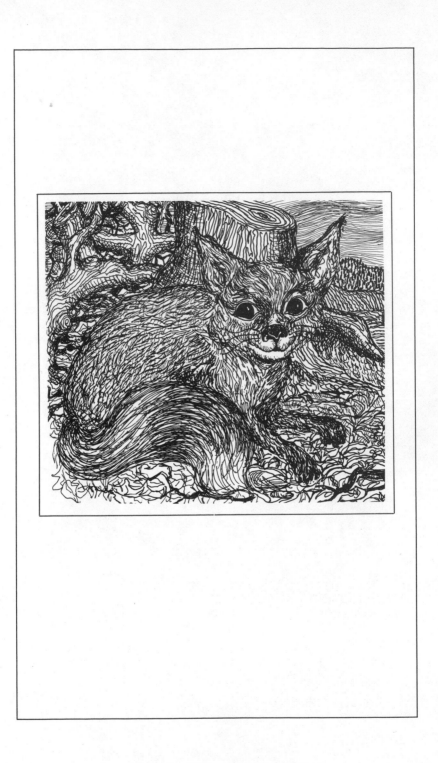

FRANKY FURBO

A NOVEL BY

William Wharton

Illustrated by the Author

HENRY HOLT AND COMPANY

NEW YORK

Copyright © 1989 by William Wharton
All rights reserved, including the right to reproduce
this book or portions thereof in any form.
Published by Henry Holt and Company, Inc.,
115 West 18th Street, New York, New York 10011.
Published in Canada by Fitzhenry & Whiteside Limited,
195 Allstate Parkway, Markham, Ontario L3R 4T8.

Library of Congress Cataloging-in-Publication Data
Wharton, William.
Franky Furbo: a novel / by William Wharton. —1st ed.
p. cm.
ISBN 0-8050-1120-X
ISBN 0-8050-1157-9 (pbk)
I. Title.
PS3573.H32F7 1989
813'.54—dc19   89–1805
                                                            CIP

Henry Holt books are available at special discounts
for bulk purchases for sales promotions, premiums,
fund-raising, or educational use. Special editions
or book excerpts can also be created to specification.

For details contact:
Special Sales Director
Henry Holt and Company, Inc.
115 West 18th Street
New York, New York 10011

First Edition

Designed by Ann Gold
Printed in the United States of America
1 3 5 7 9 10 8 6 4 2

D E D I C A T I O N

This book is dedicated to our daughter Kate, her husband, Bill, their two beautiful daughters, Dayiel, age two years, and Mia, age eight months.

They are all dead now. They were killed on August 3, 1988, at 4:00 P.M. in a terrible automobile crash and fire on Highway I-5 near Albany in the Willamette Valley in the state of Oregon.

This horrible accident was precipitated by a field fire licensed by public officials of that state. Despite this accident, in which seven were killed, thirty-five injured, and twenty-four vehicles destroyed, these field fires are still licensed with the published endorsement of the governor. The overwhelming objection to field burning by most of the residents in that valley is also ignored in the special interest of less than a thousand farmers who bring in $350 million yearly to the state at a profit of $170 million to themselves.

The first Franky Furbo stories were told by me to Kate, over thirty years ago. I told them every morning to each of my children during the next twenty years. I'd looked forward to telling them to Dayiel and Mia.

Now, due to the arrogance, shortsightedness, and greed of these grass growers with the backing of Oregon state officials, this can never be.

We hope to forgive but we can never be reconciled.

C O N T E N T S

FRANKY FURBO

GOING TO GROUND

In the center of Italy, surrounded by the rolling hills of Umbria, there is a city built on top of a hill. This city is called Perugia, an old fortress city, with tunnels under it designed to withstand sieges during the many battles that, through the centuries, have raged up and down the Italian peninsula.

A few kilometers south of Perugia is a much smaller village called Prepo. It has only twelve houses in it; these are the homes of farmers who work tiny plots of ground around the village. Mostly the farmers grow olives and grapes on their land. They also grow vegetables for themselves, and grain for their animals.

In order to plow the ground, the farmers have huge white oxen called *buoi*. These beautiful animals are usually hitched by a wooden yoke in twos to pull a plow. The wooden plows dig deep into the dark, brown earth.

Up on the side of a hill, beside Prepo, is a small forest of pine trees. At the edge of these pine trees, and above a small plot of two hectares, is a medium-sized stone house. This house has a tile roof with moss growing on it. There are five windows with wooden shutters, and a chimney. Attached to the house, on the south side so it catches the sun, is a terrace with a grape arbor. In the summer and early autumn the grapes hang over the terrace and the leaves give shade. In all, it is a beautiful place to live.

Inside this house on the side of the hill, near the forest, lives a most interesting family. The father is an American. The mother, although she speaks perfect Italian, is not Italian; she doesn't look American either. She has golden tan skin and dark red hair. The people in Prepo consider her *brutta*, or ugly, because red hair to them is a sign of the devil. Actually, almost anyone from anywhere else would call her beautiful.

This American family has lived in their house for more than forty years. The father comes out often and talks with the villagers or rides his bicycle into Perugia to shop. The mother stays home and keeps house and works in the garden. She does not talk to many people. If someone comes to visit, she is very polite, but she never invites anyone to come and never visits anyone herself. Many times she walks alone, or with her husband, through the fields, in the night. There are some in the village who have insisted she is a witch.

This American and his strange wife have four children. Three of them, when they were old enough to leave home, went elsewhere to live, but the youngest still lives with them. None of the children ever attended the Italian schools or any school whatsoever. The parents have taught these children themselves.

The man speaks some Italian but with a quite strong American accent. The children all speak beautiful Italian like their mother. It must be she who teaches them.

In addition to cultivating his grapes and olives, the American father, whose name is William Wiley, is said to write stories for children. Often he can be seen in the neighborhood pedaling around on his bicycle with a folder of paper and a box of paints while he looks for places to paint or draw. No one has ever seen anything he wrote or painted, so there is no way for them to know that the stories he writes and illustrates are published in America and England. The people in Prepo do not travel much. The farthest any of them has ever been is Rome.

It's the postman who made that journey. He also travels all over this hilly region of small villages, delivering the mail. He is considered by everyone very well traveled. He says the American often receives packages and letters from America or other places. In fact, the mail this American man, William Wiley, receives is probably about half the mail the mailman delivers from the small bag attached to the front of his bicycle.

One of the strange things about this family is they do not make wine from their grapes. They pick the grapes at the proper time, when they are filled with juices, then eat some of them, as does everyone in the village. The rest of the grapes they crush in a large wine press, as everyone knows it must be done, but then they bottle the juice and keep it tightly closed so it can never turn into the lovely light wine for which this part of Italy is famous.

They drink this juice of the grape just that way, raw. It is another thing the people in the village can never understand. But then, they say, what else can one expect from foreigners, especially when one of them is most likely a witch, or worse.

Long ago, the cardinal in Perugia sent a priest to vist the Americans. This was just after they had arrived.

This priest was thirty-five at that time, and it is said he had studied in Rome. He did not think the mother and wife, whose name is Caroline, was ugly at all. He found her quite attractive in a foreign kind of way.

He made this first visit over forty years ago. They invited him to drink with them, and it was true: it wasn't wine, it was grape juice. He told the villagers he was surprised to find how delicious it tasted, but no one in the village would believe him, even though he was a priest.

This priest discovered the Americans were not Catholic, had no religion, did not go to any church, did not intend to send their children to church or to instruct them in religion. In fact, he suspected they weren't even Christians, but he didn't tell anybody in the village this.

Finally, he talked to the family about why he'd come to visit them, how the villagers found them peculiar and thought the wife might be a witch. At this, the two strangers looked at each other and smiled. They'd just had a child born to them, a baby girl; the mother brought her out for the priest to see. He asked if perhaps he might baptize the child. It would help the villagers accept the Americans if he could tell them the baby was baptized. William and Caroline had no objection, and so the priest performed the ceremony. They named the little girl Kathleen.

With that, he left. There was no other discussion.

In the course of years passing by, he came once a year, until, years later, he became a monsignor and was assigned to another church in another part of Italy. During all that time, the American couple allowed him to bless the house and baptize their other children when they were born. This seemed to satisfy most people in the village, although many still maintained the woman was a witch.

The thing that especially bothered everyone, particularly the women in the village, was that as the years passed by, the wife, Caroline, scarcely seemed to age. She became only more mature, more beautiful. At the time when our story starts, after over forty years, she still looked younger than most forty-year-old women in the village. It wasn't natural.

Over the years, she continued with her long nocturnal walks, through the dusty fields, up into the forests, sometimes as many as twenty or thirty kilometers in different directions. When she did appear in the daytime, or when children came near her house, she was always kind, and the village children grew to love her. This, perhaps even more than the priest's acceptance, somewhat commended her to the villagers. In Italy, anyone who loves children and whom children love in turn cannot be thought of as really bad and probably couldn't be a witch.

So, now it is time for our tale. It will be told mostly by the man in the family, the American named William Wiley. It is a strange, somewhat frightening history, and I must admit I cannot actually remember now how I came to know it. Sometimes it all seems like a weird dream. At the same time, I believe it as strongly as I believe anything in this life.

At the time of our story, the three older children have left and only the young boy remains. The father, William, now has almost pure white hair and is over sixty years old. Caroline continues to look young, not girlish, but like a real woman, a strong woman of great natural beauty. The little boy is dark, thin, and tall. All the children, like their mother, seem to mature slowly, seem very young for their years.

Inside the house, on the first floor, is one large room, the room into which one enters. On one side, to the right, is a huge bed, a bed as large as three double beds; it takes up the entire width of the room. In the center of the room is a large round wooden table. It is massively thick and ample enough to seat six people comfortably.

On the other side of the room is a kitchen with a closet for dishes and food. The kitchen has a copper sink, a drainboard in wood, and a large worktable. On the rear wall of the room is a fireplace. On either side are closets for clothing, huge, hand-carved wooden chests reaching to the ceiling. Also on that back wall is a staircase, almost like a ship's ladder. It leads to the upstairs.

If we go up those stairs, we find two rooms. One is a schoolroom, with chalkboards on the walls, a wide desk and four smaller ones. In that room, the walls, where there are not chalkboards, are lined by bookshelves filled with books. It's a miniature schoolroom.

The other room is the workroom of the father, William. There is a desk with a typewriter. This desk is large and has many drawers. It also has a section with a slanted top for drawing. There is a light over the typewriter and another over the drawing board. On the board is a half-finished drawing, but we cannot quite see it.

We now go downstairs again. The mother, Caroline, is in the kitchen preparing breakfast. The father, William, and the son, Billy, are still in bed. The little boy is stretched out on his father's chest.

Let us now begin our story. I only hope I can tell this properly. Oddly enough, being a professional writer of novels can sometimes make it difficult to tell about true things so they'll be believed. People don't expect truth in novels. Once, in a book called *A Midnight Clear*, I wrote about a nineteen-year-old boy who said, "I have a penchant for telling true stories no one can believe."

I feel that way myself, now.

CHAPTER 2

DENIAL

"Aw, come on, Daddy, that's not the way it ends. You can't end the story that way."

"What do you mean, Billy? Of course that's the way it ends. That's the end of the story."

"Please, Dad, make up another ending. Make up an interesting ending with more things happening, exciting things."

Billy has his head on my chest now. With one ear he can listen to the hollow sound of my voice inside me, and with the other ear hear the sounds coming out of my mouth. All our children figured this out at one time or another, or maybe it was only one and they shared. But, in the past, when for a while there were four of them scattered on top and around me, there was hardly room on my chest for all the heads. I'm missing those wonderful mornings, those full days. I dread when Billy will grow up and leave us.

Kathy, our oldest, once told me how hearing a story that way, with her ear on my chest, made it seem to come from inside herself.

Matthew, our first boy, always said he liked to watch my eyes and mouth when I told a story, but that it was even better hearing it with his ear against me. Once in a while, in an exciting part, he'd lift his head and look into my eyes. He'd have such a wonderful glow of excitement and interest in his beautiful yellow-brown eyes. Such wonderful days.

But now I must come back to the present; I can't avoid it any longer. I know I'm only putting this off. It's something I don't want to face; I'm not prepared.

"But, Billy, you know these aren't stories I make up myself; these are stories Franky Furbo told me many years ago. I can't change the ending, you know that."

Billy lifts his head from my chest and looks me in the eyes the way Matthew used to years ago, only Billy's eyes are more knowing, more challenging. I think, what a beautiful, sensitive, intelligent, kind boy he is, as have been all our children, each different and each such a tremendous joy to us over the many years. Our lives have truly been like a dream; there's no other word to describe the way we've lived all these years.

I never have had to go off to work anywhere. The combination of my military disability pension and the money I earn from the little stories and books I write, along with the money we make selling olive oil from our trees, has more than provided us with any money we've needed. When the children were young, none of us wanted to travel. We only sent the children off from home to the university because it was time for them to know something of the everyday world, the world we've abandoned.

Caroline has insisted they have this experience with real life, the hostility, competition, violence, greed from which we've sheltered them. Caroline has been an excellent teacher, and they were each well prepared to attend any university they wanted, or do any work that interested them.

The most rewarding, incredible thing is how, during their entire lives, they've always played with one another. They've been such loving friends. They've had Italian friends as well, but mostly they've made up their own games here at home. There's been much laughter and joy in this house over these years.

Billy is still staring into my eyes as my mind wanders.

"I *know* you make up these stories, Dad. I don't really believe in Franky Furbo anymore, either. Come on, Dad, tell me, truly. You do make all these stories up, don't you? There isn't any real Franky Furbo; he's just somebody you made up in your head. You can tell me; I'm old enough now."

It had to come, sooner or later. But he's the first one to challenge me, to throw it in my face. Probably the others were too timid or too kind, or maybe they only wanted to believe more than Billy does. Also, they had one another to back up the stories. They'd repeat them over and over; they'd even play Franky Furbo games, taking turns being Franky. They'd often ask me questions about Franky Furbo, questions independent of the stories I told. They were curious; Franky was such an important part of their lives. Believing might be harder for Billy because he's been alone these past years. In some important way he's different.

The crazy thing is how hard it hits me when he says he doesn't believe in Franky Furbo. I don't know how to respond. I want him to believe with me. I want to respect his opinions, his beliefs, but I still have to be true to myself.

"But, Billy, there *is* a Franky Furbo. I've seen him. I lived with him. I know him very well. I'm not lying to you."

"I know you're not lying, Dad. You're only telling stories. That's not the same as lying. You know how you've tried to teach me, all of us, to tell stories. Telling stories is fun. I know that. I know you like to tell stories, and I like to listen to them, too. Come on, Dad. Make up another ending for me. I don't really have to believe in Franky for it to be fun."

He puts his head back on my chest and gives me a good love hug. I know how soon it will be before he's too embarrassed to come into bed with me and cuddle like this in the morning. Boys or girls, it doesn't seem to make much difference. Even though we all sleep together in this gigantic bed, it still happens. I designed this bed because neither of us, Caroline nor I, believe children should be alone in the night.

Still, there comes a time when they pull back and are less willing to be held closely. It's interesting how the farthest part of the bed from Caroline and me becomes the special prerogative of the oldest child. As they've grown older and each one, in turn, has left our nest, our private warren, the next in line would move toward that end. Little Billy has a lot of bed to himself, and he seems to pick a place according to his mood. Last night I noticed he slept on the far end, as the oldest child at home normally would. That should have told me something.

Most likely, the children sense that the bed space where Caroline and I sleep is our private property, and they feel like invaders in our personal life. There's a little curtain I insisted on putting up, which can be drawn across when we want to make love alone. Caroline says I'm silly, but she lets me draw it anyway sometimes.

However, whatever the reasons for their pulling apart, I do regret it, as does Caroline; although both of us are resigned to this inevitable pulling away, separation, parting. And we know we're lucky having them as long as we do.

I turn my mind back to the problem of Billy and Franky Furbo. Billy lifts his head up to me one more time.

"Don't feel badly, Dad. I don't believe in the Easter Bunny, or *Brufani*, or Santa Claus either. It doesn't mean anything if I don't believe Franky Furbo really exists."

How can I ever tell him?

"OK, then, if that's what you want. So, instead of the guardians for the ball of fire returning through the crack in time-space and going back to their own world in another galaxy, in another universe, they work their way through again. They force their overwhelming power of blue death through the Climus Channel and with great wickedness and malevolence set fire to everything. They burn down the forest where Franky lives with his friends. All of them are burned, turned to a white ash. Before Franky can even think to make himself big or small, change himself into something else, hide, or fly away on Bamba, it's all over.

"The denizens of Climus look over their work, their destruction, and even they are sad. This is the end. All their years of trying to stop Franky Furbo's efforts at doing good, helping people on this planet, have finally been successful. They've won! Franky is dead! His tree house and all he'd built, his magic powders—all are gone! These wicked aliens will never have anything to worry about in their conquest of the universe. The end."

I stop. I know, even as I'm telling this story, that I'm being incredibly cruel. I don't understand it myself. I've been telling this continuous story of Franky Furbo all the years we've had children old enough to listen and enjoy. I also know I've hurt myself as much as anyone.

In our family, storytelling time is always in the morning. It gives Caroline some free moments to get herself dressed, to clean up and make breakfast. I must've told thousands of stories over the years. And all these Franky Furbo stories would just come to me out of nowhere. In a certain way I really *didn't* make them up any more than the real things in life are made up.

Another reason I'd always tell these stories in the morning was because the children would go to bed at different times at night, according to their age; also Caroline was concerned they would dream about them. Some of the Franky stories are very scary. But this one I just told, this ending I gave to this story, didn't come from anywhere but my own wounded vanity. I'd struck back at my much-loved son with an unnecessary, indefensible violence.

I can feel Billy sobbing against my chest. He doesn't look up at me. I wait. He's gone limp. When he speaks it's haltingly, between sobs.

"Aw, that's not fair, Dad. You didn't have to kill off everybody, even Franky. I feel awful. Camilla and Matthew and Kathy will be sad, too, when they find out. Just because I don't believe in Franky doesn't mean he isn't really there. I feel as if I killed him myself."

I hold on to him tightly. Caroline comes over from the kitchen and looks down at me. Boy, is she ever upset! Usually she doesn't get angry easily or show much of what she's feeling unless the feelings are good. And then, somehow, she helps me feel *her* good feelings. But I know right now she has no good feelings toward me. She doesn't have to *say* anything. I don't think I ever remember her being this deeply disgusted. She's so angry she doesn't speak but turns away and goes back to her work in the kitchen.

"OK, Billy. I was only kidding. That isn't the way it ends. I was just pretending. The way it ended the first time I told you is the real ending. It's the way the story ended when Franky told it to me. I can't change it. If I change that ending, then *any* ending would be all right, could be true, even the terrible one I just made up. Do you understand? Making up stories is a tricky business. I must be

12

honest with the story even if *you* don't like it or don't believe it, even if *I* don't like it, don't believe it."

Billy hugs me harder and nods his head that he understands. At least that's what I think he's doing. I look over at Caroline. She's shaking her head, too, but not the same way. She's shaking her head as if she still doesn't understand or agree with what I'm up to. It's a head shake of incomprehension.

The tension is so great I can't take it anymore, and, besides, it's time to get up. The eggs and cereal are almost ready, and I need to wash up first. So does Billy. It used to be a madhouse around here when all six of us were trying to wash. Caroline would have hot water in bowls for each and there would be as much splashing around and spluttering as a flock of birds bathing in a birdbath. Caroline would check all of us, even me, to see if we'd washed correctly and were clean. Our toilet is in the back, behind the house, and we'd each take our turns there too. I'm really missing the other children, especially right now, just before Christmas. And Billy will have another birthday, two days before Christmas. It won't be long before we're alone. It's hard to think about.

Kathleen and Matthew are both down in the mountains of Chile now. They seem to be happy together, and each is doing work they think is important. Kathy has become what she calls an anthropologist-archaeologist and is making studies of giant rocks and strange marks on the mountains down there. Matthew works on a computer and makes up programs for solving different problems in ecological procedures, the way I make up children's stories. He says he can live anywhere he wants, and he likes living near Kathleen. I worry about them living such strange lives, but Caroline doesn't seem concerned, and, after all, *she's* the mother. I've been a pretty good father, but there's no question: the center of our family has always been Caroline. She lives her life around them and they around her. Except for the Franky Furbo part of my life, I'm not very important.

Camilla is living on one of the northern islands of Japan. She's an oceanographer and is concerned about the whales and dolphins, their survival. She keeps trying to dissuade the Japanese from killing whales and dolphins for food. Boy, our kids sure have taken up crazy things for a living. It's hard to believe it all started here in this little house.

But then, I should talk; I'm probably the wackiest one around.

Could be I'm actually not *all here*, a true loon, the way the army psychiatrists insisted. I do know I can't get myself to stare over that edge to the black hole of existence or nonexistence without help. I really like to pretend, to make believe, to live inside stories, stories I hear or read or make up, even the stories I write for a living. Also, I'm a sucker for all the group fantasies man's created— Christmas, Easter, Halloween, birthday celebrations. All those things buffer me, give me an illusion of continuity. I need something I can hold on to.

Also, the entire Franky Furbo saga, and what I believe about him, is a part of my life, my reasons for living. I just can't *consider* that he doesn't exist, that I make him up myself. He means too much to me. The deep purples of despair surround me right now, and only because Billy said he didn't believe in Franky. I don't know how to handle it. I smell the smells of dirty feet, moldy sheep, feel the slippage of entropy. I'm not ready for this unwanted clarity of perception.

After breakfast, Billy goes upstairs to the schoolroom. One of Caroline's theories of teaching is that children must learn to teach themselves. She teaches them so they read with personal joy and pleasure, then gives them books that will interest them and at the same time instruct. After they've read the books—whether they be novels, biographies, algebra, chemistry, physics, geography, any subject—she'll sit with them and discuss what they've read. When something is particularly difficult, she'll explain or, better yet, help them explain it to themselves. I've sat in when she's been teaching, and sometimes I just leave the door open from where I'm working, opening onto her classroom, and I always learn something I didn't know.

When we were at UCLA together, I knew she was an outstanding student, but I didn't know how much more she was learning than I was. She loves to teach too, and our children love her as teacher almost as much as they love her as Mother.

So, we're left alone. I'm drying the dishes and stacking them in the closet. I'm waiting for her to say something about the terrible ending to the Franky Furbo story I told, but she's holding back. It's almost as if she's thinking of something else and doesn't want to be disturbed. I'm feeling terribly depressed and want to talk with her, but I don't want to interfere with her thoughts. I find I've started whistling; it's that damned six-pence song. That's always a bad sign for me. Caroline notices and looks over. I stop. I need to talk.

"All right. I'm sorry. I shouldn't've made up that ending. It was a cruel thing to do."

"Yes it was. He's getting too old for you to insist he believe in all those things; he's growing up. I think he's going along with Santa this year because he knows how much you enjoy it, but this will be his last year. Billy is a very nice person."

I know I'm supposed to feel bad here for what I did, and I do. I really do, with *one* part of me.

"Caroline, I know I shouldn't have made up that whole bit about the fire and Franky being killed and all that, but Billy hit me where it really hurts. He said he didn't believe in Franky Furbo. I guess I was striking back."

"He was only being honest, William. You can't punish him for that. He can't go on *forever* believing in a fox who's more intelligent than human beings, who can fly, who can make himself big or small, turn himself into a man or fox, can transmigrate his body from one place to another, transmute matter—all the rest. You can't ask him to grow up believing something like that. It isn't right. You should be proud he could come right out and tell you."

"Yes I know. But the trouble is, there really *is* a Franky Furbo. You *know* that. It can't hurt him *too* much believing in something that really *is*, even if he can't see him or know him himself, can it?"

She looks at me, she looks into my eyes in that kind yet veiled way with which she can seem to see into my deepest parts.

"William, we both know, in one way, there really *is* a Santa Claus too, but in the *real* world, there isn't. You can't ask Billy to live with you in your fantasies; it isn't fair. The children need to know there's a place where they can draw a line between what is and what isn't, what can be and what can't. It's only natural."

"You're not listening, Caroline. There really *is* a Franky Furbo. Let us not forget that. We're not talking about Santa Claus or the Easter Bunny or the Little People now. We're talking about *Franky Furbo!* If he isn't true, then nothing is true."

Caroline looks at me again. In over thirty-five years, we haven't talked much in this area. I think we've been afraid of it, what it means, could mean to our relationship, to the way we live.

"You don't really believe that, William. I know you like to play with thoughts, the nature of reality and all that kind of thinking, but this is serious. You know, deep down in your heart, there's *no* Franky Furbo. There couldn't be. It's just too ridiculous."

I stare back at her. I could leave it here. We mean so much to each other and it all happened so long ago, but I can't stop myself.

"Caroline, you *do* know I had a Section Eight discharge from the army. I never lied to you about that now, did I?"

"Of course, William dear; I know that. But it never mattered to me. I love you. I loved you then and I love you now."

"But when I told you about my Section Eight, I also told you about Franky Furbo. I told you all about it then, when we were at the university, just after we'd met at one of those Friday night dances and knew right away we were in love. I told you about it *that* night. I felt you were the first person I'd ever met I could tell about Franky who wouldn't laugh or get scared or run away from me. It was the year I was released from the hospital back in Kentucky. This is true, isn't it? You *did* believe me, didn't you?"

Caroline stares at me. She has the butter in her hand, ready to slide it into the refrigerator.

"It was such a long time ago, William. Everything was mixed up after the war and you were so sad. And yet you had a fascinating way about your life, driving that impossible black, yellow, and red cut-down jeep with the birdcages built into the back, living in a tent up there on a hill in Topanga Canyon. And then building your private nest in the attic of Moore Hall and living there.

"I would have believed anything you told me; even if I *didn't* believe, I'd have *pretended* I did. I wasn't about to let you get away. I was so young. You can't imagine what it is for a young girl when she meets someone like you and knows she's in love— it's a special kind of desperation."

"Then you didn't believe me and you don't now. You've only humored me along. Is that it?"

17

"It's not so simple, William. I knew you'd had a terrible time with the war and had been hurt deeply. I guess I felt sorry for you. But more than that, I wanted to be involved in your life, the life you told me you were going to lead. It's possible I could have believed you with a part of my mind, an important part, the part related to my heart. Don't you understand—I wanted to believe so much I maybe actually *did* believe. I never *felt* I was lying to you."

She pulls the plug to let the water out of the sink. I dry the frying pan and hang it on the wall. I'm feeling empty inside, cold, lost, the way I used to feel in the hospital when no one would believe me and they'd ask the same questions over and over. Now, my own wife and youngest child don't believe in me.

"I'm not trying to blame you, Caroline. I understand. It's just during all these years, I thought you believed. It helped me hold on to what I thought was the only sanity I had left. Except for the army psychiatrists, I never talked to anyone about it. Then I started telling the children stories, some of them actual stories Franky told me, some I made up over the years to amuse them. But even those made-up stories were somehow true, true in that I believed them myself.

"You know how the doctors in the hospital put the whole Franky business down to a fantasy I'd constructed as compensation for a complete amnesia due to extreme trauma. They insisted I was only supporting a sustained delusion. That's why they gave me the Section Eight. That's why I still receive the fifty-percent disability pension—not for anything physical. I'm considered fifty percent mentally incompetent. I'm a certified half-wit. You know that.

"But, damn it, I was convinced *you* believed me. I was sure you understood about Franky and believed with me; it gave our lives some sense. Probably I should never have invented some of those stories for the kids. Maybe it was there when you stopped believing in me. But I wanted to share the magic. I wanted them to know something about why their father is the way he is, lives the way he lives, has tried to design a personal kind of life for all of us.

"Of course, some of those stories I told weren't true, didn't necessarily happen; there weren't that many stories Franky told *me*. But I wanted to tell those stories, and I didn't think it would hurt. Also, in an unbelievable, almost mystical way, I *didn't* make them up. It was almost as if Franky were speaking *through* me. Even some of the children's stories I've published came into my mind that way, like magic writing. I don't quite understand it myself.

"But, the important thing is, this doesn't mean Franky Furbo isn't real, and many of the stories I told them *were* true—true stories Franky told *me*, especially stories about how he discovered he was different from other foxes, that somehow he was a magic fox."

I dry my hands on the dish towel and go over to the rocker in front of the fire. There are only two chairs in our home, other than those in the schoolroom and my workroom. There's the rocker I'm sitting in and another rocker on the other side of the fireplace. Mostly we all just stretch out on our gigantic bed. Each of us has a reading light, and it's there, in the bed, where we spend a good part of our evenings: reading, talking, discussing what we're reading, playing word games—having wonderful times.

My sitting in the rocker is another bad sign, like the whistling. I hardly ever sit in it.

I see the fire needs more wood. I push myself up and throw two more logs into the hearth. We have all the wood cut for winter. It doesn't get very cold here, but some evenings can be bitter. We have enough for at least two winters. A good part of our wood is olive, which we get when we trim the trees. It's hard to start but then burns long and hot.

Caroline comes over behind me. She puts her hands on my

neck and shoulders and starts massaging. I don't respond. In fact, it annoys me. I don't feel she even knows me, and I'd always thought of her as my closest friend as well as my wife. I'm feeling very alone, and I don't know what to do. I'm wishing I'd just let it all go and left everything the way it was.

Caroline is very sensitive and I know she feels what I'm thinking, what I'm feeling. This somehow makes it worse. There are double-barreled guilts floating around in all directions. I sense how easy it would be for me to drift off into a deep depression, the way I would in the hospital when I felt so isolated. When I'm like that, it's almost as if I'm in a nonexistent state; I have a hard time even remembering to eat or sleep.

Caroline stops massaging and comes around in front of me. I look up at her and she doesn't smile. She just stares at me.

"Look William, what does it matter if I believe in Franky Furbo or not? It just doesn't matter. I believe in you; that's what counts. Why should something that happened more than forty years ago be so important? Don't make a big thing out of this. Please don't ask me to lie to you."

"Honest, Caroline. I really don't want to talk about it anymore. If you don't believe, after all these years living with me, living the way we've lived, the way Franky taught me to live, then how can mere talking help?

"Don't you realize that if it weren't for Franky Furbo, I wouldn't be alive? And even if I were alive, I wouldn't be anything like the person I am. In a strange way, belief in Franky Furbo has been my religion. The experience I had with him made me an artist, a writer, gave me a feeling of uniqueness, of value, such as I'd never known. He gave meaning to my life. Can't you understand that?

"Without Franky I'd definitely be dead, not just physically

dead but mentally dead, psychically dead, psychologically dead—a zombie. I'd lost confidence in the importance of living, the value of being alive, and Franky gave it back to me, helped explain some of what life is about. As a child, an orphan in an asylum, there had never been much joy or meaning in my life, and then there was the insanity of war. It all seemed so meaningless, so awful. Franky gave me a reason for living."

I look up at Caroline; tears are rolling down her face. She just stands there in front of me. What can I do?

"Caroline, please, will you listen to me one more time? I want to tell you everything I can remember. You don't have to believe if you can't, but it could be good for me to go over it all once more, to remind myself of what *did* happen, what *didn't* happen. If I can separate those things, perhaps, now so much time has passed, I can see the whole experience for what the doctors said it was—only some kind of complicated delusion.

"I think I made up many things to explain aspects of Franky I didn't understand myself. I wanted the children to believe with me. Even this morning's story, I know now, although I told it as truth, was not a story Franky told me. In a certain way, Billy was right when he said I made it up, that it wasn't true. But it *seemed* true to me, and I wanted him to feel this truth with me. I couldn't change the ending just because he wanted me to. *That* would be lying, untruth.

"I hate to think those army doctors were right and there really is something wrong inside me, that my head doesn't work right, that I can't separate reality from fantasy. But I do accept the possibility there is something different in me. I often have the peculiar feeling I'm not even myself. That's got to be crazy, doesn't it?

"If Franky Furbo *isn't* real and I can learn to believe it, I can live with it now, I think. I have you, the children, our wonderful life—that should be enough. It's been a long time, much has happened, we are so close. You're right, I shouldn't ask too much of you. It isn't right.

"But would you sit down there, dear, in our other rocking chair, and let me go over the entire experience one more time with you, and please, please, try to listen. Listen to me, knowing I'm not purposely trying to make any of this up, that I'm not lying to you. Listen as if it's all happening to you, and believe what you can believe. I need someone to hear this with me."

CHAPTER 3

FOX HOLE

As you know, dearest, I was only twenty when we hit the beaches near Palermo in Sicily. I was with the Thirty-fourth Infantry Division, and we were all scared out of our minds.

Somehow, after horrible fighting, we made our way up through Sicily and then onto the mainland of Italy. It seems so strange now, thinking of attacking this beautiful land, which has become home to us.

By some miracle, I managed to stay alive and unhurt. We were attacking Germans entrenched in an old monastery on a hill called Monte Cassino. There was ferocious fighting, small arms, mortar, artillery, bombing, much pushing forward and then retreating. It seemed as if we were never going to get past this defense position the Germans had set up. Many Italian prisoners came in, but the Germans were fighting to the last man. It looked to me as if we were going to lose the war, or at least keep fighting until either I was killed or died of old age.

Rumor spread along the lines that we were about to mass a major attack coordinated with division, corps, and army artillery. I, personally, wasn't ready. I was at the very limits of what I could endure, but then so was everyone else.

I was half asleep in a hole with a friend called Stan Cramer, when Sergeant Messer came up to our hole.

"OK, you two, haul ass outta there and follow me, the captain wants to see you."

We crawled back on our bellies, in the mud, to the company CP. The CO was as dirty as the rest of us. Somehow he'd also managed to survive. He was one of the only company commanders in our battalion who had lasted this long.

He wanted us to go on a reconnaissance patrol. The word *patrol* had taken on a special quality of its own for me. My brain, my insides shook when I heard it. I was so frightened I couldn't speak. I listened with Stan, as the CO pointed at his dirt-smeared, often-folded map and explained what was going to happen, what we had to do.

"Now, this is only going to be a 'recon' patrol, you two, so don't get your ass in an uproar. We just want to find out if a little bridge up ahead has been mined or has been set to be blown. If anyone opens fire or you see anything that looks like a serious defensive position, hustle your asses right back here. This whole battalion is supposed to attack at oh-six-hundred, right through there, and if that bridge is intact, it would sure make things a lot easier. Artillery will start coming in at oh-five-thirty, so get on back here before then. You understand?"

He explained how the bridge was over a small stream. The stream could be forded but would be hard for the antitank guns and heavy-weapons people. He wanted to know just what was there if we could find out.

He gave us C rations: hot hash and hot coffee. Then he left us. We ate leaning against a piece of broken masonry near the CP. We didn't talk much. We rested. It was good to be off the line, even if it was only a hundred yards back. We had four hours before we were to move out.

At four o'clock in the morning we started. We moved behind

our own lines, north, till we were in line with where the bridge was supposed to be. I remember the password that night was Lana-Turner. We came up to the last outpost on that part of the line. It was the Third Platoon. They challenged us and we gave the password. We slid down into the hole with them. We told them what we were supposed to do. They told us they hadn't seen any bridge but could tell us where the stream was, down the hill, just before you had to start up the next hill. They insisted the hill was absolutely infested with Jerry. They scared us with descriptions of suspected mortar emplacements here, snipers there.

We went out carefully; I could taste the coffee in my nose and in the back of my throat—sour. I should never have drunk it. We slid and slipped down the hill. It was hard mud with flat loose shale over the whole surface. We came to the stream. We stopped.

Stan had the map and was sure the bridge had to be farther to the north yet, although it was actually supposed to be more east than north. I had no idea. I was interested only in going through the motions and getting back.

We started working our way up along the draw formed by the stream. It was hard going because it was so dark. The sky had that little bit of light that always seems to come before dawn when you're on guard duty and waiting for relief. But, as usual, it didn't help much. Mostly, we guided ourselves by the sound of water running in the stream.

The sides of the draw began getting steeper, so we slipped more and more often into the water. Then Stan stopped. He pointed. There was a bridge. It had to be the bridge we were looking for. It was a typical Italian bridge one finds around this area, constructed of stone part way out on each side and the middle built with heavy wood. It was longer than the stream was wide, so the stream must have run more fully in the spring. We crept up a little closer. Stan leaned close to my ear.

"You willing to slide out on that thing and take a look-see? I'll scramble up the side of this hill to cover you."

I was willing but I didn't want to. I nodded my head. Stan put his mouth close to my ear again. He had a luminous watch he'd taken from an Italian officer.

"We have about half an hour before all that corps and division crap is supposed to hit. We sure as hell want to be far from here by then. Give me five minutes to get up in a good spot to cover, then scramble out on the bridge and give it a quick going-over."

He started off up the ridge. I sat and wondered what I was doing. I had a carbine and four grenades. Out on that bridge I'd be a dead duck if anyone were guarding it. Only the dark was in my favor. This was one of those patrols that could turn out to be only a cold, wet walk or a last walk into the final cold.

When I figured Stan had to be in place, I started. Twice, I slipped into the streambed till it was over my boots, so I figured I'd walk along in the water at the edge of the stream; it was easier and I wasn't going to get any wetter. I was reaching the point where I was not only scared but scared of being scared. When you get *too* scared, you don't do the right things at the right time in the right way; that can be really dangerous.

I wondered if I should be higher up on the side of the hill with a chance to scurry for cover. The problem is, when nothing is happening, I get careless.

Now, as I got closer to the bridge, there were bushes and reeds growing along the edge. I moved into them and looked at the bridge carefully. There seemed to be no one there. I started to worry about the time; my watch is only a normal Bulova, which doesn't glow in the dark, and I couldn't read it, no matter which way I twisted my wrist. The orphanage, St. Vincent's, gave it to me as a high school graduation present because I was first in my class. It's amazing it's still working after all it's been through. It's an ordinary watch, not waterproof, but it's been in a lot of water.

I reached the bridge on our side of the stream. I slithered under it and felt for a mine or dynamite sticks. There was nothing. I pulled myself up onto the bridge quietly and stretched out there. At this point, I began to feel that the moon, the stars, and all possible light available were concentrating on me. I looked under my arm, almost expecting I'd cast a shadow. It was too dark; my imagination was running amuck.

I pulled myself on my belly and reached over the edge of the bridge to check each of the supports. I figured if anything started, I'd just let myself drop into the water and float on downstream. I was probably not actively thinking this, but the thoughts were there.

The secret to success on any patrol is full-fledged paranoia. You have to *expect* the worst to happen and be prepared for it, at any minute. The least surrender to a sense of security is an invitation to sudden death.

I slid farther along the bridge. I tried to stay beneath the cover of the railing and reached far under to the center support where the diagonal wooden braces met. It's the place where dynamite should've been placed if somebody really wanted to blow this bridge. There was nothing. I was beginning to feel more confident. I slid farther along and now only had to check those supports where the wood fit into the stone on the other side. Stan and I had agreed that, when I was finished, and if everything was OK, I'd wave my arm so he'd know to start back to our meeting place, the place where we'd separated. This wasn't the first patrol I'd been on with Stan. We'd take turns doing the hard parts, and it was my turn.

I leaned over the edge of the bridge again, feeling for something there but not really expecting it. Then, two hands reached out from under the bridge and pulled me down! My carbine strap got caught up on the bridge, so it was ripped right off my shoulder.

There were two of them. Germans. They weren't SS, only regular field green, garden variety Wehrmacht, German GIs. The one who pulled me over the edge had a knife at my neck, the other had his rifle pointed at my head. I put my hands above my head behind me. I was on my back, half in the water. The one with the knife let me go and pointed up the hill on the other side of the draw. The one with the gun prodded me in the ribs, hard. I clambered up in front of them in the dark, stumbling, wondering if Stan could see us. He probably could, but couldn't do anything. He could never tell in the dark which were the good guys, me, and which the baddies, Krauts. I'm hoping he won't try any shooting. He's not all that great a shot; he just barely made marksman, with help from all of us.

In a few minutes we reached a hole dug in the lee of the hill on the other side of the draw. They shoved me into it. The one with the knife also had a Schmeisser, what we called a "burp gun," slung over his shoulder. He reached for my neck and yanked off my dog tags. He also used his knife to cut off my division insignia. He searched me and took my Bulova watch and wallet. This was more like a mugging than a capture. I began to be afraid. These guys must never've heard of the Geneva Convention. Or maybe they'd heard of it and didn't believe in it. Just my luck.

He jammed all my stuff into his pocket and said something to the other guy. This Kraut then braced his back against one side of the hole and propped his rifle on his knee, pointed right at my chest. The one with my things clambered out from the hole and took off up the side of the slope.

I tried smiling at the Kraut with the rifle, a smile in the dark. No smile back. I'm wondering what time it is, how soon that artillery is going to start coming in. I wonder if Stan has run all the way back to tell them I'm stuck out here, or if he even knows. Hell, they wouldn't hold up an artillery barrage for one lousy Pfc.

I slowly try to make moves with my hands over my head like

bombs coming in. I make "Boom Boom" noises. He flicks off his safety! Maybe "Boom Boom" means something different in German. I keep trying to get the message across, but he's only acting more suspicious and crouches behind his sight to let me know he's ready to shoot if I make one false move. I'm beginning to panic. They're bound to have this bridge zeroed in.

Then it comes. First one over, then one under, bracketing. The third lands about fifty feet down from us and to the right of the bridge, near the water.

Now my German comrade finally seems to have gotten the picture. Keeping his rifle on me, he looks down as bits of dirt and rocks are dropping all around us. I make moves as if to get the hell out of that hole and up the hill. He points his rifle at me again and shouts something. Another salvo comes whistling and roaring in; the bridge is blown sky high, bits of wood and stone fly around with dirt and shrapnel. So much for the attack over the bridge; everybody's going to get their feet wet anyway. If the Krauts don't blow it, we'll do it ourselves.

I crouch down deep in the hole with my hands tight on my head. I remember I don't even have my helmet. It fell off when they pulled me under the bridge and is probably floating downstream. I'm beginning to feel I'm in for it.

I'm thinking how I didn't have a chance to surrender; I've had many wonderful fantasies—walking up to some Kraut, handing over my rifle, and surrendering, like General Lee at Appomattox. But they ripped my grenades off me down there by the water before I could think, and my carbine must still be on that bridge, actually flying around in pieces with the rest of the debris.

Well, now I'm a prisoner, but not for long. I try once more to get this guy to climb out of the hole with me, but no go.

Just then, it starts truly coming down. The concussion is so great I feel as if my eyes are popping out of my head. That Kraut and I are groveling, fighting, for the lowest spot in the hole. We're both screaming. Mommy and *Mutti* are in great demand that morning but are not responding. I don't even remember my mother but I'm yelling for her anyway. The impact, the noise, the dirt falling in on us fills the air.

In the middle of everything, I see the rifle leaning, unattended, against the front edge of the hole. The Kraut has forgotten all about it. We're involved with bigger guns now; this popgun looked like a peashooter.

I decide how, if by some major miracle we get through this, I'll look a lot better if the German is *my* prisoner than the other way around; so, in a clear instant, when dirt isn't being blown into my mouth, eyes, and ears, I lean over with one arm and cradle that gun against my chest. I might as well *look like* a hero, it can't hurt. *Single-handed, in hand-to-hand combat after he'd been captured, he overwhelmed the enemy and escaped*—all that crap. It could make a fairly nice bronze star citation.

The Kraut looks at me as if I'm nuts. He probably figures we should be past all that. He's right. I try to relax, let my mind wander, think about other things, because there's nothing I can possibly do concerning what's actually happening now. I try to justify what's going on, explain it to myself.

So far, I've found out there's a big difference between recklessness, fearlessness, and bravery. The first is to be avoided, except as something from afar, say in a movie or a story. The second is also something to be avoided. If you are fearless, you probably lack some critical aspect of imagination. If you're near someone who is fearless, chances are you'll get sucked into the vortex of fearless madness and get hurt yourself, no matter how careful you are. I'd already discovered the truth of this second one *before* the crazy war, but have had it verified too often over the past few months.

Bravery is doing what has to be done even though you're afraid.

Most brave people I've known have done what they did very cautiously. They were scared, but for survival reasons, either of self or others they valued, did something that normally would require fearlessness or recklessness. But they don't do it fearlessly or recklessly. They only do what has to be done and they do it with an absolute minimum of bravado.

Then, there's another category. I could call it pragmatic sensibility. It's when one does the obviously intelligent thing, which can easily be confused with bravery, that is, if you don't look carefully. My reaching out for the rifle and cuddling it to myself fits in here somewhere.

But I don't have long to cogitate all these minor variations in human behavior. I keep telling myself that anything I can hear or feel probably isn't going to kill me. I've gotten through a few other bombardments with this specious rationale, but then the one I didn't feel or hear must have come. I don't know how close it was, but it was close enough to just fold that hole right in on top of us. Everything stops for me.

When I come to, I'm covered with mud, dirt, and blood. I can't move. I can barely see. My ears are ringing. My feet and arms are numb. I feel strangely warm and comfortable. I consider the idea that I am dead.

In front of me, stretched out on my dirt-covered lap, is the Kraut. His eyes are open and looking right at me, but he isn't seeing. His neck looks twisted the wrong way. I figure he's dead, too, and if he's seeing anything, he's seeing me dying. We're on the inside of a mass grave for two.

If I'm dead, then there's nothing to do but wait and find out what happens next. If I'm not dead, then I'm probably dying. I'm astounded at how easy it is, how I'm not as scared as I thought I'd be.

I can see enough to know, or think, that it's full daylight. Some considerable time must have passed. I feel the way you feel when somebody buries you deep in sand at the beach, or when, in a hospital, they give you an ether anesthetic, or I should say, the way I felt when they gave me an ether anesthetic to take out my tonsils and adenoids at the orphanage when I was eight years old.

I know I'm crying, but I can't hear myself. When you've been under a one-five-five artillery bombardment, you don't hear much of anything for a while.

I'm not sure how long we lie there like that. Nobody comes to check us, neither GI nor Kraut. The war seems to have passed us by. That's not too disappointing.

I drift in and out. I'm just beginning to feel some pain. Maybe I am alive, more or less. I try moving a few fingers but nothing happens. I can't even lift my head to look up over the edge of the hole, and that's when I'm conscious. When I'm passed out, we must just look like a couple of prime candidates for the grave-registrar bunch, and they won't be along till much later. Everybody's too damned busy fighting the crappy war to pay much attention to us for now. We're sort of obsolete.

It's getting to be night again when I hear a small scurrying sound. That wakes me! I'm sure it's rats come for a free nibble. We had rats in the night at the orphanage. I wonder, if I try, if I can make a noise like a cat. I try making a noise and two things happen. The "dead" Kraut starts to moan; muddy tears come out of his eyes, puddle with his muddy sweat. The other thing is I can hear myself as well as hear his moan. Of course, I'd also heard the scurrying, so my ears must be working. I try to turn my head a little, but it hurts, hard, down deep in my back, under all the dirt. My arms, hands, legs, and feet begin feeling cold—not so much cold as dead.

I'm starting to wish all of me could feel as dead as they seem. At least they don't hurt.

I look around for the rats, but there aren't any. It's a fox! It's a beautiful fox standing on two legs! He comes close and begins carefully, with small fine almost handlike paws, scraping dirt off the Kraut and me.

I watch, not knowing what's happening or what to do. Then the fox looks me in the eyes and says in a clear, calm voice:

"Stay perfectly still, William. I'll have you out of here very soon."

Now I'm sure I'm dead or crazy, or both, but there's nothing I can do. He slowly lifts off the Kraut's helmet and gently slides his head off my chest. He works slowly, carefully, pulling dirt from the both of us until we're completely uncovered. Then this little fox stares down and at me again.

"Now you do just as I say, William, and everything will be all right."

I'm *sure* I'm dead now, but how is it nobody ever figured out God was a fox? The Kraut moans again, and the fox touches him all over with his light, tender, moving paws. He speaks to him in another language. I'm not sure, but it sounds like German. In either language, his voice is a strong modulated whisper, warm and comforting, still loud enough so I hear it easily through the mud and dirt packed in my ears.

He turns back to me. His eyes are an incredible yellowish amber.

"William, you shall both die unless you do exactly what I tell you."

I'm numb, dumb with shock and fear. His eyes peer intelligently at me over his reddish black muzzle.

**"Look deeply into my eyes. Try to relax. You will have a strange
sensation, but it is the only way I can think right now to remove
you from here and to a place where I can help you."**

I stare into his eyes and slowly seem to feel myself lifting out of my
body. At the same time, I sense an intense enclosing concentration,
a compaction of all I am. The closest thing I can think of is the way
it would feel for loose snow to be squeezed into a snowball. I slowly
become as nothing. The pain and numbness leave, then I lose con-
sciousness.

CHAPTER 4

THE WARREN

The next thing I know, Caroline, I'm in a large room. I'm stretched out on a bed. My entire body is in traction, with pulleys and weights hanging from rafters in a ceiling. The ceiling, rafters, walls, and floors are made from wood, and they're not painted. It seems like a strange kind of hospital. But I'm in a clean bed and it's quiet. I don't feel any pain if I lie still, not even a headache.

I try to remember what's happened to me. I can move my hands, my arms, if I do it carefully, but it is painful. I turn my head slowly back and forth. In the bed beside me is the German soldier. He's asleep and breathing hard. I recognize him by his split front teeth. I have the same kind of teeth myself, you know, Caroline, and when I see it in someone else I always remember it. I have a feeling of family with people who have this kind of teeth.

I figure that somehow some medics, Kraut or American, have found us, and we're in a field hospital somewhere. I couldn't care too much which, Kraut or American. I'm beginning to believe I'm alive and out of the war, out of pain. I fall gently back to sleep.

When I wake again, I can't believe what I see. A giant fox is leaning over me, checking my bandages, checking the bottles and tubes hanging above my bed. He's human sized and wearing white doctorlike clothes! He has the build of a medium-sized man, taller than most bears.

He sees I'm awake and lays his paw on my forehead. The underside of his paw is soft but feels cool.

"Well, William, you are awake at last. Those were really horrible wounds you had, but you shall soon be all right. You had two fractured vertebrae, which were hard to repair without damage to your spinal cord. You also had six broken ribs and a broken collarbone. There was some damage to your liver and one of your lungs as well, but that is all repaired."

I'm beginning to wonder again whether I'm dead. But this is even more than I'd expect if I were dead; this is all just nuts. The fox is still standing there, leaning over me. The tip of his nose is wiggling so the whisker hairs dance.

"I'm sorry, William, I know it must be very confusing. I can tell you that you are not dead and you are not crazy either. I should also tell you I cannot only speak English, but that your thoughts speak to me as clearly as words."

It takes a little courage getting myself to say anything. I have an inside feeling that if I begin talking to this giant fox all dressed up in a white coat like a doctor, I would definitely be bonkers. But what else is there to do? Maybe if I start talking, he'll disappear and some real people will come running to help me.

"How did I get here? What are you? What's happening?"

The huge fox pulls a chair over from the wall. He sits in the chair beside me.

"Now you just relax and listen, William. Your questions are hard to answer and the answers will be even harder for you to believe.

"How did you get here? I brought you here from that hole

36

where you were dying. I made you very small, along with Wilhelm across there, and carried you both back with me to my home. For me, it was not a long or difficult journey. I shall tell you why later. I brought you into my home to see if I could make you well. I should tell you that my home is in the inside of a tree. You think I am a big fox right now, and I could be if I wanted to, but actually I have made you and Wilhelm small and I am the natural size of a fox. You only *think* I am big because we're the same size and you expect a fox to be smaller than you."

He pauses. It's almost as if he's watching my brain and waiting until what he's said has printed itself in there. I'm wondering how I could make this all up. In general, I'm not very imaginative. He starts talking again.

"Don't worry about it, William, just listen. You shall understand much more as time goes by. Your second question is harder because I do not understand it very much myself. 'What am I?'

"It seems easy just to say I am a fox. But you can see I am not an ordinary fox. For reasons I do not know or understand, I was born very intelligent, with many skills and abilities no fox or even humans have. I live by myself here in this tree. My mother, brother, and sisters were ordinary foxes. I don't know why or what I really am. I know that doesn't answer your question, but it is the truth.

"Now your next question. 'What's happening?' I was wondering the same thing. What's happening here in this place where I live? Humans are dashing up and down, back and forth, killing one another, making noise, destroying towns. I know it is a war, but I don't know *why* there must be all this killing, how they force all of you to do such a crazy thing.

"So, this is what is happening to you: I decided to select two samples of people who are doing the killing, acting so insanely, and find out why they're doing it. I didn't want to capture anyone who was well and healthy so I waited till I could find two humans, each speaking a different language, who were fighting each other but were about to die. When I found you and Wilhelm in that hole, I decided to take you two because I could see you would soon be dead anyway. Wilhelm is hurt even worse than you. But he is soon going to be well, too. One of the many skills I have is that I can heal others, better than any human doctor."

I watch his eyes. They show only kindness and intensity. I begin to feel myself relax, able to believe a little bit what I'm hearing. In a crazy way, it almost makes a kind of sense, at least as much sense as the dumb war does.

"That's good, William, now you are relaxing. It will help you become well sooner. I have only a little more to say now, then I want you to sleep.

"I shall be asking questions, as well as reading your mind over the next while. I want to understand why humans do some of the things they do, especially war. I want you and Wilhelm to know each other, to speak to each other. I shall teach each of you the language of the other so you can share what you know. I shall also teach you another language, one that will make understanding, for all of us, much easier. I cannot teach you to read each other's minds because it is probably impossible for humans to do that; but this language I shall teach you is the most complete communication possible for humans.

"When you are well, when you want to, you may leave here and go back to your own people. I hope you don't mind my having taken advantage of you this way, but I think it will be good for us all. Now, close your eyes and go to sleep."

With that he puts his cool paw on my forehead and slides it down over my eyes. I go to sleep, deep sleep, immediately.

I don't know how much longer it is before I wake again. I feel much better. The traction has been removed. I'm stretched out on my bed, very relaxed, warm, and with a happy feeling. I hear talking on the other side of the room.

I turn my head, without pain, and see that the fox is sitting in a chair beside the Kraut's bed, just as he had been with me before. I try to listen. They are talking German. I stare at the ceiling and want to put it all together. I'm beginning to feel nervous, frightened again.

The next thing I know, the fox is leaning over me, smiling. He pulls the covers down and begins to feel over my body with his gentle paws. His eyes, his ears, seem to be concentrating on my body. When he finds a spot that still hurts, he covers it with his hands, makes it warm, and it doesn't hurt anymore.

"You're coming along fine, William; you are almost completely healed. You will feel weak for a few days but with some good solid food you shall be on your feet soon."

I don't know how to thank him. How do you thank a fox? What should I call him, Mr. Fox? He's checking the back of my neck now.

"Don't worry about it, William. My name is Franky Furbo. At least, that's what I call myself. Foxes usually don't have names. You may call me Franky, if you will. I'd like that."

"All right, Franky. Thank you for saving my life. You saved the life of that Kraut too, right? Whose side are you on?"

"I don't take sides, except I'm on the side of life. You two are now alive and are human, the closest creatures on this earth to myself I've found so far. There's no need to thank me; my pleasure is in seeing you well."

39

There's no answer I can think of to that.

"Did I hear you speaking Kraut—I mean German—to that guy over there?"

"That's right. I can speak any language spoken on this earth; it's a hobby of mine. Do you know there are more than six thousand languages spoken on this planet alone? I find it fascinating, also the way languages come about, how they're constructed. It is easy for me to learn all these languages because of my special mind skills. Our German friend's name is Wilhelm, the same as yours only in German. His full name is Wilhelm Klug. And your name is William Wiley. Is that right?"

Of course it's right. At first I think he's read my dog tags, but then I remember the other German took them with him. It's so weird being around someone, even if it is a fox, who knows everything in your head. It almost makes it not worth talking.

"I'd like to teach you to speak German, William. It won't take any time. I can also teach you everything that is in Wilhelm's head so you can know him as well as he will know you. That way, I feel you can talk about this war and understand more of what it is supposed to be all about. Are you agreed?"

By now, I'm so confused I'll agree to anything. I nod my head.

"All right then, just relax. You will feel a strange warmness and you won't be able to see or hear for a few minutes, but then it will go away. It's best if you close your eyes now."

Franky lowers his head close to mine. I close my eyes. It's the way it was in the hole. I feel warmth, but this time going through my whole brain. There is a smell, almost of burnt almonds or the smell of the seed inside a peach stone. It seems to last only a few minutes. Then Franky leans back. He speaks to me.

"Well, how did that feel? It wasn't so bad, was it?"

"It felt warm in my head and I smelled something peculiar. How should I feel?"

"Listen to yourself."

Only then, I realize I've answered in German, and it was so familiar to me it sounded like English to my ears. I also realize I *do* know everything about Wilhelm, all he can remember about his own life. I know where he lived, about his wife, how he misses her. It's almost as if they are my own memories, but more, as if it's a movie I'm watching, only seeing it, not actually participating. I stare over at Wilhelm. I turn to Franky.

"You did it. You actually did it. But can I still speak English?"

"Certainly. Sometimes, at first, you might get confused and speak the wrong language, but that won't last long. In time, your own language will control your German. It's what you are, an American who speaks English as your home language."

"You haven't done this with Wilhelm yet, have you?"

"No. He isn't quite strong enough, but in a few days he'll be ready. I think now he would appreciate it if you would speak with him some when I am gone. He's very lonesome and frightened."

"I never thought about that. He's probably as scared as I am. In fact, I know he is, I can feel his feelings. He's afraid of *me* even."

Franky pats me on the arm while his nose and whiskers quiver again.

"Well, I'm going down to cook you a good meal. Would you like a big omelet with baked potatoes and carrots, all served with fresh homemade bread?"

He knows I would, he knows everything about me. I smile. He leaves. I look over at Wilhelm. He's staring at the ceiling and I can see tears flowing from his eyes. I speak and it comes out in German.

"It'll be all right, Wilhelm. Franky will make everything just fine. We would be dead if he hadn't saved us, you know."

He lifts his head, stares at me.

"You are German?! You are Bavarian, a Münchener?"

"No, I am American."

His head falls back. He stares at the ceiling, the wooden ceiling.

"But you speak perfect German, the German I speak, the German from my part of Germany. What is this? Are you an American spy?"

I try to explain how Franky taught me, how, by some magic way, he put part of Wilhelm's brain into mine.

"But that is not possible. None of this is possible. Who is it who wears the big fox suit? Is this some American trick?"

I don't know whether to try explaining it or not. It seems impossible. How can one explain what one not only doesn't understand but doesn't even really yet quite believe himself? But Franky wanted me to talk to Wilhelm. I try.

"This fox we see is a real fox, a special fox. He calls himself Franky Furbo. He is not a giant fox; he only looks big to us because he has made us little as foxes. He has saved us from death with his magic medicine and special skills."

My God, it sounds just as crazy in German.

"He made us small, took us from the hole, and brought us here. We are in the inside of a tree, which is where this fox lives."

"Yes, he told me these things. But do you believe him? It is not possible. Perhaps *you* are crazy, but I am not."

I know how he feels.

"Yes. I think I believe him, although it is very difficult. When he gave me your language, he also gave me a good part of your life. Let me tell you some things and maybe then you will believe."

I wait. I have a sensation of a Peeping Tom, looking at this film that is in my brain, at the life of this man who a few hours ago was a stranger to me, the enemy I was trained to fight and kill.

"Wilhelm, you are married. You have a wife named Ulrika whom you call 'Riki.' You miss her very much and are worried for her because of the bombs. Your father's name is Heinrich. Your mother's name is Heidi. You had a brother named Hans, but he was killed in Russia. You were studying to be an engineer but were taken into the army."

As I talk, Wilhelm twists to look at me. There is pain on his face. It is the pain of his body and the pain of his emotions.

"Stop. This is all a trick. I must have been talking out loud when I was unconscious. How do you know these things? This is very cruel of you to treat me like this!"

"I know much more, but it will not help to say it now. Let us talk about other things. You play chess, yes? Perhaps Mr. Furbo will find us a chessboard and we can play. How are you feeling? Do you still hurt? Mr. Furbo took away all my pain yesterday and says that soon I shall be able to stand and walk."

I stop. Wilhelm is quiet.

"All this craziness must be true then. Do you know that you speak with my voice? When you speak it is almost as if I am speaking myself. How can that be?"

"It's as I told you."

Wilhelm is quiet; he lies back. I'm feeling tired myself. I drift off to sleep. When I wake, Franky has placed a table beside my bed. He helps me swing up so I can sit at the table. He puts slippers on my feet. I look over and see that Wilhelm is asleep. Franky pulls up a chair for himself across from me.

"Ah, William, it will be nice to sit at a table with someone, to have conversation and eat. I do not often have the chance. Most of the time I am alone. I make friends with some of the other animals in the forest, and once there were two children with whom I was friendly, but now they have grown and gone off to the university, taken work in another part of Italy. I don't see them anymore. We write to one another and I hope someday they will come back to live near here."

The omelet is delicious, the carrots cooked just right, not too soft, not too hard. Franky tells me wonderful tales of his life as a fox, how he writes children's stories to gain the little money he needs for books and necessities. He has a post office box, a bank account, and mostly he orders the things he wants by mail to be delivered at his P.O. box.

"I used to have one or the other of my two young friends pick up those packages for me, but then I discovered I could transmute matter and make myself look more or less like a human, or even be invisible. This simplified life for me, and also I could travel by transmigration of my body. Would you like to see me as a man? It must be somewhat uncomfortable for you sitting here, eating with a fox. I'm sorry I didn't think of it. I try not to enter

your mind unless I feel it is necessary. It confuses conversation when only one is a telepath.

"By the way, I hope you don't mind, but I am a vegetarian; it seems very unfoxlike, but it is my preference. If you want meat while you are here, I can obtain some for you."

"To be honest, if you cook vegetables and eggs like this all the time, I won't need meat, Franky. Also, I hardly notice you're a fox anymore, so you don't need to do anything about that either."

I'd practically forgotten I was sitting there on the edge of a bed, at a table, eating cooked eggs, potatoes, carrots, and homemade bread with someone who looks like a gigantic fox. Perhaps Franky Furbo has entered my mind to make me more comfortable. No, I don't think he'd do that without telling me.

But then, right there, he actually does it. As I watch, he gradually changes: his fur disappears, his muzzle shortens, his arms and legs thicken, and he's practically a human. There's still something foxlike about him, but this is probably because I *know* he's a fox. A stranger would only think he was a slightly thinner-than-usual human.

"This is amazing, Franky. I wouldn't have believed it. And are you little, the way we are?"

"Of course; if I made myself the size of a human I wouldn't fit in my own house."

His nose wiggles and he begins eating. Franky stays in his human form for the rest of the meal. He says tomorrow he will work with me and try to help me get out of bed and walk around.

"You need to regain some tone in your muscles and loosen up the area where I repaired those vertebrae. Now I think you should slide back in bed, stretch out, and try to sleep. Your body has been through much and needs all the rest it can get."

He gathers up our dishes from the table and carries them downstairs. I realize more than just my *body* has been through much; I definitely need rest. My brain feels as if it's sizzling from so many new thoughts.

Two days later, Franky does the same thing to the mind of Wilhelm he'd done with mine. When he's finished, Franky leaves us alone. Wilhelm starts talking to me in English. His eyes are wide; his face white.

"But I speak with your voice, the voice you use when you speak English. I know all about you as if we were brothers. How can this be?"

"I don't know. You'll have to ask Franky Furbo. He's the one who can perform this miracle. I think only he can know."

Now we talk easily. Wilhelm is less scared, more willing to believe. At first, we avoid the situation under which we met. Me sliding out on the bridge, his sergeant and he underneath waiting for me. We switch back and forth from English to German, at first, but then he begins speaking German and I speak English. We understand each other perfectly, and, at the same time, we feel like ourselves speaking our own languages.

It turns out they'd seen me from the time I stepped out of the stream. I told him about Stan up on the hill. They hadn't seen him. I make the motions of the bombs over my head and go "Boom Boom" again. He remembers and I tell him what I was trying to do. We both get to laughing. We laugh the hardest when we talk about my grabbing his rifle in the middle of the bombardment when we were being killed.

"I thought you were really crazy then, William. First you're waving your hands over your head going 'Boom Boom,' then

you take the rifle when we both know we're going to be killed, anyway."

He tells me about his experience in the war, how he wouldn't have been too disappointed if I had captured him. He says his sergeant was a very hard man and I'm lucky he didn't kill me. He only saved my life because he thought some officer might want to interrogate me. The Germans knew there was going to be an attack soon but didn't know where it would be. I told him I'd been looking for a way to get captured since Palermo. It turned out we'd been in the same area several times in the battle up the Italian peninsula. We agree we're both glad to be out of it.

We're also curious about what's happening to us. We keep reassuring each other we aren't crazy. Two people couldn't be crazy about the same situation at the same time, could they? There's only one thing to do and that's wait to see what happens. He wants very badly to get some message to his wife, Riki, so she will know he is all right, because he knows the sergeant will report him dead or captured. I suggest he ask Franky when we see him again about the possibility of getting word to her.

During the next days, both Wilhelm and I start getting out of bed and exercising. Franky has individual exercises for each of us to help us gain our strength. He also has different potions and medicines he gives us along with our food. We eat only vegetarian food and Wilhelm says he wants meat, so, at first, Franky brings him chicken, steaks, roasts—things like that. But Franky is a good cook and likes to eat. The way he prepares the vegetarian meals for us is so tasty, the meat Wilhelm's eating begins to look like animal food.

After about two weeks, Wilhelm shifts over to vegetarian food with us. Once in a while he'll have a Wiener schnitzel, but the main part of his food is vegetables. Franky has all kinds of spices he adds to the vegetables, so it's hard to tell them from meat sometimes.

He says this is one thing from his fox background that has stayed—he really enjoys eating; but he can't justify killing animals, especially because he can talk to them.

We have many conversations about ourselves. It is pleasant sharing our ideas, our experiences. Franky does manage to get a message to Wilhelm's wife, and even brings a letter to him after a few days, written in what Wilhelm recognizes as her handwriting. She says she is well and staying with her family in the country. She tells him his mother and sister are well, also. She was very surprised to find his letter in her mailbox, even without a stamp or a Wehrmacht seal, because how could Wilhelm know where she is, that she is staying with her mother?

But Wilhelm is even more surprised. How could Franky deliver the letter and bring back an answer in only two days? It isn't possible. Franky only wrinkles his nose, which I now begin to suspect is his way of smiling. I'm ready to believe anything, but Wilhelm has a harder time with believing. It's not his way; he always wants to *know* things.

Finally we're both in such good condition, it isn't necessary for us to stay in bed. I don't know where our uniforms are. We are both wearing blue pajamas.

One morning Franky comes in with clothes for us. They are not our uniforms, at the same time they aren't regular clothes. There is a jacket, or jerkin, which slips over our heads, and trousers almost like knickers, only tighter. There are heavy socks and light leather boots. There's a wide leather belt to go over the shirt and to help hold up the trousers. He also has brought us light blue underwear, three pair each, the same color as our pajamas. I can't help wondering where he gets these things, but I'm too embarrassed to ask. I see he no longer wears his white coat but is wearing the same kind of clothes himself.

We put on the costumes. There is also a hat. The clothes are all the colors of the forest, different greens and browns. The hat is dark green, pointed front and back like the kind of hat we used to make from old newspapers at the orphanage. I must say, we look fine in our new costumes, a bit like Robin Hood's forest rangers, but Wilhelm seems worried. Franky twitches his nose.

"I know, Wilhelm. You are worried because you are out of uniform and it is against the German military laws for a soldier to wear any other clothes. But your other uniform was so dirty. When you leave, you may have it back. In the meantime, if you want, I can make it so you will be invisible to anybody but William or myself. Please don't worry so much."

"Yes, Franky, but I feel so strange in these soft clothes, these soft boots. What kind of uniform is this? It's somewhat like Bavarian clothes but much softer. What is this?"

"Let's just say it is a peace uniform, Wilhelm, that, for a while anyway, we three are in an army for peace."

Franky wrinkles his nose again. I smile, then laugh, and Wilhelm joins us. I smile at Wilhelm. It seems a great idea to me. I would definitely not be happy putting on my old dirty olive drabs and going out to war again. Wilhelm looks down at himself in his peace costume.

"Well, it's better than being dead, I must say. I was tired and scared by the war, anyway. I'm proud to be a member of our peace army. Can you really make us invisible?"

"If you want."

"But we will be able to see each other?"

"Oh yes. You won't feel a thing. We won't know we're invisible unless somebody else tries to see us."

49

"OK, let's be invisible. I'm ready."

Wilhelm rises and stands at attention. I stand up, too, just to be sociable. Franky wiggles his nose and laughs.

"OK, you're invisible, both of you. I am too."

Wilhelm looks down at himself.

"How do I know I'm invisible? I can see myself."

"OK, if you want to be invisible to yourself, fine."

Franky waves his hand as if he's brushing away a fly. I think he's failed for once, because Wilhelm is still standing there. Then I watch Wilhelm. His face is pale. He's holding out his hands, touching them together; they're shaking. He looks down at his legs.

"Where am I? I'm gone. You did it. I'm invisible!"

"Only to yourself. We see him, don't we, William?"

"That's right. Are you sure you can't see yourself, Wilhelm? You're right there."

"Right where? I'm nowhere, I'm nothing! Mr. Furbo, *Gott in Himmel*, make me come back, make me visible again."

"Do you want to be visible to everybody, just to the three of us, or only to yourself?"

"The way you said, just to the three of us, the peace army."

He stands at attention again. Franky waves his arm at that truly invisible fly. Wilhelm looks down and smiles.

"You *are* marvelous, Franky Furbo. Now I believe everything. You are some kind of miracle man."

50

"No, I'm a fox. Would you like me to be a man?"

Wilhelm is confused again, I can't help but laugh.

"I saw him as a man, Wilhelm. You were asleep and we were eating. He can really do it."

"No, just stay the way you are, Franky. This is fine."

As I said, Wilhelm tends to talk in German and I talk in English, but I can understand when he speaks and he understands me. Franky talks in either language depending on who's asked a question or with whom he's speaking. Franky looks down at the table where we are sitting, then looks up.

"I am going now to bring up the food I have been cooking for us. Tomorrow I hope we can eat downstairs at my regular table; it will be easier and more comfortable. After our meal, there are many things I want to talk about with you, but for now we eat. Today we are having pizza with spaghetti and a special cheese sauce I make. It is a very famous Italian dish."

He stands and goes downstairs.

After we've eaten, Franky looks in turn at both of us.

"As I said before our meal, I have many things I want to speak with you about. It would be much more convenient and easier for all of us if I spoke to you in my language, 'Fox.' This is a language I created for myself.

"It combines the best of all the six thousand human languages I have learned, including sign languages, plus some methods of expression—using the eyes, the nose, the mouth, even the ears—that allow for a clarity and an intensity just short of telepathic. In human speech there are some ninety phonemes, or

can destroy one another at a faster and faster pace, perhaps destroy the entire planet, before those children can grow up and take charge. He's also interested, through us, in helping humans see their failings and adjust to them, in helping them improve the quality of their lives. He's convinced we still have many primitive urges that are appropriate only to the apes from which we've come, and if we're to continue as the dominant creatures on this earth, we must learn to curb those urges.

We tell him everything about ourselves we can. He knows most of it, but with the two of us there, he can ask questions. He wants to know why humans are so competitive, always wanting to get ahead of the other person, to gain the advantage, to win. He still isn't sure if this is something left over from our evolution when we had to fight like animals or if it's something we've been taught. He says it could only be left over from those earlier days, like his enjoying food so much, but he suspects strongly that it's part of the way our society trains us.

He tells us many things about how humans could live together. He shows us how stupid it was that we, Wilhelm and I, had tried to kill each other when we didn't even know what the war was about. Wilhelm and I smile at each other. It seems impossible to us now that we could ever have been enemies, sworn to kill each other. We agree that probably we were seduced into going to war because we were bored, restless with our own lives, and wanted adventure, wanted to appear brave when we knew we weren't.

Franky insists we learn to think for ourselves and share our ideas, but not to follow blindly or try to have others follow us. He keeps saying we must learn to trust ourselves, know our own value.

We have many discussions that would sometimes be almost like arguments. Wilhelm is convinced there are some races or breeds of people that are superior to others. Franky gives example after example of how this is not true, that Wilhelm has been fooled, given false information by wrong-thinking people. Franky says people are different, and this is necessary and good, but that no one race or group is better or less than another. Finally, Wilhelm admits that probably Franky is right. I think he actually comes to believe this, too.

We ask how we can live as humans in a way that would be intelligent and sensible to Franky. Franky talks much about this. He says he is convinced from his observations of the war and of human life that the main thing is to make the most of one's self, not to value yourself by comparisons with others but by what you know of your own individual capacities, your personal nature. He says also that the need to possess, both things and other people, exclusively, is crippling to good human relationships and to the development of the species.

He's convinced most human adults do not know how to play anymore and that playing is one of the best ways to think. Franky finds children, by far, much more pleasant and intelligent than most adults, but they are easily ruined by their families, schools, and society. He says one of the ways they are ruined is by being forced to think of all the tasks that need to be done as *work*, not as play. It takes the joy out of living.

He believes schools are usually very dangerous places for children. It's there where they are trained to do as they are told without asking questions. It's there where they are taught that answers are more important than questions. They are taught to remember— memorize—so many answers others think are important that they lose confidence in their own questions. He says it is why he writes children's books, trying to encourage children to play, to trust themselves and their imaginations. Franky feels that trust and tolerance both for self and for others is the basis upon which a good life can be built. It allows for the joy of personal innocence.

Franky believes in imagination, in fantasy, in the value of believing. Some days he'd talk about this, only, for the entire day.

It is very difficult to explain all we are doing. I find I'm looking forward each day to the talks we will have. Talking in Fox is such a joy, and talking with Franky, who invented it, is even more joyful. Wilhelm and I carry on discussions long into the night sometimes and it is very stimulating, but when Franky is there, it is always more lively, more important. He seems able to transfer his enthusiasm, his strength of knowledge to us.

Often we walk through the forest as we talk. We see the animals and they are not afraid of us because they cannot see us. If we come close to a human, we duck back into the forest, even though we are invisible.

Because we are so small, the forest seems very large. Rabbits are large as dogs, small birds large as turkeys. It's amazing how being so small makes everything so much easier to see. It's like seeing the world through a magnifying glass. Our walks are always different and always enjoyable.

At first, Wilhelm and I play some chess or a German card game called *Schafskopf*. In the beginning it's fun, but then we find we enjoy more just talking. Also, as Franky teaches us, the idea of winning becomes unimportant. But still we play sometimes; when no one tries to win, it can be fun.

Also, for the first time, I begin to enjoy chess. It's a lovely game when you don't want to win but only want to see beautiful plays unfold. Sometimes Wilhelm and I would laugh or almost cry at 'some especially convoluted or complicated set of moves. It becomes a way of getting closer to each other rather than, as is so often the case with games, of being pulled apart.

One morning at breakfast, Franky tells us there is something important we should know. Wilhelm and I look at each other, then at Franky.

"The war is over. It has been over here in Europe for several days. The Americans, British, and French have won over the Italians and Germans.

"Wilhelm, you can go straight home when you want. I don't think you will have too much difficulty; there is much confusion. You can go directly home. Your wife is fine. I can get you there quickly and easily. There will be hard times in your country, but remember all we've talked about and try to live a life of love."

I'm amazed at my feelings. I'm very glad the war is over, but I don't like to think of leaving Franky and Wilhelm. I have no parents, I have no one waiting for me when I come back.

"William, with you it will be more difficult. Your country is continuing to war with the Japanese. I do not think that war will last long. Your country has developed a dreadful, powerful weapon that will kill and maim thousands of people.

"But you will have a difficult time explaining where you have been for the last long while. I think it would not be wise to try to go back secretly. It will be best for you to go to some American soldiers here in Europe and tell them what happened. They will not believe you, but insist *that it really did happen, that you lived with Wilhelm and me, just as you remember it. Have faith in me. This will not be an easy thing to do, but it will be best."*

I'm shocked. I sit there not believing it is happening, that this wonderful life we've been living is ending.

"Can't I stay here with you, Franky? I have no one I want to go back to in my country."

"Please, William. One of the reasons I have spent so much time trying to teach you and Wilhelm is so that you can go back and show by example how humans should live. If you stay here with me it would help nothing. Do you understand?"

I nod my head. I do understand. It is one of the things Franky has taught us—how to understand and accept even things we do not want to hear.

"You have both been good companions to me. I am sorry to see you go, too. You must understand that. You gave me much information about humans I needed to know, and I feel I am much closer to your species now. But it must end. I shall take Wilhelm home first, then come back for you, William."

Wilhelm has stood. He holds his head down.

"Thank you for all you've done, Franky. Thank you for saving my life, thank you for helping me be a better human. I will try to live with Riki the kind of life you have described to us. I feel no pain that the war has been lost by my country. It was a war that was not meant to have been won."

He looks up, first at me, then at Franky.

"I shall miss very much our comradeship, these were beautiful days. But I also miss my wife terribly. I shall be very happy, Franky, when you can take me to her again and I can help her through these bad times."

Franky goes over and puts his paw in Wilhelm's hand.

"It was good for all of us, Wilhelm.

"Now, I have cleaned and repaired your uniform. I shall bring it up to you. If there is anything here you might want, take it with you."

Wilhelm looks at me.

"Would it be all right if I took your chessboard and the pieces, as souvenirs of these good times?"

Franky nods his head. Wilhelm leaves the room and goes upstairs.

"Now, William, when I come back I shall give you your uniform, too. I have not cleaned it, purposely. I have brushed it off, but I want you to go back to your people as if you have had very difficult times. Of course, I shall turn you and Wilhelm back to your regular size and make you visible just before we leave one another."

He stares into my eyes.

"Remember, I am counting on you to keep alive this last chance for humans to save themselves. I have a terrible feeling that important things are about to happen that could destroy the entire planet, and it will come from humans."

I stare back into Franky's eyes and try to take strength from him.

That next day Franky and Wilhelm leave. It is painful to see them go. I stay alone in the house, then take a long walk through the familiar forest. It is quiet. Only the animals rustle around me. I've almost forgotten what it is to live in real life. What I remember of it, of my parents' death when I was six years old, of foster parents, orphan asylums, school, then working in a garage until I was drafted—none of it draws me back. I don't want to leave the peace of this place.

When I come back, Franky is already there. I'm so accustomed to the impossible, I don't even question it. We have a quiet meal together. Franky says that Wilhelm is with his wife, and, although things are difficult in Germany, he is in the country, for the time being, and there is food.

When I wake, the next day, my old uniform is at the foot of my bed. I put it on. The cloth seems rough, hard, unbending after the softness of the clothes I've been wearing all these months. Franky is waiting for me downstairs. I have a hard time not begging to stay.

"I know how you are feeling, William. I know all about your life, of course, but, if you live as I've told you, you will know great beauty and it will be a beauty you will have created for yourself. Be brave. You have some difficult times coming first. Remember, don't ever deny me or Wilhelm or all we've had, no matter how great the pressure might be.

"Also, you are an intelligent human with many skills in drawing, and you express yourself well. Yes, I've seen the drawings you have done in private. You should go to a university to study and learn to become a painter, a writer, or perhaps a poet. Since you speak Fox, being a poet will come easily to you."

And those were his last words of advice. By some way I do not yet understand, he transported me to the edge of a field where everything suddenly seemed to get smaller, including Franky himself. It was almost as strange a feeling as being small had been. I realized I was growing larger, coming back to my normal size.

In the distance I could see two American soldiers standing under a bridge along a large autobahn. There were no cars, but people walked along the autobahn with bundles on their shoulders or pulling small carts. Some pushed baby carriages.

"Go to the soldiers and tell who you are. Now good-bye, William. Please don't ever try coming back to my house in the forest. We have had our time and now it is over."

With that, he made himself disappear, and I was alone at the edge of the field. I started across to the soldiers.

And so, dearest, I came back into this world. I was in the hospital a long time. I had no dog tags, but they finally believed I was who I said I was. I had been listed as missing in action, thought to be dead. They'd notified the orphanage, my foster parents. My body had been reported as seen in that hole where I was with Wilhelm, but then the grave registrars had never found it. Now they were convinced I had deserted.

When I told them about being with Franky, all that I'm telling you now, they began to think I was crazy, that the wounds I had received, which they could see from my scars and by X ray and which had somehow miraculously healed, had given me a terrible trauma that had brought on an amnesiac condition. They were convinced I'd made up this whole fantasy to explain to myself the loss of time involved. Either that, or I had deserted.

They sent me back to America, where I was put in a hospital for soldiers who had combat fatigue or were insane. I talked to many psychiatrists and was given many tests. They wanted me to forget what they thought was only a temporary delusion, but I did as Franky told me and insisted.

I was asked by different psychiatrists to tell everything I could remember from being in the bombardment until now. I told them over and over.

One psychiatrist was very kind. I told him every detail, from being pulled under the bridge to being brought to the edge of the field by Franky. He kept saying, "Yes, yes, and then . . . ," so I really thought he was listening to me. I even spoke some Fox for him. He called it "gibberish" and said I had quite an imagination.

Another psychiatrist, a major, accused me of making everything up, that I really *was* a deserter.

But all my tests showed that, except for this delusion, I was normal. I was quite a bit above normal in intelligence, as Franky had told me, and other than my weird story, there was no reason to keep me in a hospital.

The last psychiatrist I saw, before they discharged me with a medical, Section Eight, discharge, told me I would receive a permanent disability pension of 50 percent. Then he paused.

"Come on, now. You've got what you want. Just between us, this whole cockeyed story, although it's imaginative, isn't true, is it? A fox who flies, transmutes matter, has his own language? Nobody could believe that kind of crap. You don't actually believe it now, do you?"

"Yes, but I do, sir. It really happened."

"Are you sure you weren't just wandering around hurt, confused, lost, looking for help and made up this fox in your mind to give you some security?"

"No. Except for when I was unconscious in that German foxhole and then in Franky's house, I know where I was all the time. I've told all about it. It's there in that folder on your desk.

"You know, it's all there. I had terrible wounds, wounds that should have killed me and now they're healed. Doesn't that mean something? I tell you, Franky Furbo healed me."

He closed the folder and pushed himself back.

"I knew the mind was a powerful thing, but this is the most impossible construct I've ever come upon."

And so I was given a Section Eight medical discharge. I was declared 50 percent disabled, mentally. I was let out and given my discharge money and all the back salary for the time I was with Franky Furbo. I had over a thousand dollars. They agreed to send me by train to Los Angeles because it was where I wanted to go. I didn't want to go back to Philadelphia, where I'd had such a terrible life. I wanted to start all over again. I went to UCLA and registered. It was there I met and fell in love with you, Caroline, dearest.

I felt it was only fair to tell you I had a mental medical discharge from the army. I told you all about Franky Furbo and what had happened. I spoke to you in Fox and tried to teach you but found it virtually impossible to teach this beautiful language to a human, even you.

You said you couldn't believe there was anything wrong with

my mind because I did well in my classes. I also told you how I was
an orphan and had no relatives I knew of. But you didn't seem to
mind any of this. We were happy together. I fell more in love with
you every day, and I think you were in love with me.

I decided to study literature, poetry, because I wanted to become a writer; my minor was art. Franky was right, poetry was the
closest thing to Fox, and I could write simple, clear poetry that was
well received because of the paths in my mind that Fox had made.
You were studying business administration and were Phi Beta
Kappa. I was somewhat better than an ordinary student and enjoyed
my classes immensely.

I talked you into living the life with me that Franky had told
me to live. We would do what I'd wanted to do since I had left him,
which was come back to Italy. We came here, and I hunted with
you until we found the area that seemed most like the place where
I had lived with Franky. You agreed to all this. You said you believed
with me in Franky Furbo and all that had happened. It helped me
hold on to the faith I felt I owed him.

I'd saved most of the money I received when I was discharged,
by living in a tent part of the time and then camping in the attic of
the art building. We bought our little house on a hill where we live
now and fixed it up. You know all this.

We've lived here ever since and had our wonderful children,
our beautiful life. I wrote and sold my children's stories, really poems
with simple illustrations. That, along with the pension, was enough
for us. We taught the children ourselves, and everything was as it
should be.

"But I always thought you believed in Franky Furbo, Caroline.
You told me you did. I thought you understood we were carrying
out everything he had told me. Tell me, dearest one, that you believe
me, that for some reason, you've only temporarily forgotten the

reason for our lives. It's so beautiful, so hard to believe it's true, I can understand if you lost faith in it after all these years."

Caroline looks me in the eyes and she's crying. She'd been crying through a good part of the tale, especially when I was most lost in the story, when I was living it all again as if it were right now.

She comes close and puts her hands on both sides of my face. She looks me in the eyes.

"I want to say I believe you, William. But I'd be lying. I've never lied to you and I don't want to lie now. Please, don't make me lie!

"It doesn't matter if I believe you. It just doesn't matter. We love each other and that's all that counts. Can't you see that?"

Caroline kisses me gently, but with felt purpose, on the forehead, then leaves the room.

I sit there and try putting it together. I can't believe Caroline doesn't believe me. Everything my life has seemed to be about is slipping from under me. How could a man delude himself so thoroughly? It just isn't the belief in Franky Furbo, but the seeming delusion of my whole life, everything I believe, all I live by.

I try pulling myself together. If it really *is* true—what the psychiatrists had insisted—then Caroline has every right, in fact, she has an obligation to be honest with me. When I *thought* I was speaking, teaching Fox to her, to the children, perhaps it did sound like gibberish. No wonder they had such a hard time trying to learn.

I try going over in my mind all my memories, try separating what I think I remember and what I've made up. I realize I've been so anxious that Caroline and the children understand, believe, participate in the magic of it all, that I've made up explanations for aspects of Franky I don't understand myself, or which would be almost impossible to explain. I think it's the same with most of the major religions; those who feel responsible for transmitting that which they *know*, that which they *believe*, make up stories to simplify complicated concepts. I'm certain I've done the same with Franky. Maybe it isn't fair or the right thing to do, but it's what seemed right at the time.

Then I remember the book I'd written and illustrated for the children at Christmas almost twenty-five years ago. It was a children's book, just for them. In it I put a good part of what Franky had told Wilhelm and me about the beginnings of his life, how he learned English, how he realized what a special being he was. I also invented simple stories to explain some of his incredible gifts.

Now, I know I wrote this as fiction, just as I write children's stories for children all over the world. But there was something different. For one thing, it was for my children alone. I made only six copies—one for myself, another for Caroline, and one for each of the children. At that time, Billy hadn't yet been born, but I felt, in the way I feel things sometimes, without understanding, that he would come along, and I wanted a copy for him too.

Perhaps by reading this book, I can gain some insights into this self-built mixture of conviction, belief, desire to share, fantasy, and what could be called, just plain lying.

I go upstairs to my writing room and take down my copy from the shelf. I can hear Caroline going about her business cleaning house, washing clothes, downstairs. Billy is outside playing in the haystacks. I sit down in my favorite chair, a big overstuffed job beside my work chair. I open the book and start to read.

THE STORY I

A GOOD TIME AGO, IN THE UMBRIAN HILLS OF ITALY, A FOX WAS BORN. HIS FATHER WAS A GRAY FOX WHO HAD ESCAPED FROM THE

LABORATORY OF A SCIENTIST, AND HIS MOTHER WAS AN ORDINARY RED FOX. THIS BABY FOX WAS PALE PINK WITH A DARKER PINK TAN, AND HAD AMBER-YELLOW-BROWN EYES.

HE HAD ONE BROTHER AND TWO SISTERS WHO WERE BORN AT THE SAME TIME AS HIM, BUT THEY WERE NOT LIKE HIM. THEY WERE GRAY LIKE THEIR FATHER AND NONE OF THEM HAD THE SAME KIND OF EYES.

NOW, THIS LITTLE FOX WAS VERY SPECIAL BECAUSE HE WAS SO INTELLIGENT. HE WAS NOT ONLY EXTREMELY INTELLIGENT FOR A FOX BUT ALSO EXTREMELY INTELLIGENT FOR A HUMAN BEING. HE WAS A MOST EXCEPTIONAL FOX IN MANY WAYS. BUT, AT FIRST, HE DIDN'T REALIZE HE WAS ANY DIFFERENT FROM OTHER FOXES.

IT WAS A STRANGE THING THAT SUCH A SMART FOX SHOULD BE BORN. EVEN HIS MOTHER DIDN'T REALIZE HOW DIFFERENT HER NEW LITTLE FOX WAS. HOW COULD SHE?

MANY PEOPLE THINK FOXES ARE GENERALLY CLEVER, BUT MOST OF THE SMART THINGS FOXES DO ARE DONE BY INSTINCT. AN INSTINCT HELPS YOU DO THINGS WITHOUT THINKING. IT'S AS IF YOU DON'T HAVE ANY CHOICE, AND IT SAVES YOU FROM HAVING TO FIGURE THINGS OUT.

TO BE HONEST, ORDINARY FOXES DON'T THINK VERY MUCH AT ALL. THEY SPEND MOST OF THEIR DAYS TRYING TO CATCH BIRDS AND MICE, OR LITTLE RABBITS, ALMOST ANYTHING THEY CAN EAT. EATING IS ABOUT THE ONLY THING FOXES SEEM TO EVEN *TRY* THINKING ABOUT.

OUR LITTLE FOX, WHO EARLY ON BEGAN CALLING HIMSELF FRANKY JUST BECAUSE HE WANTED A NAME—EVEN THOUGH NO OTHER FOX HE MET EVER *HAD* A NAME—WAS TAUGHT TO HUNT AND HIDE BY HIS MOTHER. HE MET AND PLAYED WITH OTHER FOXES HIS AGE AND HUNTED WITH THEM. IN A CERTAIN WAY HE WAS SLOWER THAN OTHER LITTLE FOXES BECAUSE HE ALWAYS

THOUGHT ABOUT THINGS BEFORE HE DID THEM. IN FACT, THE OTHER FOXES CONSIDERED HIM A BIT STUPID. I'M SURE FRANKY'S MOTHER WORRIED ABOUT HIM. THAT IS, AS MUCH AS FOXES COULD EITHER "CONSIDER" OR "WORRY."

THIS LITTLE FOX SPENT TOO MUCH TIME INVESTIGATING THINGS FOXES HAVE NO BUSINESS BEING CURIOUS ABOUT. HE WAS CONSTANTLY TRYING TO FIND OUT ABOUT THINGS HE NOTICED.

HE WANTED TO KNOW WHY IT WAS DARK SOMETIMES AND LIGHT OTHERS. WHY WAS IT COLDER WHEN IT WAS DARK? WHAT WAS THE BIG BRIGHT BALL ROLLING ACROSS THE SKY? WHAT MADE IT ROLL?

WHY DID THE LEAVES FALL OFF THE TREES, AND WHY WEREN'T LEAVES GOOD TO EAT? WHAT WAS THE DIFFERENCE BE-TWEEN UP AND DOWN? FRANKY HAD THOUSANDS OF QUESTIONS, BUT THERE WAS NO ONE TO ANSWER HIM. FOXES DON'T ASK QUESTIONS; ACTUALLY, THEY HARDLY EVEN TALK. THEY HAVE WAYS OF SAYING YES OR NO TO ONE ANOTHER AND A WAY TO SHOW THEY ARE MAD OR SAD, AND THAT'S ABOUT ALL. FOXES AREN'T MUCH FOR CONVERSATION. IT IS ALSO CONSIDERED VERY UNFOX-LIKE TO WASTE TIME THINKING ABOUT THINGS THAT AREN'T GOOD TO EAT. FOXES DON'T EVEN HAVE ANY IDEA ABOUT WHAT "TIME" IS; TO A FOX, EVERYTHING JUST RUNS TOGETHER IN ONE BIG CLUMP.

CONCERNING THINGS TO EAT—THE FAVORITE FOOD OF THE FOXES ON THIS PARTICULAR HILL WAS THE CHICKENS IN THE CHICKEN YARD OF A FARMER WHO LIVED IN THE VALLEY ON THE WAY TO TOWN. ALTHOUGH ONE MUST ADMIT THAT CHICKENS ARE DELICIOUS, IT WAS A VERY DANGEROUS KIND OF FOOD FOR THESE FOXES. YOU SEE, THIS FARMER WAS A CLEVER FELLOW, FAR CLEV-ERER THAN THE FOXES ON THE HILL, EXCEPT FOR FRANKY, OF COURSE. HE DIDN'T INTEND THAT FOXES SHOULD GROW FAT ON HIS CHICKENS.

MORE OFTEN THAN NOT, HE CAUGHT THE FOXES IN HIS TRAPS AND SHOT THEM WITH HIS GUN, OR HIS DOGS KILLED THEM. SOME-TIMES, HOWEVER, BECAUSE FOXES ARE REALLY QUITE GOOD AT THAT KIND OF THING, AND BECAUSE THERE WERE SO MANY CHICK-ENS, A FOX WOULD COME BACK WITH A FULL STOMACH AND PER-HAPS AN EXTRA CHICKEN IN HIS MOUTH.

NOW FOXES AREN'T GOOD AT COUNTING EITHER. THEY NEVER

KNEW HOW MANY FOXES WERE REALLY LIVING ON THE HILL. WHEN A FOX SNUCK OFF FOR A CHICKEN AND DIDN'T COME BACK, IT WAS HARDLY NOTICED. IF QUITE A FEW FOXES WERE BEING CAUGHT, I THINK THE ONLY THING THE OTHER FOXES MIGHT NOTICE WOULD BE THAT THERE WERE MORE WILD MICE, RABBITS, AND BIRDS TO GO AROUND.

IF SOME FOX THEY DID KNOW, PERSONALLY (I GUESS THAT SHOULD BE "FOXILY"), DISAPPEARED, OR THEY EVEN SAW HIM SHOT OR CAUGHT IN A TRAP OR TORN TO PIECES BY THE DOGS, THEY FORGOT ABOUT IT ALMOST IMMEDIATELY. FOXES DON'T HAVE VERY GOOD MEMORIES, ESPECIALLY ABOUT THINGS THEY DON'T WANT TO BELIEVE.

HOWEVER, ON THE OCCASION WHEN SOME FOX CAME BACK FULL OF CHICKEN AND LICKING HIS WHISKERS, THE OTHER FOXES KNEW ABOUT IT RIGHT AWAY. THIS FOX WOULD STRUT ALL OVER THE HILL. THIS WAS THE KIND OF THING THAT WAS HARD TO FOR-GET, EVEN FOR A FOX. SO, THE POOR FOXES KEPT SNEAKING DOWN AT NIGHT TO CATCH CHICKENS AND WERE MORE OFTEN CAUGHT THEMSELVES.

NOW, FRANKY LEARNED TO COUNT QUITE EARLY, AND HE WAS *ALWAYS* NOTICING THINGS. ONE OF THE THINGS HE NOTICED WAS HOW MANY OF HIS FOX NEIGHBORS WOULD SEEM TO DISAP-PEAR IN THE NIGHT. ONE DAY THEY WERE THERE, THE NEXT, THEY WEREN'T.

HE TRIED ASKING HIS MOTHER ABOUT THIS, AND ALTHOUGH HE WAS PROBABLY THE FIRST FOX IN THE WORLD TO FIGURE OUT HOW TO ASK A QUESTION IN FOX, HIS MOTHER COULDN'T UNDER-STAND AND SO JUST BRUSHED HIM AWAY WITH HER BIG BUSHY RED TAIL. FRANKY CRAWLED INTO A CORNER OF THE DEN AND BROODED.

ONE NIGHT, FRANKY WENT OUT ON THE TRAIL LEADING TO THE CHICKEN YARD. HE COUNTED SIXTEEN FOXES WHO WENT

DOWN ALONG THE PATH TRYING FOR A FREE CHICKEN DINNER. BY MORNING, ONLY SEVEN HAD COME BACK, AND THREE OF THOSE HAD ONLY ESCAPED WITH THEIR LIVES, BUT NO CHICKEN.

FRANKY RAN ALL THE WAY HOME AND TRIED AGAIN TO TELL HIS MOTHER, BUT SHE ONLY BRUSHED HIM HARDER WITH HER BIG TAIL. WHAT DOES SIXTEEN MEAN TO A FOX WHO CAN'T COUNT PAST TWO? ONE COULD SAY IT WAS EIGHT TWOS, BUT THEN WHAT'S EIGHT? IT WAS MOST DISCOURAGING TO FRANKY.

HE MADE MARKS ON THE FLOOR. HE GATHERED PEBBLES IN HIS MOUTH AND PILED THEM IN THE CENTER OF THE DEN, TRYING TO SHOW HIS MOTHER WHAT SIXTEEN WAS. ALL HE GOT WAS A GOOD SHOVE OUT THE DOOR. HIS MOTHER GROWLED AND BRUSHED THE FLOOR OF HER DEN NEAT AND CLEAN AGAIN. WHAT WAS SHE GOING TO DO WITH THIS LITTLE KIT OF HERS WHO SCRATCHED THE FLOOR OF THE DEN AND DROPPED PEBBLES IN THE MIDDLE? SHE WAS MOST DISCOURAGED. YOU CAN IMAGINE HOW DISHEARTENED OUR LITTLE FRANKY WAS.

THE NEXT EVENING, FRANKY INSISTED HIS MOTHER COME WITH HIM TO SIT BY THE TRAIL AND WATCH THE FOXES GO DOWN TO THE CHICKEN FARM. HIS MOTHER DIDN'T WANT TO GO BUT SHE REALLY DID LOVE HER STRANGE LITTLE KIT DEARLY AND WENT ALONG TO HUMOR HIM.

IT WAS A LOVELY STARRY NIGHT. EACH TIME A FOX PASSED ON THE WAY TO THE FARM, FRANKY GATHERED ANOTHER PEBBLE AND PUT IT AT HIS MOTHER'S FEET. HE TRIED TO CALL HER AT-TENTION TO THE PEBBLES BUT HE HAD A DIFFICULT TIME. WHEN-EVER A SOFT EVENING BREEZE BLEW, THE DELICIOUS SMELL OF CHICKEN CAME WAFTING UP THE HILL. HIS MOTHER WANTED TO DASH DOWN TO THE FARM HERSELF.

BY THE TIME IT WAS REALLY DARK, ONLY ELEVEN FOXES HAD PASSED. THERE WERE GETTING TO BE LESS AND LESS FOXES LIVING ON THE HILL. FRANKY'S MOTHER WANTED TO GO HOME. SHE WAS

TIRED OF WATCHING ALL THIS BUSINESS WITH THE PEBBLES. NO
MATTER HOW OFTEN FRANKY POINTED TO HIS PILE, IT DIDN'T
MEAN ANYTHING. SHE JUST COULDN'T UNDERSTAND. ONE TIME
SHE PUT HER NOSE DOWN TO THE PEBBLES AND LICKED ONE OF
THEM, TRYING TO BE AGREEABLE AND PERHAPS PROVING TO
FRANKY THAT YOU CAN'T MAKE CHICKEN OUT OF PEBBLES, BUT
THEN SHE GAVE UP AND, WITH A LONG SIGH, SETTLED DOWN.

IT WAS ABOUT AN HOUR LATER WHEN THE FIRST OF THE SUC-
CESSFUL HUNTERS CAME BACK. UNFORTUNATELY, HE CARRIED AN
EXTRA CHICKEN IN HIS MOUTH. FRANKY PICKED ONE PEBBLE OUT
OF THE PILE TO SHOW THAT ONE FOX HAD COME BACK. HE LOOKED
OVER AT HIS MOTHER TO SEE IF SHE UNDERSTOOD WHAT HE WAS
DOING. BUT SHE WAS STANDING UP HIGH AND HER LONG FOX NOSE
WAS QUIVERING. BEFORE FRANKY COULD MOVE, SHE'D DASHED
DOWN THE HILL TOWARD THE CHICKEN FARM! FRANKY BARKED
AND TRIED TO FOLLOW, BUT SHE WAS TOO FAST. HE PUT ONE MORE
PEBBLE ONTO HIS PILE. IT WAS THE PEBBLE FOR HIS MOTHER.

FRANKY WAITED ALL THAT NIGHT, AND SIX MORE FOXES
CAME BACK BUT NOT ONE OF THEM WAS HIS MOTHER. HE ASKED
EVERY FOX IF THEY'D SEEN HER, BUT NO FOX WANTED TO ADMIT
THAT FOXES WENT DOWN TO GET CHICKENS AND DIDN'T COME
BACK. IT WAS TOO MUCH TO THINK ABOUT.

AND SO THIS WAS HOW FRANKY LOST HIS MOTHER. HE'D LOST
HIS FATHER BEFORE HE WAS BORN. EITHER HIS FATHER HAD BEEN
CAUGHT BY THE FARMER, TOO, OR HE'D JUST FORGOTTEN ABOUT
FRANKY AND HIS MOTHER. REMEMBER, FOXES HAVE TERRIBLE
MEMORIES.

THE NEXT DAYS WERE VERY SAD FOR FRANKY. HIS BROTHERS
AND SISTERS DIDN'T SEEM TO MISS THEIR MOTHER AT ALL. THEY
JUST HUNTED AND HID AND PLAYED WITH THE OTHER FOXES.
FRANKY KEPT HOPING HIS MOTHER WOULD COME BACK, BUT SHE
NEVER DID. FINALLY HE ACCEPTED THAT SHE NEVER WOULD, THAT
SHE'D PROBABLY BEEN KILLED BY THE FARMER.

FRANKY DECIDED HE COULDN'T LIVE WITH FOXES ANYMORE;
IT WAS TOO SAD. IT WAS TERRIBLE SEEING HIS MOTHER, HIS
FRIENDS, HIS SISTERS AND BROTHERS KILLED BECAUSE THEY WERE
SO STUPID, AND HE KNEW HE COULD DO NOTHING TO HELP THEM.
HE'D TRIED SO HARD WITH HIS MOTHER, AND LOOK WHAT HAD
HAPPENED.

THE WARREN

ONE MORNING, BEFORE THE SUN WAS UP, FRANKY LEFT THE HILL
AND WALKED WELL AROUND THE CHICKEN FARM AND UP ONTO
ANOTHER HILL WHERE THERE WAS A GREAT FOREST. HE WALKED
DEEP INTO THE FOREST UNTIL HE FOUND A LARGE HOLLOW TREE.
HE CLIMBED INSIDE, INVESTIGATED, AND DECIDED HE WAS GOING
TO BUILD HIS HOUSE INSIDE THIS TREE. HE DIDN'T WANT TO LIVE
IN THE DAMP GROUND ANYMORE; IT WAS TOO WET AND DARK. HE
DIDN'T REALLY KNOW HOW HE WAS GOING TO DO IT, BUT HE WAS
DETERMINED TO TRY LIVING IN THE TREE ABOVE THE GROUND. IT
WAS THE BEGINNING OF A NEW LIFE.

I put down the book and remember with such pleasure how much
fun it was for the children when I gave them the book, how much
I'd enjoyed writing and illustrating it. This entire part I knew was
from the stories that Franky had actually told to Wilhelm and me
when we were living in his tree house. Franky made us feel how
sorry he'd been losing his mother, the strangeness of being so different from his brothers, sisters, the other foxes. He transmitted to
us his deep sense of loss, estrangement, when he moved away from
the foxes and decided to live another kind of life, so different from
that of the foxes. He felt he was a stranger to the entire world. I
look at the illustrations and pick up the book again.

FRANKY HOPED TO BUILD HIS NEW HOUSE IN THE TREE WITH
FOUR FLOORS. HE WANTED WINDOWS LOOKING OUT THE SIDE OF
THE TREE ON EACH FLOOR AND LITTLE LADDERS GOING FROM ONE
LEVEL TO THE OTHER. HE THOUGHT HE'D USE THE GROUND FLOOR
FOR STORAGE. ON THE SECOND FLOOR HE'D HAVE HIS LIVING AND
DINING ROOMS, AND ON THE THIRD FLOOR HE'D SLEEP. HE WOULD
RESERVE THE TOP FLOOR FOR THINKING.

FRANKY WASN'T EXACTLY SURE WHAT IT WAS TO THINK, BUT HE KNEW IT WAS THE THING HE MOST LIKED TO DO, SO HE WANTED A SPECIAL ROOM JUST FOR THINKING. HE DIDN'T EVEN KNOW THE WORD FOR THINK, NOR, FOR THAT MATTER, DID HE HAVE WORDS FOR ANYTHING—HOUSES, LADDERS, WINDOWS—BECAUSE HE COULDN'T *REALLY* TALK MUCH YET. IT JUST GOES TO PROVE YOU DON'T NEED WORDS TO KNOW THINGS. BUT THEY DO HELP.

NOW THE PROBLEM WAS THAT EVEN THOUGH FRANKY COULD KNOW THESE THINGS, HE DIDN'T HAVE THE FIRST IDEA HOW TO BUILD THEM. HE WAS SURE, TOO, NO FOX OR ANY OTHER ANIMAL HE'D EVER MET KNEW HOW TO MAKE THEM EITHER. FRANKY THOUGHT ABOUT THIS FOR TWO DAYS.

THEN HE HEADED BACK DOWN THE HILL TOWARD THE FARMER'S HOUSE—NOT TO CATCH A CHICKEN; HE WAS TOO SMART FOR THAT. FRANKY'S IDEA WAS IF THE FARMER COULD BE CLEVER ENOUGH TO CATCH THE FOXES, AND CLEVERER YET TO HAVE ALL THOSE CHICKENS FOR HIMSELF, HE MIGHT JUST BE SMART ENOUGH TO KNOW HOW TO BUILD A HOUSE WITH FOUR FLOORS, FOUR WINDOWS, AND THREE LADDERS.

IT WAS NIGHT WHEN FRANKY WENT SOFTLY DOWN THE HILL. HE STAYED FAR AWAY FROM THE CHICKENS, WHERE THERE WERE TRAPS AND DOGS. HE CREPT CAREFULLY UP TO THE HOUSE WHERE THE FARMER LIVED. HE SCRAMBLED INTO A TREE AND LOOKED THROUGH A WINDOW. ALREADY HE'D FOUND TWO OF THE THINGS HE WAS LOOKING FOR—A HOUSE AND A WINDOW. HIS QUICK LITTLE FOX MIND MEMORIZED ALL THE DETAILS.

INSIDE, THERE WAS LIGHT COMING FROM A BRIGHT BALL, A BALL LIKE THE ONE IN THE SKY, ONLY SMALLER. THERE WERE BIG HAIRLESS ANIMALS IN THE HOUSE WHO WALKED ON THEIR BACK LEGS! FRANKY ALMOST FELL OUT OF THE TREE.

HE SAW MORE THINGS INSIDE THAT HOUSE THAN HE COULD

EVER HAVE DREAMED. HE FELT LIKE A VERY DUMB LITTLE FOX INDEED. FRANKY STAYED UNTIL THEY STOPPED THE LITTLE BRIGHT BALL AND NO ONE MOVED ANYMORE, THEN HE WENT HOME.

THE NEXT DAY HE WISHED HE HAD HIS NEW HOUSE FINISHED WITH HIS TOP FLOOR FOR THINKING BECAUSE HE HAD *MUCH* THINKING TO DO. IT WAS SO COMPLICATED FOR A LITTLE FOX TO UNDERSTAND.

EVERY EVENING HE WENT DOWN AND WATCHED. EVEN IN THE DAY HE SAT ON THE SIDE OF THE HILL AND WATCHED THE FARMER AND HIS SON WORK IN THE YARD WITH THE CHICKENS. FRANKY LEARNED MANY THINGS.

THE FIRST THING HE LEARNED WAS HOW TO BUILD HIS HOUSE. WITH HIS SHARP TEETH HE FASHIONED TOOLS FROM HARD-WOOD AND NAILS HE FOUND IN THE FARMER'S SHED. WITH THESE, HE CUT AND SMOOTHED BOARDS FROM TREES. IT WAS QUITE DIF-FICULT WORK AND TOOK A LONG TIME. A FOX'S TINY PAWS ARE NOT REALLY MADE FOR THAT KIND OF THING.

SOMETIMES FRANKY, WORKING BY HIMSELF, GOT DISCOUR-AGED. HE DISCOVERED ALSO WHY MEN STOOD ALL THE TIME ON THEIR HIND LEGS; IT WAS TO KEEP THEIR HANDS FREE SO THEY COULD WORK.

FRANKY'S BACK WOULD BE SO SORE AT NIGHT HE COULD HARDLY SLEEP. FINALLY, HOWEVER, AFTER MONTHS OF WORK HE HAD THE JOB FINISHED. ALSO, HIS BACK HAD STOPPED HURT-ING, AND NOW HE WALKED ON HIS HIND LEGS MOST OF THE TIME.

HE HAD SCRAPED DOWN THE INSIDE OF THE HOLLOW TREE WITH HIS TOOLS AND WITH HIS CLAWS SO THE SIDES WERE QUITE SMOOTH. THEN HE'D INSERTED STRONG LENGTHS OF WOOD TO

HOLD UP EACH OF THE FLOORS. ACROSS THESE HE'D FASTENED
THE FLOORBOARDS. BETWEEN EACH FLOOR HE'D LEFT A HOLE AND
THEN CAREFULLY CUT A LITTLE LADDER STAIRCASE FITTING
AGAINST THE SIDE OF THE TREE.

AFTERWARD, HE CUT SMALL HOLES IN THE TREE ON EACH
FLOOR FOR HIS WINDOWS AND DESIGNED SHUTTERS OUT OF BARK
SO THEY COULD BE CLOSED AND HIDDEN. HE ALSO BUILT A DOOR

WITH A BARK COVERING, WHICH SWUNG ON TINY LEATHER HINGES BETWEEN THE SPREADING ROOTS OF THE TREE.

ALL TOGETHER, FRANKY WAS MOST PLEASED WITH HIS HOUSE. NOW HE HAD A PLACE TO STORE, A PLACE TO REST OR EAT, A PLACE TO SLEEP, AND HIS PRIVATE ROOM TO THINK. WHAT MORE COULD A SMART LITTLE FOX WANT?

BUT FRANKY WAS LEARNING MANY NEW THINGS. HE WATCHED THE MEN SIT AROUND A HOLE IN THE SIDE OF THEIR HOUSE, AND THEY SEEMED HAPPY. FRANKY WANTED TO KNOW WHY.

ONE NIGHT, AFTER ALL WERE ASLEEP, FRANKY CRAWLED IN THROUGH AN OPEN CELLAR WINDOW AND WAS INSIDE THE HOUSE OF THE MEN. HE WAS VERY SCARED. HE CAREFULLY WENT ACROSS THE CELLAR FLOOR AND UP THE LARGE STAIRS INTO THE BIG ROOM. IT WAS WARM AND SMELLED OF FOOD AND MEN. THERE WERE MANY THINGS HE WANTED TO TOUCH AND EXPLORE, BUT HE SCURRIED ACROSS TO THE HOLE IN THE WALL.

ORANGE, YELLOW, AND RED—SOMETHING DANCED OUT OF THE WOOD IN THE HOLE AND WAS WARM. FRANKY TRIED TO TAKE SOME IN HIS HAND AND ALMOST HOWLED FROM THE PAIN. THIS WAS FIRE. IT WAS THE FIRST TIME FRANKY HAD SEEN ANY. HE CAME CLOSE AND LOOKED AT THE SMOKE GOING UP THE CHIMNEY. HE WENT OUTSIDE AGAIN AND CLIMBED ONTO THE ROOF. HE WATCHED THE SMOKE COMING OUT. FRANKY KNEW THIS WAS A THING HE MUST HAVE IN HIS HOUSE—FIRE. IT WOULD BE NICE TO BE WARM, EVEN IN THE WINTER.

IT WAS A TRICKY THING TO CONSTRUCT. FRANKY USED SOME OLD TIN CANS, WHICH HE CHEWED AND BENT INTO THE CORRECT SHAPE. THEN HE CAREFULLY PILED STONES AROUND THE CANS. IN THIS WAY, HE MADE THREE CHARMING LITTLE FIREPLACES, ONE FOR EACH FLOOR, EXCEPT THE GROUND FLOOR, WHERE HE STORED HIS FOOD. HE ALSO BUILT A CHIMNEY, WHICH CAME OUT HIGH IN

THE TREE WHERE NO ONE BUT THE SQUIRRELS COULD SEE THE
SMOKE. FRANKY PUT WOOD IN EACH OF HIS FIREPLACES AND CARE-
FULLY CARRIED HOT COALS FROM THE FIRE IN THE MEN'S HOUSE.
HE VERY QUICKLY LEARNED TO BUILD AND KEEP HIS LITTLE FIRES
BURNING. NOW HIS HOUSE WAS COZY AND WARM. HIS FIREPLACES
DIDN'T SMOKE AT ALL.

NEXT, FRANKY BUILT SMALL PIECES OF FURNITURE—A CHAIR, A TABLE, AND A TINY SOFA, JUST RIGHT FOR A FOX. FRANKY EVEN WENT SO FAR AS TO LEARN HOW TO SIT AT THE TABLE AND EAT. HE WANTED *SO* MUCH TO BE LIKE A MAN. YOU SEE, FRANKY HAD BEEN THINKING UP IN HIS THINKING ROOM, AND THIS IS WHAT HE THOUGHT:

FOXES ONLY DID THINGS THEY ALREADY KNEW HOW TO DO. THEY DIDN'T TRY TO LEARN NEW THINGS AT ALL. THAT WAS WHY SO MANY OF THEM WERE KILLED WHEN THEY TRIED TO CATCH CHICKENS. THE FARMER ALWAYS KNEW WHAT FOXES WERE GOING TO DO, BECAUSE FOXES DIDN'T CHANGE. IT WAS EASY FOR THE FARMER TO CATCH THE FOXES.

FRANKY WATCHED THE FARMER AND HIS FAMILY. THEY WERE CONSTANTLY DOING DIFFERENT THINGS. MORE IMPORTANT, THEY DID THESE THINGS TOGETHER; THEY HELPED ONE ANOTHER. FOXES HARDLY EVER DID ANYTHING TO HELP ONE ANOTHER.

MEN ATE THE SAME FOOD TOGETHER AND DIDN'T FIGHT OVER IT. FOXES COULD *NEVER* DO THAT. MEN MADE QUIET NOISES TO ONE ANOTHER ALL THE TIME, AND IT SEEMED TO MAKE THEM HAPPY. FRANKY WAS SURE THEY WERE ASKING QUESTIONS AND ANSWERING THEM.

THERE WAS A TALKING BOX THAT ASKED AND ANSWERED QUESTIONS, AND ANOTHER SOFT BOX, WHICH OPENED, FROM WHICH ONE COULD BOTH ASK AND ANSWER QUESTIONS. THE FARMER OFTEN SAT IN FRONT OF THEIR FIRE. HE'D PUT HIS FINGER IN THE BOX AND MAKE QUESTIONS FOR THE OTHERS.

FRANKY WANTED MORE THAN ANYTHING ELSE TO DO THESE THINGS. HE HAD SO MANY QUESTIONS. EVERY NIGHT HE LISTENED, BUT HE COULD UNDERSTAND NOTHING. FRANKY THOUGHT MUCH ABOUT THIS. HE WANTED TO HAVE ONE OF THE BOXES, SO HE DECIDED TO TAKE ONE. FRANKY WAS STILL TOO MUCH A FOX TO

KNOW THIS WOULD BE STEALING. FOR A FOX, STEALING IS AS NAT-
URAL AS TALKING IS FOR YOU AND ME.

THE NEXT NIGHT, FRANKY TOOK ONE OF THE LITTLE BOXES.
IT WAS A CHILDREN'S BOOK ABOUT FARM ANIMALS. BACK UP IN HIS
THINKING ROOM NEXT MORNING, FRANKY TURNED THE PAGES
AND LOOKED AT THE PICTURES. IT WAS A KIND OF MAGIC. HE SAW
LITTLE ANIMALS, ANIMALS HE KNEW, LIKE CHICKENS AND THE
COW, ONLY THEY WERE FLAT. HE'D TURN A PAGE AND THE
CHICKEN OR COW WOULD DISAPPEAR. THERE WAS ALSO A PICTURE
OF A FARMER AND A HOUSE. FRANKY STUDIED THE PICTURES CARE-
FULLY.

FRANKY PUT HIS PAW ON THE BOOK AND OPENED HIS MOUTH,
BUT NO QUESTIONS OR ANSWERS CAME. HE COULDN'T UNDER-
STAND WHAT HE WAS DOING WRONG, WHY HE COULDN'T MAKE
THE PICTURES TALK AS THE FARMER DID.

HE SPENT THE ENTIRE DAY LOOKING AT THE BOOK AND
TRYING TO MAKE QUESTIONS OR ANSWERS, BUT NOTHING HAP-
PENED. HE WAS SURE IT HAD SOMETHING TO DO WITH THE LITTLE
BLACK MARKS NEAR THE PICTURES. FRANKY RAN HIS PAWS OVER
THOSE MARKS AND EVEN TRIED LICKING THEM ONCE, THE WAY
HIS MOTHER DID THE PEBBLES, BUT IT DIDN'T HELP.

THAT NIGHT HE TOOK THE BOOK BACK AND PUT IT WHERE
HE'D FOUND IT. THIS WAS A WONDERFUL THING FOR A FOX TO DO.
FOXES NEVER GIVE THINGS BACK. FRANKY WAS CERTAINLY AN EX-
CEPTIONAL FOX.

THE NEXT DAY, FRANKY THOUGHT FROM MORNING TO
NIGHT; HE EVEN FORGOT TO EAT. THIS IS SOMETHING FOXES
HARDLY EVER FORGET. HE DECIDED THERE WAS ONLY ONE THING
TO DO. HE MUST ASK HIS QUESTIONS TO ONE OF THE MEN. OF
COURSE, HE COULD ASK HIS QUESTIONS ONLY IN FOX, HIS OWN
PERSONAL LANGUAGE, WHICH NOBODY IN THE WHOLE WORLD
COULD UNDERSTAND EXCEPT FRANKY. IT WOULDN'T HELP AT ALL.

BUT WHAT ELSE COULD HE DO? HE DECIDED TO ASK HIS QUESTIONS TO THE LITTLEST MAN, WHO WAS ACTUALLY A SMALL SEVEN-YEAR-OLD GIRL NAMED LUCIA.

Again I look up from my reading. It's interesting to me how I'm not only translating from Fox as Franky had told the stories to us, but I'm translating from "adult" to "child," trying to make his fantastic accomplishments seem real to my kids by using the language reserved for them by adults when telling stories. Perhaps I should have tried telling the story more naturally, but this was twenty-five years ago and they were very young. I was too. But still, all that's in this book so far is close to the tales Franky told us of his beginnings.

I look up. Caroline has come quietly into the room. She sits in my work chair at my desk.

I close the book. Caroline's only looking at me, watching to see how I'm reacting. I smile.

"I thought I might discover some things I don't understand."

"And what did you find, William?"

She's crying. It's the first time I've noticed. She has a way of crying without making any noise, only the tears roll down the outside of her face. I go over to her.

"I find I *still* believe in Franky Furbo, Caroline. I also realize how some of this story and the stories I told the children aren't true. So Billy was right, or at least partly right, when he said he didn't believe in Franky Furbo anymore. I must explain myself, apologize to him. Most of what he knows about Franky Furbo, through me, *isn't* necessarily true; it just seems that way to me.

"The same with you, dearest. It's been so long since we've talked about the *real* Franky Furbo, you must have thought I was insane asking you to believe these wild, fantastic stories I made up. It wasn't fair to you, and I'm sorry."

I've begun crying myself. I want to tell her what I believe without being too emotional, but I can't help myself.

"But, dearest one, that doesn't mean there *isn't* a Franky Furbo. I still believe in him, probably always will. I don't have any choice, he's so much a part of me. I hope you'll try to understand."

CHAPTER 5

A SUGGESTION

Caroline stares at me a minute, her eyes still wet with tears. Then, without a word, she puts her hand gently on my head, holds it there, looking all the while in my eyes.

"Dearest William, I'm going to give Billy his lessons now; I'll close the door behind me. You just sit here and think some more. Remember, I do love you, and I never said you shouldn't continue to believe in Franky Furbo. He means very much to you and I know it."

She stands, walks past me and out of the room. I go back to my chair, hold the book on my lap. I take a deep breath and try looking inside myself. What kind of creature am I?

I remember how much the children loved this book when I gave it to them so long ago. Now, already, the pages have begun to yellow on my copy. I wonder if the other children have kept their copies, if they ever look at them. I know Billy has his and usually pulls it out to read just before Christmas, the way I like to read *'Twas the Night Before Christmas* and *A Child's Christmas in Wales*.

English is our family language. Because of Franky, I can still speak Bavarian German, but I'll never be good with Italian, even after all these years. It's a family joke. I'm sort of the family's private village idiot.

Caroline speaks beautiful Italian and has taught the children. I've taught them German. Caroline learned to speak German when I taught the children, so we have three languages in the family. Four if you count Fox. But, I really don't think any one of them believe Fox is an actual language. They keep asking me to *write* something in Fox, but Fox is so dependent on small movements, tips of the head, movements of the eyes, the mouth, the way you hold your mouth, even wiggle your nose, and intonations of the voice, it would be impossible for it to be put down in the little marks people learn to read.

Probably the only way there could ever be a "literature" in Fox would be to have people tell stories, read poetry, perform plays, on film, or on videotapes.

Franky Furbo, himself, claimed the printing press was most likely more responsible for severe limitations in virtually every written language than any other invention by man. This is because it quickly narrows any language so only those aspects that can be translated into print survive.

He could be right. Living language is real sounds, real words, the whole essence of one being trying to communicate thought to another.

There I go, believing in Franky again, assuming he really is. *He is!* How is it I know German if it weren't for Franky? I'm terrible at languages. It's because of me, my trouble learning Italian, more than anything else, that we speak English at home. My German is limited to the German Wilhelm knew when he was nineteen years old and had only *Überschule* experience. I feel tied to it and don't like to read it. I imagine that's because Wilhelm himself didn't like to read books, and when I speak German, in some strange way I *become* Wilhelm. The kids have never liked it when I speak to them in German because I'm not myself. And none of them, not even Caroline, are ever comfortable with my Fox. All the face twisting and movements just look silly to them.

I always write my children's stories in English. It's still my home language even after more than forty years here in Italy. I don't have any of them translated into Italian, even though my agent in New York has a publisher for them in Milan. One of the reasons is I want to keep my privacy. The other is, I feel Franky Furbo wouldn't be happy if I did this. I write with a pseudonym. As a tribute to my teacher, I use the name Franky Furbo on my children's books.

But now I've got to think more about this story I wrote that Christmas long ago. As I said, all the parts dealing with Franky's birth, his moving away from the other foxes, building his house in the tree, sneaking down to watch the farmer's family, imitating them— all those parts I know Franky told me as much as I know anything.

I left out all the business about how Franky could read minds, how he could transfer things from one mind to another, the way he did with Wilhelm and me. I thought it was just too much for them then. When they were older, I told them those parts.

I sit there in my chair and look over the illustrations. They're much different from the way I usually illustrate the stories I write now. The people who sell children's books today want globs of color and simple fuzzy drawings, but I knew this wasn't the way Kathleen, Matthew, and little Camilla would want to see Franky—clearly but not realistically.

So, now I have to decide whether Franky Furbo is only a myth, a fantasy I'd constructed to give some meaning to my life at a time when all meaning seemed to have been taken away from me. Or is he a real experience, an unbelievable experience, an experience I can never even completely understand myself? I can't help but think of the prophets in all religions, disciples, who had these kinds of overwhelming experiences and tried to pass them on to others. It can be so discouraging.

Am I, as Caroline insists, like a child who cannot let go of unbelievable stories, a mental cripple, as the U.S. Army medical authorities insisted? Am I trapped in a delusion, an unsustainable delusion, which is ruining my life and the lives of those around me? It's difficult to accept. I realize that deep inside me I'm dependent on this "myth," Franky Furbo, as my reason for living, just as any fanatic is convinced in a particular God or political system as a reason for life, something worth more than life itself.

But, I don't *feel* crazy. I like very much the life we live. I think Caroline and the children like it too. So what if our first child is probably married, in all practical senses, to our second one? They're old enough. Caroline is convinced Camilla is only waiting for little Billy to grow up so he can join her, too. Camilla's probably up there in northern Japan getting the nest ready.

We *have* lived special lives, all of us so close, but isn't that the way a good life is supposed to be? Am I so wrapped up in the things I think Franky told me I can't think for myself anymore? Am I a menace to the ones I love most?

I know I changed my Franky Furbo stories according to the ages of the different children and to their different natures. For a while there, Franky was sort of a Sherlock Holmes of the forest. People and animals of all kinds would come to him for help. There was a while there that he worked with a detective snake in New Mexico named Sam Sidewinder. This was related to the stories an artist friend of mine, Morris Byrd, told. He came to Perugia with his children and told them about this snake. Sam Sidewinder was the hero of all his stories. But I don't think Morris really believed in Sam Sidewinder, and he didn't insist his children did. They were only stories.

Then there was a policeman in Paris, Monsieur Le Blanc. He was constantly contacting Franky for help in international crime cases. Sometimes the stories would go on for a long time, continuing from morning to morning. Other times it would only be stories about animals in the forest, the kinds of stories I write professionally, for other children.

Then there were always trolls and witches, fairies, elves, dwarfs, monsters—all those mysterious creatures. There were some stories along the lines of science fiction, when people would come to Franky from other planets or other solar systems or other times. The kids loved those. I know I was teaching them with the stories. There was usually built in, somehow, some kind of idea I wanted them to think about.

All I would start with was a title: *Franky Furbo and*. . . . The story would take off by itself. I didn't feel as if I were telling it myself at all; I listened to the stories with as much interest as the children did. These stories came into my head from nowhere. It really was as if Franky Furbo *were* telling them. This was why I thought it was all right to try keeping Franky Furbo alive as a real fox, somebody who truly existed, and that Franky wouldn't mind my insisting these were *his* stories and were true.

I know all this sounds crazy. I sit. I can hear Caroline downstairs again, probably cooking up lunch. School time must be over. She manages to teach with such joy and effectiveness, it's always been the highlight of the day for our kids, being with her and learning. I'd sort of light the torch with our Franky Furbo story and then she'd take over. I really can't understand why she doesn't believe in Franky, or maybe even more, I can't believe I thought she believed all these years when she didn't.

I go down to lunch with Caroline and Billy. Billy is very excited about a small turbine he's building, using a stream that runs beside the house. I don't really feel like talking much myself but I listen to him. He's got it fairly well worked out. I give him a few suggestions.

Caroline is watching me. Whenever I look over at her, she looks down at her soup. I can feel she's as concerned about our morning discussion as I am myself. Maybe she's going to insist I go see a psychiatrist or something like that. I don't really think it would do much good. I had enough of that kind of treatment when I came home, when I was only twenty years old.

After lunch, I go back up to my workroom. I look at the story I'm working on. The text is finished; it's about a robin mother teaching her children how to listen for worms with their feet and about one of her children who doesn't like worms. It all ends up with that little robin becoming an Italian robin and learning to cook and eat spaghetti. He eats strands of spaghetti as if they were worms.

I've started on the illustrations. I have two other stories I'm working up. One is about a tree that's forgotten how to grow and is gradually turning into a bush. I'm not sure just where it's going to go. The other is about a canary who escapes and has experiences with the other birds. They're jealous of his yellow color and the way he can sing. He's looking for kinds of foods he can eat and for kinds of birds with whom he can live. I have a canary in my workroom here. His name is Birdy—not very original. He's singing in the background behind me. Most of the time when I'm working, I let him fly freely around the room.

I sit down to write, but my heart isn't in it. One thing about writing children's books is you have to be part child yourself and get enthusiastic about the story, just as a child does—not only in the writing and illustrations but in the story itself. I sit back.

Then I hear Caroline come into the room. This is twice this

morning, and she rarely comes into my room in the daytime when I'm working. She knows how part of what helps me become the kind of man-child who can write these stories is concentration, a sense of being isolated, totally immersed in what I'm doing.

She moves between me and my worktable and looks down at me.

"Please, William, let's not go on like this. You know I love you. I'd do anything I can for you, but please don't make me lie."

I sit there. I don't think I'm ready to talk about it.

"What does it matter if I say I believe in Franky Furbo or not? I could say I did and still not believe. What difference would that make? I could say I don't believe and really believe in him myself but not want you to be so terribly lost in all that time, in the memories it must bring back to you. What difference does it make? It just *doesn't matter.*"

I'm afraid I might cry again. I want to talk now but don't know what will come out if I open my mouth. If I start bawling all over the place, Caroline will be more convinced than ever I'm some kind of neurotic or psychotic who doesn't have it together. I sit there. Then I look up at her concerned face leaning over me.

"It matters to me, Caroline."

She stands there, looking down. Her lovely brown-yellow eyes showing all the love I know she has for me. She's crying herself. I take a deep breath and try to talk.

"Maybe I shouldn't have started reading this book I wrote for the children about Franky Furbo all those years ago. It didn't help; all it did was make me realize how much I'd lose of myself, if it weren't for Franky Furbo. Do you remember how excited they were when they found the books in their stockings?"

"I'll never forget it, William. I can't even imagine a more beautiful Christmas present any child could ever have. I still have my copy and take it out to read often. I sometimes think you should publish it, share it with the world; then I think, 'Oh no, it's so much better this way, just a family book, only for us.' "

"I went through it all in my mind, Caroline. I tried to remember the parts Franky told me and the parts I made up myself. I really tried. I wanted our children to understand something of what Franky meant to me. The stories I remember him telling me weren't enough.

"Now I begin to wonder if I was right. Is it fair for me to want them entering into and living in *my* craziness? It must be craziness, because no matter how carefully I go over everything, I still come up believing in Franky Furbo. I truly believe in the super fox who can fly, read minds, transfer thoughts from one brain to another, transmute matter, invent and speak a language so complex, so subtle, that all other languages in the world, including my own, sound like sterile whinings and gruntings. I know it makes you unhappy, but I do believe. I'll never stop believing."

Tears are flowing down her face now. She slides into my lap, slips her arms around my neck, looks into my eyes. God, she's so beautiful. How did I ever get so lucky with all that's wrong with me to have such a beautiful, intelligent, wonderful wife? She hugs me hard, then pushes herself away.

"William. Listen to me. There is one way you can prove or disprove this whole idea."

I watch her eyes. The intensity in them can almost be frightening sometimes, but I know she isn't trying to frighten me.

"You've told me you have all of Wilhelm's memories in your head. I've never been able to understand how you speak such perfect, simple German with no American accent. The only thing I can think is that in the time you think you were with Franky, you were actually a prisoner of the Germans. Nothing else makes sense. Perhaps Wilhelm is someone you got to know during that time. Also the fact that you had such terrible injuries and they were repaired. You must have been in a German hospital where they treated you. German medicine is supposed to be quite good."

I start to speak, to explain again how Franky pulled me back from death, but she puts her fingers on my lips.

"Hear me out, William. One deep part of me knows, after watching you with your troubles in Italian—a much easier language to learn than German—that you could never have learned German in such a short time. It is one portion of your story I've never been able to figure out. Also, it's so strange how when you speak German you become someone else. This could be some strong survival thing in you that helped you escape, if you were a prisoner. I don't know. I'm only trying to tell you some of the things I've been thinking."

"It would be so much easier if you would only believe, Caroline. Do you really think that when I'm speaking Fox, trying to teach it to you and the children, that I'm just wanting to fool you, spouting some kind of drivel as part of a monstrous hoax?"

"I'm sure you wouldn't do any such thing on purpose, William, dear. It's another thing that totally baffles me. It's so strange. But it leads me to what I want to talk with you about."

I'm transfixed by her eyes, the smoothness of her lips, the soft burnt honey color of her skin, the clean straightness of her nose, the deep auburn hair with only a soft haze of gray to lighten it. Hell, I'm totally white now, even my beard, and she's almost the same as the day I met her. I try to smile.

"OK, Caroline, come out with it. But I warn you, I'm not going to any psychiatrist or psychotherapist or anything like that. I want, *need* to believe in Franky Furbo. He's part of my life."

"I understand. But would you be willing to take a little trip, for a week or a month—whatever it takes?"

"You mean to some kind of sanatorium or something; let the mad writer of children's books take off for a while and chase the demons from his soul? No!"

"Listen to me, William. Stop being silly. You tell me you know everything about Wilhelm up until he was twenty years old, right?"

"That's right. It's more like a dream I can remember in every detail than real experience or real memory, but I can still call up most of the things he knew about before Franky made the transfer of our minds."

"OK, then. You *must* know where he lived. Go find him. See if you can talk to him, if he exists; check out what reality there is that can be checked.

"I've always been surprised, William, considering how close the two of you were, that you've never hunted for him. He'd have had a hard time finding you because we're so far from where you grew up and because you have no parents, brothers, or sisters. But the chances are, since he was supposed to be married, he's somewhere near where he was before the war."

I stare at her harder. Why didn't this ever occur to me? It's so logical. Maybe deep inside myself I know Franky is all only a fantasy and by doing this, searching things out, I would tear it down, destroy it. Caroline slowly stands up. I stand beside her and take her in my arms.

"Thank you, dearest. You're right, it's the one way I can find out. Even if he's moved somewhere else, I should be able to trace him down. He can't just have disappeared. And I promise, if I don't find any trace of him, I'll never mention Franky Furbo around here again."

"Please don't say that, William. Franky is important to all of us; he's like another member of the family. The only thing I'm saying is, don't ask us to believe he's a *real* creature. If it makes *you* happy believing, that's fine. Do you know what I mean?"

She looks down at her feet. She's wearing soft bedroom slippers she made herself. Inside the house we all wear these slippers; they're soft and comfortable. We leave our outside shoes by the front door. She looks up at me again.

"Will you go?"

"Yes, Caroline, and thank you. Tomorrow I start on my trip to look for Wilhelm Klug in the village of Seeshaupt at the foot of the Alps and at the head of the Starnberger *See* in Bavaria. Do you want to come with me?"

"No, William, this is your search. I'll stay here with Billy. All I ask is that you don't give up looking until you're absolutely sure that Wilhelm Klug doesn't exist or . . . that you find him."

CHAPTER 6

THE SEARCH

So, from the attic, I pull down one of our old pieces of luggage. It's a bag we used when we left California and came here—old-fashioned, heavy, canvas. I dust the bag off and stuff it with the things I think I'll need. I don't know how long I'll be gone.

Caroline is a big help, remembering all the little things I forget, like toothpaste and nail clippers. This is the first trip of any length I've made since we moved here to Italy over forty years ago. Neither of us has much desire to be a tourist.

Every year we'll take a trip either to Florence or Rome with the kids and stay a few days. This is at Caroline's insistence. She says she wants the children to see what good things people have created both in the distant past, in Rome, and in the more recent past, in Florence. She's a great tour guide, and, as often as I've gone with her, each time I learned new things. I don't know how she knows so much about architecture, history, painting: I don't ever remember seeing her read anything on those subjects, and it wasn't her major at the university. She just seems to absorb information the way she did German, then has the ability to make it all come alive and exciting for us.

I ask her again if she won't come. Billy is quite capable of taking care of himself, thanks to Caroline's training. I must admit I'm beginning to be anxious about leaving. When you've lived in the same place as long as we have and you've always had the support of a loving wife and wonderful children, it isn't easy to just walk away from it all. Also, I'm almost sixty-three years old.

In a strange way, I have the feeling I'm abandoning them, running away. Or maybe it's more the other way, even though I'm the one leaving: they're abandoning me.

But I really need to find out about Franky Furbo. I have to search out Wilhelm and settle things once and for all. At the last minute, I pack the Franky Furbo book I'd been reading.

I ride my bicycle to Perugia with my bag on the back. Caroline comes with me on her bicycle. She says she'll go home after the train leaves; we'll leave my bicycle here at the train station; it's such an old beat-up no-speed bike no one will steal it, but I lock it. Caroline says she'll walk out here if I'm not back soon and ride home. She has a key to the lock. We've never had a car, don't want one, feel no need for one.

We kiss good-bye and I climb into the train. Caroline smiles into my face. It's almost as if she has some secret she isn't telling me.

"Now, William, don't you come back until you're absolutely sure. Let's not have all this between us the rest of our lives, OK?"

I nod yes. I can't trust myself to speak. I feel the distance between us growing even before the train starts. I find a seat, throw my bag up on the luggage rack, and look out the window. She's still standing there, not waving, just looking at me. She has the look of someone who's come to see the train only out of curiosity, not to see someone special off, someone she hasn't been separated from, for even one day, in over forty years.

The train starts. I wave and only then does she wave, just once, and turn away. I watch as she goes through the station and out of sight.

The trip is long. I take out the book but can't concentrate at first. I try drawing some of the people around me in a little sketchbook but can't concentrate on that either. It's a strange feeling, as if I'm going out of myself, like a snake leaving its skin.

As I go farther north, changing trains, I start hearing more and more German being spoken around me. Although I speak German, I've never been in a country where the language is spoken. I can feel myself changing; it's as if I'm becoming someone else. I am. In some strange way, I'm becoming Wilhelm. I can hardly think of any words in Italian. My American English is there, deep inside me, but the German all around becomes more and more familiar as we come closer and closer to Munich. I can finally concentrate enough to read my book.

THE STORY II

THAT NIGHT, FRANKY WENT THROUGH THE OPEN WINDOW AND INTO THE ROOM WHERE HE KNEW THE LITTLEST MAN SLEPT. LUCIA WAS FAST ASLEEP. FRANKY TOOK ONE OF HER BOOKS FROM THE SHELF AND OPENED IT JUST AS HE'D SEEN THE FARMER DO. HE SAT ON THE BED IN HIS BEST MAN FASHION, WITH HIS LEGS CROSSED, THEN BARKED A TINY FOX BARK TO WAKE THE LITTLE GIRL.

YOU CAN IMAGINE HOW SURPRISED LUCIA WAS TO SEE A FOX ACTUALLY SITTING ON THE EDGE OF HER BED WITH A BOOK OPEN ON HIS LAP. HIS BIG BUSHY PINK TAIL WAS WRAPPED OVER HIS SHOULDER LIKE A SCARF AND GLEAMED IN THE BRIGHT MOON-LIGHT COMING THROUGH THE OPEN WINDOW BEHIND HIM.

FRANKY STARTED TALKING FOX TALK AS FAST AS HE COULD, TRYING TO MAKE IT SOUND AS MUCH LIKE MAN TALK AS POSSIBLE.

OF COURSE, LUCIA DIDN'T UNDERSTAND A THING. SHE SAT UP IN HER BED, STILL HALF-ASLEEP, AND LISTENED. FRANKY POINTED WITH HIS PAW TO A PICTURE IN THE BOOK. IT WAS A PICTURE OF A BIRD. LUCIA LOOKED AT THE PICTURE AND SAID "*UCCELLO*" SEVERAL TIMES. THAT'S THE WORD FOR "BIRD" IN ITALIAN. FRANKY REPEATED THE WORD UNTIL HE COULD MAKE A REASONABLE IMITATION OF THE SOUND LUCIA MADE.

"OH MY, YOU CAN TALK. YOU ARE A LITTLE FOX WHO CAN TALK."

SHE SAID THIS IN ITALIAN, NATURALLY, BECAUSE SHE WAS AN ITALIAN GIRL.

FRANKY DIDN'T KNOW WHAT SHE WAS SAYING. HE POINTED TO ANOTHER PICTURE, A PICTURE OF A HORSE. LUCIA TOLD HIM WHAT IT WAS IN ITALIAN AND HE TRIED TO SAY THAT WORD.

LUCIA NOW UNDERSTOOD THAT THIS LITTLE FOX WANTED TO LEARN HOW TO SPEAK, BUT I'M SURE SHE STILL FELT AS IF SHE WERE DREAMING. EVEN THE MOST REAL THINGS CAN SOMETIMES SEEM LIKE DREAMS, THE SAME WAY DREAMS CAN SEEM REAL TO US.

FOR QUITE SOME TIME, THEY SAT IN THE MOONLIGHT AS SHE TAUGHT FRANKY THE NAMES OF ALL THE PICTURES IN THE BOOK. IT WAS FUN, AND LUCIA WAS SURPRISED HOW FAST FRANKY COULD LEARN.

WHEN HE FINALLY LEFT, JUST BEFORE THE BIG BALL CAME UP OVER THE HILLS, SHE MADE FRANKY TAKE THE BOOK WITH HIM.

LUCIA WAS VERY TIRED THE NEXT DAY, BUT SHE DIDN'T TELL HER PARENTS ABOUT THE LITTLE FOX. FOR ONE THING, SHE KNEW NO ONE WOULD BELIEVE HER, AND FOR ANOTHER, SHE DIDN'T THINK THE FOX WOULD LIKE HER TO TELL. THERE IS A KIND OF TALKING AND UNDERSTANDING THAT IS NOT IN WORDS.

FRANKY SPENT THE WHOLE OF THE NEXT DAY PRACTICING THE WORDS IN THE BOOK. IT WAS MOST TIRING TO MAKE THE MAN

SOUNDS WITH HIS FOX THROAT, AND HE WENT OFTEN TO THE STREAM FOR A DRINK OF WATER AND TO WASH HIS FACE. HE WAS VERY TIRED BUT HE WAS HAPPY TO BE LEARNING. SOON, HE FELT HE COULD ASK QUESTIONS WITH MEN. HE WAS SURE THEY KNEW MANY THINGS HE WANTED TO KNOW.

ALMOST EVERY NIGHT FOR THREE MONTHS, FRANKY CREPT DOWN TO THE HOUSE AND THEN, JUST WHEN LUCIA WENT TO BED, HE CLIMBED UP INTO HER WINDOW AND SHE TAUGHT HIM. SOME NIGHTS LUCIA WAS TOO TIRED, AND FRANKY WOULD GO HOME AND WORK ON THE BOOKS BY HIMSELF.

HE LEARNED QUICKLY ALL THE WORDS FOR THE PICTURES AND THE WORDS FOR EVERYTHING IN THE ROOM. HE AND LUCIA COULD BEGIN TO HAVE SHORT CONVERSATIONS. FRANKY ASKED MANY QUESTIONS, BUT LITTLE LUCIA COULD NOT ANSWER ALL OF THEM BECAUSE SHE WAS ONLY SEVEN.

IT WAS NOW WHEN LUCIA TOLD HIM HER NAME: IT WAS LUCIA BIANCHI. SHE ASKED FRANKY IF HE HAD A NAME. IT WAS THEN FRANKY STARTED CALLING HIMSELF FRANKY FURBO. *FURBO* MEANS "CLEVER" IN ITALIAN. IT'S WHAT LUCIA KEPT CALLING HIM WHEN SHE WAS TEACHING HIM, AND FRANKY THOUGHT IT WOULD MAKE A NICE NAME.

LUCIA WAS LEARNING TO READ IN SCHOOL, AND SHE SHOWED FRANKY THE WORDS IN THE BOOK AND HOW THEY TALKED, TOO. THIS WAS MOST INTERESTING TO FRANKY. EVERY NIGHT HE WOULD TAKE HOME A NEW BOOK, AND VERY SOON HE COULD READ QUITE WELL. IN FACT, HE COULD READ MUCH BETTER THAN LUCIA HERSELF. HE WAS, INDEED, A VERY SMART FOX.

NOW, FRANKY STARTED READING THE BOOKS IN LUCIA'S FA-THER'S LIBRARY. SHE WOULD BRING THEM UP INTO THE ROOM FOR HIM AND HE WOULD BRING THEM BACK THE NEXT MORNING. THERE WASN'T A BOOK FRANKY COULDN'T READ IN ONE DAY. HE

WAS VERY SURPRISED AND PLEASED WITH HIMSELF AND HE LOVED READING. IT WAS ALMOST AS GOOD AS THINKING, AND READING GAVE FRANKY MUCH TO THINK ABOUT.

ONE EARLY MORNING, AS FRANKY WAS CARRYING ONE OF THE FARMER'S BOOKS HOME AFTER HIS LESSON WITH LUCIA, HE WAS CAUGHT IN A TRAP. IT SEEMS THAT THE FARMER'S SON HAD NOTICED THE FOX TRACKS ALONG THE TRAIL FRANKY USUALLY TOOK FROM HIS HOME IN THE WOODS TO THE FARMER'S HOUSE. THE BROTHER HAD SET HIS TRAP QUITE CLEVERLY SO FRANKY DIDN'T SEE IT. BEFORE HE KNEW WHAT HAPPENED, THERE WAS A LOUD SNAP AND HIS BACK LEG WAS GRIPPED IN THE SHARP TEETH OF THE TRAP. FRANKY FELT A TERRIBLE PAIN BUT DARED NOT MAKE A NOISE FOR FEAR THE DOGS WOULD HEAR HIM.

GETTING CAUGHT IN A TRAP WAS SUCH A DUMB, FOXLIKE THING TO DO. FRANKY FELT LIKE CRYING, HE WAS SO DISCOURAGED. HE TRIED TO THINK WHAT HE COULD DO TO ESCAPE, BUT THE TRAP WAS TOO STRONG FOR HIM TO OPEN WITH HIS PAWS. SOMETIMES A WILD FOX WILL CHEW OFF HIS TRAPPED LEG TO GET AWAY, BUT FRANKY WAS MUCH TOO CIVILIZED TO DO A THING LIKE THAT. HE HAD TO THINK, AND THINK HE DID, BUT TO NO AVAIL.

SOON IT WAS DAYLIGHT, AND DOWN THE HILL THE FARMER CAME OUT OF HIS HOUSE. THE FARMER'S SON WAS BEHIND HIM. THE TWO OF THEM WENT OVER TO FEED THE CHICKENS. THE DOGS WERE RUNNING AND JUMPING AROUND THEM. FRANKY WISHED WITH ALL HIS HEART THAT LUCIA WOULD COME OUT AND HE COULD SOMEHOW SIGNAL HER.

AFTER THE FARMER AND SON FINISHED WITH THE CHICKENS, THE SON PUT HIS RIFLE OVER HIS SHOULDER AND CAME UP THE HILL TOWARD FRANKY WITH ONE OF THE DOGS. HE WAS CHECKING THE TRAP TO SEE IF HE HAD CAUGHT ANYTHING. FRANKY COULD SEE ALL THIS AND THERE WAS NOTHING HE COULD DO.

WHEN THE BOY FINALLY CAME TO THE TRAP WHERE FRANKY

WAS CAUGHT, HE SAW A FOX SITTING ON THE TRAP READING A BOOK. THE DOG RAN AT THE FOX, BUT THE FOX ONLY LOOKED UP FROM THE BOOK AND SAID, IN A MOST MANLIKE VOICE:

"DOWN DOG!"

NATURALLY, HE SAID IT IN ITALIAN. THE POOR DOG STOPPED IN HIS TRACKS AND STARTED TO WHINE. HE LOOKED OVER AT HIS

MASTER, BUT HIS MASTER HAD DROPPED HIS GUN AND HIS MOUTH WAS WIDE OPEN.

THE FOX STOOD AND POINTED AT HIS FOOT.

"WOULD YOU BE SO KIND, SIR, AS TO REMOVE THIS TRAP FROM MY FOOT? IT IS MOST UNCOMFORTABLE."

WELL, AS YOU CAN IMAGINE, THE BOY WAS FRIGHTENED. HE ALMOST RAN RIGHT BACK DOWN TO HIS HOUSE. IN FACT, HE STARTED TO DO JUST THAT WHEN FRANKY CALLED OUT.

"DON'T RUN AWAY, YOUNG MAN. I NEED HELP TO REMOVE THIS TRAP."

THE DOG LOOKED BACK AND FORTH FROM HIS MASTER TO THE FOX. THE BOY STOPPED AND CAME BACK. HE CAME A LITTLE CLOSER TO FRANKY.

"ARE YOU A FOX WHO CAN TALK?"

"YES, CERTAINLY; CAN'T YOU HEAR ME?"

"BUT, DO *ALL* FOXES TALK?"

"OF COURSE NOT. PLEASE, WOULD YOU HELP ME REMOVE THIS TRAP? I'VE BEEN HERE FOR OVER THREE HOURS."

THE BOY LEANED DOWN AND SPREAD THE JAWS OF THE TRAP SO FRANKY COULD GET HIMSELF FREE.

IT HAD BEEN FRANKY'S PLAN TO DASH OFF AT THIS POINT, BUT NOW HE FOUND HE COULDN'T BEND HIS LEG. WITH THE DOG THERE, HE COULDN'T POSSIBLY GET AWAY USING ONLY THREE LEGS. BESIDES, HE HAD LUCIA'S FATHER'S BOOK TO CARRY. HE KNEW HE COULDN'T RUN VERY FAST ON HIS HIND LEGS EITHER; IT WAS ONE OF HIS HIND LEGS THAT HAD BEEN CAUGHT IN THE TRAP.

"THANK YOU VERY MUCH, SIR; THAT WAS VERY KIND OF YOU."

"YES, BUT I SET THE TRAP."

"THAT IS TRUE, ISN'T IT?"

"I WANTED TO CATCH THE FOXES WHO ARE STEALING OUR CHICKENS."

"QUITE A GOOD IDEA. THE FOXES ARE FOOLISH TO COME DOWN AND STEAL YOUR FATHER'S CHICKENS."

FRANKY WAS HOPING HIS LEG WOULD GET BETTER, BUT IT WAS STILL NUMB, UNTIL HE PUT HIS WEIGHT ON IT AND THEN THERE WAS A STRONG PAIN NOT UNLIKE A TOOTHACHE.

"BUT *YOU* ARE A FOX. YOU TOO MIGHT BE HERE TO EAT FATHER'S CHICKENS."

"NOT AT ALL. I COME TO VISIT WITH YOUR SISTER, LUCIA."

THE BOY SCRATCHED HIS HEAD AND LOOKED AROUND.

"I DON'T UNDERSTAND ALL THIS. HOW CAN A FOX TALK, AND WHAT ARE YOU DOING WITH MY FATHER'S BOOK?"

"YOUR SISTER LUCIA LENT ME THE BOOK TO READ. YOU SEE, I AM NOT AN ORDINARY FOX. FOR SOME STRANGE REASON, I AM A VERY SMART FOX. I DON'T UNDERSTAND IT MYSELF."

FRANKY WAS BEGINNING TO SUSPECT HE WAS A QUITE REMARKABLE CREATURE, PROBABLY MORE CLEVER THAN ANY HUMAN. THAT'S ANOTHER REASON HE'D TAKEN THE NAME *FURBO*. THE BOY CAME CLOSER.

"BUT WHERE DO YOU LIVE?"

"IN THE FOREST ON THE HILL THERE."

FRANKY POINTED. HE WAS FEELING VERY UNCOMFORTABLE BECAUSE OF HIS HURT LEG. HE WANTED ONLY TO GO HOME AND SLEEP.

"BUT THE FOXES LIVE ON THE OTHER HILL. WHY DO YOU LIVE IN THE FOREST?"

"THE FOXES WERE TOO FOOLISH AND I WANTED TO LIVE ALONE."

"PLEASE, MR. FOX, WON'T YOU COME DOWN TO OUR HOUSE? YOU MUST HAVE SOME WASHING AND A BANDAGE ON THAT LEG."

"THAT IS VERY KIND OF YOU, SIR, BUT I AM AFRAID OF YOUR DOGS. ALSO, I THINK YOUR FATHER WOULD NOT BE HAPPY TO HAVE A FOX SO NEAR HIS CHICKENS."

"I WOULDN'T TELL ANYBODY BUT LUCIA, AND SHE ALREADY KNOWS. WE COULD KEEP YOU IN A SECRET PLACE."

FRANKY WASN'T SURE WHAT TO DO. HE WAS FEELING VERY

WEAK SUDDENLY AND DIDN'T THINK HE COULD WALK ALL THE
WAY TO HIS HOUSE. AS HE WAS PONDERING THIS, THINGS BECAME
DARK AND HE DIDN'T REMEMBER THE BOY PICKING HIM UP AND
CARRYING HIM BACK DOWN THE HILL.

I stop again. This story is also one that Franky actually told Wilhelm
and me. He showed us the scar where he had been caught in the
trap. I skip through the rest of the chapter. Lucia and Dominic put
Franky in a box in their attic and nurse him back to health. Franky
reads the rest of their father's books, including books of algebra,
geometry, history, science, and other more complex books than those
Lucia had been lending him. Franky began to realize that Lucia's
father was a very well informed and intelligent farmer. No wonder
the foxes got caught by him.

Lucia sews up some clothes for Franky, while Dominic makes
boots and a cane. I think I put in that part to amuse our kids.

Then, when Franky goes back to his home in the tree, he asks
Dominic to open a post office box in the name of Franky Furbo and
to bring him some baby chicks. Franky had to assure the children
that he would not eat the chicks, that he only wanted them so later
on he could have his own eggs.

I read some more. It helps pass away the long train ride.

WHEN HE GOT HOME, FRANKY WENT UP TO HIS THINKING ROOM
AND THOUGHT FOR A LONG WHILE. IT IS ALWAYS NICE TO COME
HOME, NO MATTER HOW PLEASANT THE VISIT MIGHT HAVE BEEN.
FRANKY HAD A LOT OF THINKING TO DO. THERE WAS MUCH HE
DIDN'T UNDERSTAND ABOUT THE WORLD. MOSTLY HE DIDN'T UN-
DERSTAND ABOUT HIMSELF. WHAT WAS HE? WHY WAS HE SO

SMART? HE COULD NEVER LIVE THE LIFE OF A FOX, AND HE COULD
NEVER BE A HUMAN EITHER. HE BEGAN TO SUSPECT THAT, AL-
THOUGH HE LOVED LITTLE HUMAN CHILDREN LIKE DOM AND
LUCIA, THERE WERE CHARACTERISTICS ABOUT GROWN HUMANS
THAT FRIGHTENED HIM. MANY OF THE THINGS HE'D READ ABOUT
IN THE BOOKS WERE NOT GOOD.

FRANKY REALIZED HE NEEDED MONEY FOR MANY THINGS HE WANTED TO HAVE. IT IS VERY DIFFICULT FOR A FOX TO GET MONEY. FRANKY DECIDED HE COULD BEST EARN MONEY BY WRITING STORIES FOR CHILDREN'S MAGAZINES. HE THOUGHT HE MIGHT ALSO WRITE BOOKS FOR CHILDREN AND DRAW PICTURES TO HELP TELL THE STORIES. HE'D MAIL THESE STORIES AND BOOKS TO PUBLISHERS.

DURING THE NEXT WEEKS FRANKY WORKED VERY HARD LEARNING HOW TO WRITE AND ILLUSTRATE HIS STORIES. FIRST, HE WROTE ABOUT HIS MOTHER AND THE OTHER FOXES ON THE HILL. THEN HE WROTE A STORY ABOUT THE SQUIRRELS WHO LIVED IN THE TOP OF HIS TREE. ANOTHER STORY WAS ABOUT A PAIR OF BLUE JAYS HE COULD WATCH FROM HIS WINDOW. IT WAS EXCITING MAKING UP WHAT THESE ANIMALS WERE THINKING, WHAT THEY SAID TO ONE ANOTHER, IMAGINING THE THINGS HE WOULD HAVE HAPPEN IN THE STORIES. IT MADE HIM FEEL NOT SO ALONE.

HE MAILED ALL HIS STORIES AWAY TO DIFFERENT MAGAZINES AND WAITED. THE STORIES WERE ACTUALLY VERY GOOD, AND AT THE END OF A MONTH, DOMINIC FOUND THREE CHECKS FOR MONEY IN THE POST OFFICE BOX. FRANKY SIGNED THEM AND DOMINIC PUT THE MONEY IN THE BANK UNDER AN ACCOUNT IN FRANKY'S NAME. FRANKY NOW HAD A BANK ACCOUNT AND A CHECKBOOK. HE COULD WRITE AWAY AND HAVE THINGS HE WANTED DELIVERED TO HIS POSTBOX. MOSTLY HE BOUGHT BOOKS. SO, HE WAS WRITING BOOKS TO BUY MORE BOOKS.

THE FIRST THING FRANKY DID WAS PAY FOR THE CHICKS AND THE POST OFFICE BOX DOMINIC HAD GOTTEN FOR HIM. HE'D ALREADY BUILT CAGES FOR THE CHICKS; THEY'D GROWN UP AND WERE LAYING EGGS FOR HIM. HE GAVE DOM MONEY TO BUY A NEW HAT FOR HIMSELF AND A NEW DOLL FOR LUCIA. IT WAS SUCH A THRILL FOR FRANKY TO GIVE PRESENTS AND HAVE HIS OWN BOOKS. HE BUILT SHELVES ALL AROUND THE SIDES OF HIS THINK-

ING ROOM AND LOOKED FORWARD TO THE DAY WHEN THESE SHELVES WOULD BE FILLED WITH BOOKS HE HAD READ AND OTHER BOOKS HE COULD READ WHEN HE WANTED TO.

SO, FRANKY PASSED HIS DAYS, READING, THINKING, TENDING TO HIS CHICKENS, WRITING STORIES FOR CHILDREN, GRADUALLY IMPROVING AND ENLARGING HIS HOUSE.

HE BUILT A PLATFORM HIGH UP IN THE TREE AND ON THE PLATFORM BUILT A SPACIOUS AND AIRY SUMMERHOUSE BIG ENOUGH FOR LUCIA AND DOMINIC TO VISIT. HE FASHIONED A LADDER FROM ROPE WITH WHICH THEY COULD EASILY CLIMB UP THE SIDE OF THE TREE. THEY WOULD PULL THE LADDER UP AFTER THEM SO THEY WERE COMPLETELY ALONE IN THE TOP OF THE TREE NEXT TO THE SKY. ON CLEAR EVENINGS IT WAS WONDERFUL TO LOOK UP AT THE STARS THROUGH THE LEAVES OF THE TREE.

OFTEN FRANKY INVITED LUCIA AND DOMINIC TO COME VISIT WITH HIM AND HAVE LUNCH. THEY SAT AT A LITTLE TABLE WITH DISHES AND GLASSES, EVEN SILVERWARE. FRANKY RAPIDLY WAS BECOMING AN EXCELLENT COOK. AS I SAID, FOXES LOVE TO EAT, AND, AFTER ALL, FRANKY REALLY WAS A FOX EVEN THOUGH HE WAS SO SMART. FRANKY HAD ALSO STARTED A GARDEN AND THERE HE GREW THE MOST WONDERFUL VEGETABLES. IT WAS MOSTLY THESE HE COOKED FOR HIMSELF TO EAT. BECAUSE HE WAS AN ITALIAN FOX, HE ALSO LIKED SPAGHETTI AND ALL KINDS OF PASTA. LUCIA AND DOM LOVED THE FOOD FRANKY COOKED.

FRANKY DUG A DEEP HOLE UNDER HIS TREE AND DESIGNED A BEAUTIFUL CELLAR IN AND AMONG THE BIG ROOTS. THERE HE KEPT HIS FRUITS, POTATOES, AND OTHER VEGETABLES—ANYTHING HE WANTED TO KEEP COOL. HE ALSO THOUGHT IT MIGHT BE A GOOD PLACE TO HIDE IF ANYBODY EVER TRIED TO CATCH HIM. THIS WAS ANOTHER VERY FOXY THING FOR FRANKY TO DO. WE ARE ALL WHAT WE ARE BORN TO BE, NO MATTER HOW MUCH WE MAY CHANGE OR HOW DIFFERENT WE ARE FROM THOSE ABOUT US.

FRANKY CONTINUED TO WRITE STORIES, WHILE MORE AND
MORE MONEY GATHERED UNDER HIS NAME IN THE BANK. HE BE-
CAME SUCH A FAMOUS WRITER HIS BOOKS WERE TRANSLATED INTO
MANY LANGUAGES AND HE RECEIVED LETTERS IN HIS POSTBOX
FROM BOYS AND GIRLS ALL OVER THE WORLD WHO HAD ENJOYED
THEM. FOR FRANKY, READING THESE LETTERS WAS THE MOST FUN
PART OF BEING AN AUTHOR. HE TRIED TO ANSWER AS MANY AS HE

COULD. THIS IS HOW HE GOT STARTED LEARNING SO MANY DIF-
FERENT LANGUAGES.

THE ONLY SAD THING FOR FRANKY WAS THAT AS HE LEARNED
MORE AND MORE ABOUT THE WORLD, HE REALIZED THAT HUMANS
WERE STRANGE CREATURES, OFTEN CRUEL TO OTHER ANIMALS
AND TO THEMSELVES. THEY WERE STUPID ENOUGH TO KILL EACH
OTHER IN GREAT WARS AS NO OTHER ANIMALS DO. THE MORE
FRANKY LEARNED ABOUT GROWN PEOPLE, THE MORE HE LOVED
CHILDREN.

FRANKY STARTED HAVING MANY ADVENTURES. CHILDREN
WOULD WRITE TO HIM FROM ALL OVER THE WORLD WITH THEIR
SPECIAL PROBLEMS, AND SOMETIMES HE WOULD GO TO SEE IF HE
COULD HELP THEM.

I know that up to here I'm still staying close to the stories Franky
told me. The next parts are where I begin trying to explain to my
children aspects of Franky Furbo that I knew about but couldn't
quite understand myself, such as his being able to go from one place
to another so quickly, read minds, make himself big or small, change
from a fox to a man—all his special skills that no human has. It was
here, I started making things up.

I close the book and think about this. Maybe I even fall asleep,
because the next thing I know, we're coming into the München
Bahnhof.

C H A P T E R   7

COMING HOME

There, in the *Bahnhof,* so much seems familiar. I don't need to ask directions how I get down to the town where I'm going, Seeshaupt. My body automatically turns to the small station beside the *Haupbahnhof* to the Starnberger Bahnhof where I find the train to Seeshaupt.

There, in Seeshaupt, I get off the train and know I'm going to walk down a small street called Pfeffenkäufer Allee, into the part of town where Wilhelm lived. It's such a weird feeling, like watching a film you've seen before, a long time ago.

When I get to the main street through town, I look across the road, and there it is—a big yellow-orange house with dark green trim. I really don't need to look at the number on the wooden, natural-stake fence to see it's number 10. This is the house where I lived—the place I've called home.

I look up automatically at a huge sundial built under the eaves. It's a smiling face, the face of the sun, with the gnomon coming out where the nose would be. Under it, there's printed in Gothic print the motto:

MACH' ES WIE DIE SONNENUHR
ZAHL DIE HEIFERN STUNDEN NUR

110

This is the house where I grew up. This is the house where I brought my wife home after we married. This is the house I had to leave when I went off to war all those years ago. We didn't live in the whole house; it was divided into apartments. We lived on the ground floor on the left. Frau Fürst, the owner, lived on the right, Fräulein Hindelmeier lived over us; she taught at the village school. Over Frau Fürst lived her daughter, Hilda. Her husband had been a pilot in the Luftwaffe, and she had three small children.

But this isn't true. This is what Wilhelm knows, or what I think Wilhelm knows; these are somebody else's forty-five-year-old memories. I walk up and knock on the door where Wilhelm lived; I knock again. No one comes. I step back. The shutters are closed, so I cross to what was Frau Fürst's door. The shutters are open on this side. There's a bell and I ring. I hear footsteps coming down the stairs.

A woman opens the door. I must be wrong; I've been imagining the whole thing: I don't remember this woman at all.

German comes as naturally to me as English, maybe more naturally here in Germany.

"Excuse me. Does Frau Fürst live here?"

The lady raises her eyebrows, leans back, and looks at me carefully. She's curious but suspicious.

"No, she's been dead for fifteen years. Why do you ask?"

"I'm sorry. You see, I used to live on the other side and I wanted to ask her some questions."

"You lived on the other side? There?"

She leans out the door and points, incredulous. I nod my head.

"I'm Frau Fürst's daughter and I don't remember you. Are you sure?"

"Hilda. Don't you remember me? I'm Wilhelm Klug."

111

Then I remember, I'm not Wilhelm Klug. What can I say? I'm feeling very foolish.

"I mean I'm *not* Wilhelm Klug, I'm a friend of his from long ago, and I'm looking for him. This is the last address I have."

"Oh, my goodness, that was a *long* time ago, from before the war, even.

"I understand Wilhelm came back from the war after having been a prisoner or something for some time, but he never came back to this house to live. However, he does live not too far from here now, I'm told, near Hohenberg."

I'm standing there with my mouth open. I put down my suitcase. Tears spring into my eyes. Hilda leans forward.

"Are you all right? Are you his brother? I haven't seen Wilhelm since he was a young man, but you look somewhat like him."

"No, I'm only a friend. I'd so hoped to see him, to find him."

"Much can happen over such a long time. However, perhaps you can find him in Hohenberg. May I ask your name, please?"

"Yes, I'm William Wiley. Wilhelm and I were friends during the war.

"Excuse me, may I ask, Frau Schwegler, did your husband, Herr Schwegler, come home safely?"

"No, he never came back. He was declared missing in action, probably killed."

"I'm terribly sorry, Frau Schwegler. How difficult it must have been for you rearing three children by yourself, especially after the war."

"I had my mother to help me, and it was difficult for everyone. We were lucky to have this house. But how do you know so much about our family? Do you live near here?"

"Wilhelm told me. He told me about his life, how much he loved this house, the people who lived here. We had much time to-

gether, and you know how soldiers will talk. We were *very* good friends."

I'm not about to try explaining to a total stranger anything about Franky Furbo. I'm having enough trouble, even with my family. It wouldn't help.

Hilda steps aside.

"I am Frau Doctor Demmel now. My husband is upstairs. Won't you please come in and have tea with us?"

"Thank you, Frau Doctor. It is most kind of you. Are you sure I won't be imposing?"

"No, of course not. Please come in."

I follow her up a pair of steep wooden steps just inside the door. It's all so familiar—the turns of the stairs, even the small window on the wall of the stairwell—only, of course, because it is the other side, everything is the opposite way. We go through a wide hall and into a large room facing the back. I'm hardly polite as I look out over the familiar view of the Starnberger *See* across the large garden.

Herr Doctor Demmel is standing. I pull my eyes away from the view to look at him. He doesn't look well. I find out later he has recently had a heart attack and is retired. All these things are easier for William to comprehend and accept than they are for Wilhelm. I have a hard time keeping my mind where it's supposed to be, hunting for Wilhelm, not succumbing to *his* emotions.

We sit, and Frau Doctor Hilda Demmel serves tea in a beautiful tea service. They are very kind to me. I'm sure I must look quite peculiar to them in my combination of Italian and American clothing with my raggedy suitcase. As I've gotten deeper into Germany I've been feeling more and more conspicuous, but I was in too great a hurry to find Wilhelm—find myself—to take time to stop and buy new clothes.

I listen and find out from Doctor Demmel that Wilhelm does indeed live nearby, in a hut, on the other side of the *Alte Eiche* outside Hohenberg. It seems his wife died just after he came home and he's never married again. He lives out there alone in the forest and works sometimes at different jobs, helping build roads or gardening. His parents, who moved to Ulm, are also dead now.

As Wilhelm, I'm shocked to hear all this, but as William I'm overjoyed to find Wilhelm is still alive and living not far from where I am right now. Frau Hilda Demmel looks over her teacup at me.

"Yes, it is really most strange. He has very little to do with anyone and only takes work when he needs money. They say he walks through the forests and fields in the evenings and nights. Most people think he is somewhat crazy from the war and from his wife and baby dying. But he doesn't hurt anyone. There are many who never recovered from the war.

"My son, Florie, has gone to visit where his house is and says it is very unique but quite comfortable."

Herr Doctor Demmel leans forward.

"The war was hard on some of the men. As a doctor, I've seen many, only fifty or sixty years old, dying of heart attacks and strokes. It's terrible. I myself blame the war for my condition. It was too much of a strain for young people. War is crazy."

He waggles his hands, shakes his head. I nod. I've found what I wanted to know. But the Wilhelm in me wants more. It's as if he's not finished, needs to be completed somehow.

"Thank you for all your help, Herr Doctor and Frau Doctor Demmel. You've been most kind. I shall go to Hohenberg and look for Wilhelm.

"But may I ask one more favor? Wilhelm talked so much about the *Garten* and the *Steg*, the beauty of the *See* and the lovely walk behind your house. Would it be possible for me to see these places?"

Frau Doctor Demmel looks quickly at Herr Doctor Demmel, then at me.

"Why, of course, naturally. Would you like me to come along with you? Oscar here can't walk as much as he would like to."

"Is it all right if I go alone? I have pictures of these places in my head and I would like to see them as Wilhelm told me about them."

"But you speak *Bayerisch*. Where do you come from? You can't live too far from here and speak such *echt Bayerisch*."

It's time to go into fiction again. It can't hurt anything. Besides, I'm getting completely confused as to what really is and what isn't. What I say isn't that far from the truth anyway.

"You see, Frau Demmel, I did live near here, but then ten years after the war I went to America to live. I had an uncle living there, and I went to stay with him. I've been living there for the past thirty years."

Then, in only slightly accented English, American English, she says:

"Oh. Then you speak English. I don't have much chance to practice my English. Would you like to speak some with me?"

She smiles. I almost have a hard time coming out with it. But it's there. I wonder if she's testing me some way. No, she really wants to speak in English.

"You speak very well, Frau Doctor. Where did you learn to speak such fine English?"

"In school. Then, of course, we were occupied by the 'Amis' for some time after the war. It was then I practiced my English, perhaps more than I would have liked."

She takes another quick look at Herr Doctor Demmel, who is following our conversation with his eyes but obviously isn't understanding. She turns back to me.

"Please feel free to walk in the garden and along the *Weg* and down into the *See Garten*. None of it has changed much since Wilhelm lived here. You may leave your bag here."

She points to my battered luggage by the door. I bow my way out as if I'd bowed my way through doors all my life. I go out the front door and around the side of the house. There is a large tree I remember swinging in as a child, as Wilhelm. I look up and can still see the marks of ropes on a high branch. I walk down a stone walkway in back of the garden and reach over to open the scrollwork iron gate. It's all so familiar.

There is the *Weg*. I look up and down it, then cross to open another gate into the *See Garten*. I continue down a curving stone walkway until I come to the *Steg*, a small dock sticking about five meters out into the water. I walk out on the *Steg*. The water is incredibly clear, just as I, that is, Wilhelm, remembers it.

I look to my right and there is the *Fischerei* just as it always was and, beyond it, the onion steepled church and the *See* Hotel. It's all the same. It's exactly like strolling through somebody else's dream.

I can look across the smooth *See* and see the blue hills on the other side. Way off to my right are the outlines of the Alps. On a clear day when the *Föhn* is blowing, I know, from Wilhelm's remembrance, those gigantic mountains seem to move right up so close you think you could walk to them in half an hour.

I look at my watch. It's five o'clock. I take one last heartrending glance around, then turn back to the house. When I ring the bell, Frau Demmel shouts down for me to come up.

They invite me to join them for their evening soup, but I now feel how much I want to get away. I begin to have the sensation I'm being swallowed by Wilhelm, by all that Franky put in me of being German. I make excuses and say I must leave, that I want to go see Wilhelm before it is too late. They tell me the way to Hohenberg and then what path I should take, just past the *Alte Eiche*, the old oak, to Wilhelm's house. Frau Doctor Demmel says to me in English:

"I've heard it said that often Wilhelm Klug plays *Schafskopf* at the *Bier Stube* in Hohenberg on Friday evenings; it is the one time when he has anything to do with anyone. If he isn't at his hut, you might check there. Today is Friday; he could be there to play this evening."

I thank her both in German and in English, say good-bye and *Auf Wiedersehen* to Herr Doctor Demmel, and back my way out of the house. I go down to the *Seeweg* and walk along it, lost in nostalgia for times I've never actually known. But I'm more sure than ever that Wilhelm really *is*, that I will find him, and that there *is* a Franky Furbo!

It's a long and beautiful walk to Hohenberg. The posted yellow-and-black sign just outside Seeshaupt, on the small road Hilda pointed out for me, says it is seven kilometers.

My bag isn't too heavy, and I have a piece of rope so I can tie it across my back. After all that's happened, is happening, I want time to walk and just think. Also, the country around is deep dark woods, so different from our own country at home in Prepo. I pass a small shrine with a statue of the Sacred Heart at an intersection, and after that, it is only fields with brown cows and forest.

The road turns to dirt and I continue up a long curving hill. All again is familiar, more familiar, more like coming home, than anything in Philadelphia. I can't really say I have any nostalgia for the orphan asylum where I lived as a child. To be perfectly honest, I don't think I have a single memory of my early childhood, little of my parents. It must have been so traumatic, so lonely, my mind has blocked it. My earliest remembrances are from the junior high school where the St. Vincent de Salles orphan asylum sent me. Before that, it's all vague.

The forest deepens and the road twists in soft curves. On one side of the road is a peaceful small lake. The path winds along beside it. I see no one else, but there are path markers cut or painted on the trees for hikers and, often, small arrows pointing the way to Hohenberg. The trees are mostly pine but with a scattering of enormous oaks. I wonder which is the one Hilda called the *Alte Eiche*. I know I'll recognize it when I see it. Wilhelm knows it well, but I have no exact memory of where it is. There is a small bench placed on a knoll overlooking the lake. I go up to sit down. My bag is beginning to cut into my shoulders.

It is all so quiet, calming. At the same time there is an ominous quality. It has the scariness of Grimm's fairy tales. When I write children's stories I try for a slight quality of this. I don't want the stories to be frightening, but the minor sense of danger, of the unknown, is something children like; they quiver in anticipation of what comes next. I always try out my stories on our kids when I'm not sure if I've gotten the right balance of fun and fear.

Just then, looking out, I remember skating here on this *See*, building a fire beside it, playing ice hockey, practicing figures, racing. I remember men with large metal weights sliding them across the ice in a game like curling. It all comes back. I try to think of a children's story with this locale, some creature that comes out of the lake and wants to play with the children, perhaps an elf. But my mind isn't conceiving well that way. This isn't the way Wilhelm's mind must work. I try getting back inside myself, seeing this as it really is, as if I'm seeing it for the first time.

I readjust my bag and start on my way again. I come out of the forest to more fields, cows grazing. Under a tree in the middle of the field is a small shrine. I know from Wilhelm's mind that the cows are supposed to pray at this shrine.

Then, up ahead I see the steeple of a very small church, more a chapel. I come down a slight incline and there's a sign saying HOHENBERG. I've arrived. Somehow I've missed the *Alte Eiche*, or perhaps it's on the other side of town.

There's a large barn, big as a movie theater, and on one end of it is what looks to be a tavern. I try the door and it's open. There are wooden tables and chairs set on scrubbed, wide-board floors. Along the walls and in the corners are benches grouped around tables. I sit in one of the chairs. There is no one else there.

The walls are covered with small mounted sets of what look like antelope or tiny deer horns. On one wall is a heavy, dark tapestry of two deer browsing in a forest beside a stream. Along one side is a bar. While I'm looking, a heavy woman comes out, drying her hands on her apron. She looks right at me, through me.

"Grüss Gott!"

"Grüss Gott."

She asks what I want and I say, in that Wilhelm voice that is becoming so familiar, I want a *halbes dunkel*. William is interested to see what this is. The Wilhelm part answered automatically, but the actual memory of what I've ordered is gone.

In a few minutes, she comes out with a huge stein of very dark beer. I haven't had any alcohol for over forty years! She asks if I'd like anything else and I ask for a menu.

Without a word, she turns and reaches over the bar. It's a single card, a *Speisekarte*. I try to tap Wilhelm's memory to read and understand it. I haven't read all that much German in the past forty-some years. But I recognize sauerbraten, as William would, and order it. I hope I've changed enough lire into deutsche marks at the *Bahnhof*. I'm sure I have. I sit back and drink the beer. It's the first German beer I've ever had, but Wilhelm remembers. It's a beer almost as powerful as Italian wine.

When the woman comes back with my sauerbraten, along with a salad and potatoes, I ask which way it is to the *Alte Eiche*. She looks at me as if I'd asked which way the sky is. She points over her shoulder, that is, in the direction I was heading, out the other side of town.

"Five hundred meters. It's on the side of the road; you can't miss it. Do you come from around here?"

I tell her no, that I'm only visiting a friend. This seems to be enough and she leaves me to my meal. The food is delicious, the meat sour and tender, the potatoes perfectly cooked and salted. The salad is not very interesting but good enough. At home we rarely eat meat, almost as rarely as we drink alcohol, but, as Wilhelm, I enjoy this.

I finish and pay. I go out the door. I think of asking which way it is to Herr Klug's but decide with Hilda's directions I can find it myself.

On the other side of the wide place in the road, which serves as the center of town, is a long building open on the sides. I walk over to see what it is. This is a wooden bowling alley. There are wooden pins and small wooden balls. There's a wooden runway to return the balls. On a slate over the alley is a sign saying ONE STEIN OF BEER PER LINE OF BOWLING in German. It looks like just the kind of alley where Rip Van Winkle might have bowled.

I step back and continue my way through the town. It's then I notice a large castle on the hill. It looks lived in. I wonder who could keep up such a place, and if all the fields and forests around it are part of the castle's grounds.

About half a kilometer outside town I come on the *Alte Eiche*. It's precisely where the lady at the *Bier Stube* said it would be, but seems to have changed some from the way Wilhelm remembers it. I sense disappointment. It is no longer alive. Most of the trunk is hollowed out, and large sections of wood rotting on the ground testify to relatively recent collapsing of this ancient tree.

The trunk standing in the ground is enormous. I walk around it in the soft leafy underfooting. The highest parts of the trunk and branches, unbroken, can't be more than thirty or forty feet high. I step back on the road.

Now, according to Hilda, I continue along this road and take the second path leading to the left. I start out again. I'm getting close to my first meeting with Wilhelm, the Wilhelm of my memories. I find the path and walk into the forest more than two hundred meters before I see a hump in the ground grown over with grass. It brings back William's memories, my own memories, of German pillboxes dug in and camouflaged. It even has a small dark chimney sticking out from the grass-covered roof.

This is where Wilhelm lives. It fits. In a strange way, it is something like Franky Furbo's house, close to nature, not too visible, comfortable, as much a hiding place as a home.

It is built into a hill. The hill has been dug out and it looks as if a corrugated curved roof was fitted over the hole, then dirt piled on top of it. Grass grows on the roof. The front wall, the only free wall, is built with adobe brick, probably also made from the dirt dug out of the hill. There is a door and a small window on each side of the door. It's most likely quite dark inside. It's dark for sure, now, because the shutters on each window are closed. There is also a shutter on the window cut into the door; it's closed, too. There's no smoke coming from the chimney and no sound within.

There's a bell hanging beside the door. I pull on the rope attached to the clapper and ring it. The sound is muffled as if the bell is cracked. I ring it several times.

If this is Wilhelm's house, then he isn't home. I put my bag down on the stone step in front of the door. From what Hilda told me, he shouldn't be gone for long; perhaps he's working. I climb around behind his house and find a storage shed, a lean-to filled with cut and stacked wood. I hide my bag there. I take my book out of the bag. It's now about seven-thirty in the evening. I decide I'll go back down to the *Bier Stube*, where I ate, and wait for Wilhelm.

I stop for a while at the old oak tree. It makes me think of Franky's home. Franky's tree was oak also, and big. It must have been hollow when he found it. Because Wilhelm and I were always small when we were living with Franky, his tree house seemed enormous to us, but it was probably about the size this tree must have grown to before it died.

The evening is starting to fall and the forest seems magical. I'm reminded more and more of our life with Franky, of our walks, our conversations. Wilhelm has tried to find something as close as possible to the life we lived, only here, in Germany.

At the *Bier Stube*, there are other men now. There are no women. Most of the men wear the typical Bavarian dress, with dark green trousers and jackets, small hats sometimes with feathers. Some wear the lederhosen, characteristic of the region. They look at me when I come in. I take a chair near the back of the room in the darkest corner. I order another *halbes dunkel*. I'll become an alcoholic before I find Wilhelm. Some rolls and pretzels are put in a basket before me. They're big pretzels, almost like the kind I used to love in Philadelphia as a kid. I pull out my book and start to read again.

THE STORY III

FRANKY HAD ONE BIG ADVENTURE EARLY ON THAT GAVE HIM SPECIAL POWERS TO HELP OTHER CHILDREN.

HE RECEIVED A LETTER ALL THE WAY FROM AMERICA FROM A LITTLE GIRL NAMED KATHY. IT SEEMED HER BROTHER, MATTHEW, HAD TURNED INTO A FOX AND NO ONE WOULD BELIEVE KATHY WHEN SHE TOLD THEM WHAT HAD HAPPENED, NOT EVEN HER PARENTS.

OF COURSE, THIS FASCINATED FRANKY. HE SMUGGLED HIMSELF INTO AN AIRPLANE AND THROUGH CUSTOMS. HE MANAGED TO FIND THE LITTLE GIRL'S HOUSE AND WENT TO VISIT HER IN THE

NIGHT, AS HE HAD WITH LUCIA. SHE SHOWED HIM HER BROTHER, MATTHEW, WHO WAS IN A BOX UNDER HER BED.

IT SEEMED THE TWO OF THEM, MATTHEW AND KATHY, HAD FOUND A SMALL CARVED STONE BOX IN AN INDIAN MOUND NEAR THEIR HOME. INSIDE THE BOX WAS A GREEN POWDER AND A SMALL CARVED STONE FOX, SMALL AS A TOOTH. MATTHEW, FOOLISHLY, PUT SOME OF THE POWDER IN WATER AND DRANK IT. HE IMMEDIATELY TURNED INTO A FOX AND COULDN'T EVEN SPEAK ANYMORE.

FRANKY QUICKLY DETERMINED THAT THE POWDER WAS "ESSENCE OF FOX." SOME CLEVER AND CRUEL INDIAN, YEARS AGO, HAD KILLED, BOILED, AND DRIED THOUSANDS OF FOXES TO MAKE IT. ANYONE WHO SWALLOWED ANY BECAME A FOX.

FRANKY TOOK THE POWDER TO A NEARBY UNIVERSITY LABORATORY AND MANAGED TO CONCOCT ANOTHER POWDER THE OPPOSITE OF THE GREEN POWDER. THIS POWDER WAS RED. HE GAVE SOME OF IT TO MATTHEW, WHO TURNED BACK INTO A LITTLE BOY, BUT A LITTLE, LITTLE BOY, THE SIZE OF A FOX.

FRANKY WENT BACK TO THE LABORATORY AND WORKED SOME MORE UNTIL HE'D DEVELOPED A FLUID THAT WOULD MAKE THE LITTLE BOY GROW. IT WORKED. IT WORKED *TOO* WELL AND LITTLE MATTHEW BECAME *BIG* MATTHEW, MUCH BIGGER THAN HIS SISTER. IT WAS ALL SO COMPLICATED.

FRANKY WENT BACK AGAIN TO THE LABORATORY AND THIS TIME HE JUGGLED BACK AND FORTH WITH THE TWO FLUIDS, A DROP HERE, A DROP THERE, UNTIL, AFTER MUCH WORK, HE'D INVENTED A FLUID TO MAKE MATTHEW HIS OWN SIZE AGAIN.

KATHY AND MATTHEW WERE VERY HAPPY.

WHEN FRANKY LEFT, KATHY AND MATTHEW SAID HE COULD TAKE THE GREEN "FOX" POWDER WITH HIM, AND FRANKY TOOK THE OTHER POWDERS AND FLUIDS HE'D INVENTED, TOO. NOW HE COULD MAKE HIMSELF INTO A HUMAN OR A FOX OR MAKE HIMSELF BIG OR SMALL. IT WAS A WHOLE NEW THING TO THINK ABOUT.

FRANKY HAD MANY OTHER ADVENTURES. BETWEEN WRITING AND SOLVING PROBLEMS ALL OVER THE WORLD, HE WAS VERY BUSY. HE KEPT IMPROVING HIS TREE AS HE SAW NEW THINGS IN HIS TRAVELS.

BUT DESPITE ALL THIS, FRANKY WAS SOMETIMES LONELY. AS TIME WENT BY, LUCIA AND DOMINIC GREW UP AND WERE OFTEN AWAY AT SCHOOL. HE HAD SOME ANIMAL FRIENDS, AND

EVEN THOUGH HE LEARNED THEIR SIMPLE LANGUAGES AND COULD HELP THEM WITH THEIR PROBLEMS SOMETIMES, IT DIDN'T HELP HIS LONELINESS MUCH. FRANKY WANTED SOMEONE LIKE HIMSELF WITH WHOM HE COULD TALK AND SHARE HIS THOUGHTS, LEARN NEW THOUGHTS FROM. WITH ALL HIS EFFORTS, HE WAS STILL LOOKING FOR ANSWERS TO IMPORTANT QUESTIONS, AND NOT EVEN HUMANS SEEMED TO HAVE FOUND SOME OF THE ANSWERS.

SEVERAL WEEKS PASSED AND FRANKY FINISHED ANOTHER STORY ABOUT THE SQUIRRELS. IN HIS SPARE TIME HE CARVED A HIDING PLACE IN THE WALL BEHIND ONE OF HIS BOOKCASES AND HUNG A LITTLE DOOR ON IT WITH A GOOD LOCK. THERE HE PUT ALL THE MAGIC POWDERS AND LIQUIDS SO NO ONE COULD ACCIDENTALLY HURT THEMSELVES. POWERFUL CHEMICALS LIKE THAT CAN BE VERY DANGEROUS.

HE ALSO FASHIONED A SMALL LOCKET TO WEAR AROUND HIS NECK ON A CHAIN. IT WAS CAREFULLY CARVED FROM A PIECE OF STONE AND HAD FOUR COMPARTMENTS, EACH WITH A TINY CORK. ONE COMPARTMENT, MARKED S, CONTAINED THE FLUID THAT MADE ONE SMALL. THE COMPARTMENT MARKED F CONTAINED THE GREEN POWDER TO MAKE ONE INTO A FOX. THE COMPARTMENT MARKED B CONTAINED THE FLUID TO MAKE ONE BIG, AND THE COMPARTMENT MARKED H HAD THE RED POWDER TO MAKE ONE INTO A HUMAN. FRANKY HAD DETERMINED TO WEAR THIS LOCKET AROUND HIS NECK AT ALL TIMES. ALSO ON THE SAME CHAIN USED FOR THE LOCKET, HE HAD THE SMALL TOOTH-SIZED FOX THAT HAD BEEN IN THE STONE BOX LITTLE KATHY AND MATTHEW FROM AMERICA HAD FOUND. FRANKY SOMEHOW FELT IT WAS A LUCKY CHARM.

ONE MORNING, NOT LONG AFTER HE HAD FINISHED HIS SQUIRREL STORY, FRANKY WENT UP TO FEED HIS CHICKENS AND GATHER EGGS, ONLY TO FIND THAT ONE OF HIS CHICKENS WAS GONE. THE TOP OF THE CAGE WAS TORN OFF AND THERE WAS NO CHICKEN. FRANKY WAS TRULY MYSTIFIED. HOW COULD ANYONE POSSIBLY CLIMB SO HIGH INTO THE TREE, PAST HIS HOUSE, WITH-OUT BEING HEARD OR SEEN? HE KNEW THE SQUIRRELS DIDN'T DO IT, BECAUSE HE'D BEEN WATCHING THEM WHILE HE WAS WRITING HIS STORY. ALSO, THE CAGES WERE TOO STRONG FOR THEM, AND WHAT WOULD A SQUIRREL WANT WITH A CHICKEN?

FRANKY REPAIRED THE CAGE AND DECIDED TO GET A NEW CHICKEN. THAT EVENING HE THOUGHT AND THOUGHT ABOUT THE ROBBERY BUT COULDN'T SOLVE IT.

THE NEXT MORNING, ANOTHER OF HIS GOOD CHICKENS WAS GONE. THE CAGE WAS TORN OPEN IN THE SAME WAY. THIS WAS TOO MUCH! FRANKY DECIDED HE'D HAVE TO DO SOMETHING.

FIRST, HE REPAIRED THE CAGE. THEN HE WENT DOWNSTAIRS TO A SACK IN HIS CELLAR. IT WAS FILLED WITH CHICKEN FEATHERS FRANKY'D BEEN SAVING FROM THE BOTTOM OF THE CHICKEN CAGES, WITH THE IDEA OF MAKING A SOFT PILLOW FOR HIMSELF. FRANKY HATED TO WASTE ANYTHING.

HE GLUED ALL THESE FEATHERS ONTO A BURLAP CLOTH AND COVERED HIMSELF WITH IT. HE LOOKED IN THE LITTLE MIRROR LUCIA HAD GIVEN HIM AND DECIDED THAT IF IT WERE DARK HE MIGHT BE MISTAKEN FOR A CHICKEN.

THAT NIGHT, AFTER HE HAD EATEN HIS DINNER, FRANKY CLIMBED UP THE TREE AND CRAWLED INTO ONE OF THE EMPTY CAGES. HE CURLED UNDER HIS CHICKEN-FEATHER CLOTH AND WAITED. IT WAS A NICE NIGHT AND THE STARS WERE OUT. FRANKY PEEKED UP THROUGH THE CAGE AND THE LEAVES OF THE TREE TO WATCH THE STARS PASS SLOWLY BY.

AFTER ABOUT TWO OR THREE HOURS, THE STARS WERE SUD-

DENLY BLACKED OUT BY A BIG OBJECT FLYING OVERHEAD. THERE
WAS A RUSH OF FEATHERS AND THE CHICKENS CLUCKED NER-
VOUSLY. FRANKY LOOKED OUT FROM UNDER HIS COVER AND SAW
A HUGE EAGLE DESCEND UPON ONE OF THE CHICKEN CAGES AND
START TEARING IT APART WITH ITS SHARP CLAWS!

FRANKY JUMPED OUT FROM UNDER HIS CHICKEN CLOTH AND OUT OF THE CAGE. HE DASHED TOWARD THE EAGLE. THE EAGLE SAW HIM AND STARTED TO FLY AWAY, BUT FRANKY CAUGHT IT BY ONE OF ITS LEGS. THEN HE FELT HIMSELF LIFTED OUT OF THE TREE, AS THE EAGLE STRAINED ITS MIGHTY WINGS TO FREE ITSELF.

FRANKY LOOKED DOWN AND SAW HIS TREE HOME GET SMALLER BELOW IN THE MOONLIGHT. HIGHER AND HIGHER THEY FLEW, AND FRANKY BEGAN TO WISH HE'D STAYED IN BED. MORE THAN THAT, HE WISHED HE HAD SOME WEAPON WITH WHICH TO FIGHT THE EAGLE. HE WAS LIKELY TO BECOME EAGLE FOOD HIM-SELF IF HE WEREN'T CAREFUL. A LITTLE FOX IS NOT REALLY MUCH OF A MATCH FOR A BIG EAGLE. THIS WAS GETTING TO BE MORE ADVENTURE THAN FRANKY WAS LOOKING FOR.

THEN FRANKY THOUGHT OF HIS MAGIC LOCKET. HOLDING ON WITH ONE HAND, HE CAREFULLY REACHED UNDER HIS JACKET WITH THE OTHER AND PULLED IT OUT. HE COULDN'T SEE VERY WELL IN THE RUSHING DARK. HE TOOK A SMALL DRINK OF THE FLUID HE THOUGHT WOULD MAKE HIM BIGGER, BUT HE MADE A MISTAKE.

HE DRANK THE WRONG FLUID AND STARTED TO GET SMALLER, SO SMALL, IN FACT, HE FOUND HIMSELF SITTING ON ONE OF THE LARGE CLAWS OF THE EAGLE! HE HELD ON TIGHT TO HIS LOCKET, WHICH NOW SEEMED BIG AS A BARREL.

BEFORE HE COULD CORRECT HIS MISTAKE BY DRINKING THE RIGHT FLUID, THE EAGLE STARTED TO DESCEND AND LANDED IN A TREE. FRANKY SAW THERE WAS A NEST WITH A BABY EAGLE IN IT. SCATTERED AROUND WERE THE FEATHERS OF FRANKY'S CHICKENS.

FRANKY JUMPED OFF THE EAGLE'S FOOT AND TRIED TO HIDE IN A CRACK OF THE TREE. HE HAULED HIS LOCKET WITH HIM AL-THOUGH IT WAS VERY HEAVY. IT WAS THE ONLY CHANCE FRANKY HAD.

THE EAGLE SAW FRANKY AND HOPPED SIDEWAYS OVER TO THE CRACK IN THE BARK WHERE FRANKY WAS HIDDEN. SHE STARTED TO PECK AT IT. FRANKY REALIZED THAT WITH A FEW PECKS HE WOULD BE TAKEN AND FED TO THE BABY EAGLE, SMALL A BITE THOUGH HE MIGHT BE. THAT BABY EAGLE WAS HUNGRY.

FRANKY FINALLY MANAGED TO GET THE CORK OFF THE COMPARTMENT MARKED *B*. IT WAS QUITE A STRUGGLE. FRANKY TIPPED THE BARREL-SIZED LOCKET AND TOOK A BIG DRINK, WHICH WASN'T REALLY VERY MUCH BECAUSE FRANKY WAS SO LITTLE NOW. FRANKY TOOK SEVERAL DEEP SWALLOWS.

IN JUST SECONDS, FRANKY SWELLED OUT OF THE CRACK—ALL EXCEPT ONE FOOT, WHICH WAS CAUGHT. HE'D ACTUALLY COME BACK ONLY TO HIS REGULAR SIZE.

AT FIRST, THE EAGLE HOPPED BACKWARD A FEW STEPS BUT THEN CAME FORWARD TO FINISH OFF THIS EVEN MORE INTERESTING BIT OF MEAT FOR HER BABY. FRANKY WAS AFRAID TO DRINK ANY MORE MAGIC FLUID UNTIL HE'D GOTTEN HIS FOOT OUT OF THE CRACK. HE TWISTED AND PULLED WHILE THE EAGLE ADVANCED. HERE FRANKY WAS IN A TRAP JUST LIKE THE ONE DOM HAD SET SO LONG AGO.

AT THE LAST POSSIBLE MOMENT, FRANKY GOT HIS FOOT LOOSE AND DRANK TWO MORE DROPS FROM THE LOCKET. NOW HE WAS BIG AS A TIGER, AND WHEN THE EAGLE CHARGED, FRANKY STRUCK OUT WITH HIS SHARP CLAWS AND KILLED HER. SHE REELED AND FELL OUT OF THE TREE TO THE GROUND.

FRANKY WAS GLAD TO HAVE ESCAPED, BUT FELT SORRY FOR HAVING KILLED THE EAGLE, WHO WAS ONLY TRYING TO GET FOOD FOR HER BABY.

WHILE THE BEAUTIFUL EAGLE LAY DEAD ON THE GROUND, THE POOR BABY IN THE NEST WAS MAKING SAD NOISES, CALLING HER MOTHER TO FEED HER. FRANKY PICKED THE BABY OUT OF THE NEST. IT HAD ALL ITS SOFT FEATHERS BUT NONE OF THE

HEAVY LONG FEATHERS IN THE WINGS AND TAIL THAT WOULD LATER ENABLE IT TO FLY. FRANKY DECIDED TO TAKE THE BABY EAGLE HOME WITH HIM AND SEE WHAT HE COULD DO.

IT WAS SURPRISING HOW FAR HE AND THE MOTHER EAGLE HAD FLOWN IN SUCH A SHORT TIME. IT WAS DAWN BEFORE FRANKY GOT HOME AGAIN.

THE FIRST THING HE DID WAS FIX A WARM NEST FOR THE BABY EAGLE BESIDE THE FIRE AND MAKE HER A MEAL WITH SIX OF HIS CHICKEN EGGS. THEN FRANKY WENT UP TO HIS OWN BED AND WAS MORE THAN GLAD TO FALL ASLEEP AFTER HIS NIGHT'S ADVENTURE.

DURING THE NEXT DAYS, FRANKY SPENT A GOOD PART OF HIS TIME CATCHING MICE AND SMALL ANIMALS TO FEED THE BABY EAGLE. WHEN LUCIA AND DOMINIC CAME, HE ASKED THEM TO BUY HIM SOME TRAPS. THAT SAVED QUITE A BIT OF TIME CHASING MICE AND MOLES AND LITTLE ANIMALS. LUCIA GAVE THE EAGLE THE NAME *BAMBINO,* WHICH IS "BABY" IN ITALIAN.

BAMBINO GREW RAPIDLY AND SOON WAS TOO BIG FOR HER NAME. FRANKY SHORTENED IT TO BAMBA. IT WAS ABOUT A MONTH AFTER BAMBA HAD LEARNED TO FLY AND CATCH HER OWN FOOD THAT FRANKY DECIDED TO TRY OUT AN IDEA. HE HAD LEARNED ENOUGH EAGLE LANGUAGE, AND BAMBA HAD LEARNED ENOUGH FOX AND ITALIAN—ALTHOUGH SHE COULDN'T ACTUALLY SPEAK THOSE LANGUAGES—THAT THEY COULD UNDERSTAND EACH OTHER. FOR AN EAGLE, BAMBA WAS QUITE SMART.

FRANKY MADE A LITTLE SADDLE AND HARNESS TO FIT BAMBA. BAMBA THOUGHT SHE LOOKED QUITE ATTRACTIVE WITH IT ON. THEN FRANKY DRANK ONE DROP OF HIS GET-SMALL MAGIC FLUID UNTIL HE WAS ONE-QUARTER HIS SIZE, OR ABOUT THE SIZE OF A VERY LITTLE KITTEN. HE CLIMBED INTO THE SADDLE AND

GAVE A SIGNAL FOR BAMBA TO FLY. THEY FLEW UP OVER THE TREES
FAST, HIGHER AND HIGHER. AT FIRST FRANKY WAS AFRAID, BUT
AFTER A WHILE BECAME ACCUSTOMED TO IT AND ENJOYED RIDING
BAMBA VERY MUCH. SOMETIMES, HOWEVER, BAMBA WOULD FOR-
GET AND DIVE AFTER A MOUSE OR A BIRD FLYING BELOW. FOR
FRANKY THIS WAS VERY SCARY, AND HE'D HANG ON FOR DEAR LIFE.

FRANKY FELT NOW HE COULD GO ANYWHERE HE WANTED WITHOUT HAVING TO USE TRAINS OR AIRPLANES. AS BAMBA GREW OLDER AND STRONGER, THEY TRIED FARTHER AND FARTHER VOYAGES, UNTIL SOMETIMES THEY WOULD FLY THOUSANDS OF MILES IN A FEW DAYS.

FRANKY VISITED ALL THE PLACES HE WANTED TO GO. HE WOULD FLY WITH BAMBA TO THE OUTSIDE OF A CITY WITH HIS MAN CLOTHES ROLLED TIGHTLY INTO A BUNDLE BEHIND THE SADDLE. THEY WOULD LAND AT NIGHT. FRANKY WOULD GET OFF, DRINK SOME OF HIS MAGIC BIG FLUID, AND TAKE SOME OF THE MAGIC MAN POWDER. HE WOULD PUT ON HIS MAN CLOTHES AND VISIT THE CITY. THERE HE WOULD GO TO MUSEUMS, LIBRARIES, BUY THE BOOKS AND THINGS HE WANTED, THEN COME BACK TO BAMBA AND DO EVERYTHING BACKWARD AGAIN UNTIL HE COULD FLY HOME.

FRANKY NOW HAD ALL THE ADVANTAGES OF BEING A HUMAN PLUS THOSE OF BEING A SMART FOX. BESIDES THAT, WITH BAMBA HE COULD FLY. LITTLE DID HE KNOW HE WAS BEING WATCHED AND THAT SOON ALL HIS SPECIAL TALENTS AND INTELLIGENCE WOULD BE NEEDED!

CHAPTER 8

THE MEETING

I put down my book. I look around the *Bier Stube*. Men keep coming in, dressed in hunting costumes. Some of them store shotguns in racks by the door. Many have their own beer steins, which they take from wooden racks by the bar and push forward onto the bar to be filled.

As each comes in, he is greeted by the others. There are no women except for the woman behind the bar. It's almost like some kind of private club. I begin to feel out of place, the way I'd felt most of my life until I met Franky Furbo, then Caroline. There never seemed to be any place for me before.

I try again to remember my childhood, but there's nothing. This could be another proof I really *am* crazy. I remember in great detail a whole tale everybody insists never happened, even two complete languages, but I can't remember my own life. The theories of the army psychiatrists make some sense.

They were always trying to get me to remember my past. All I could say was I lost my parents, was an orphan, grew up in an orphan asylum. Even under hypnosis, there was nothing. It was one of the proofs to them that I could block or repress large important parts of my experience in some kind of survival system.

After another beer and two more pretzels, the *Stube* is almost full. The men are settling down to cards and other games at different tables. I can tell easily how the same people tend to play the same games with one another. One table in a corner has a sign on it in German saying it is reserved; it's called *Stamtish*. This must be for the real regulars. I wonder if these men have homes, what their wives do while they're out playing games. Outside, I can hear the whoops and shouts along with the crashing of wooden balls against wooden pins as others are bowling. Through the window in the wall across from where I'm sitting, I can see lights along the length of the bowling alley.

About an hour later, Wilhelm comes in the door. I recognize him immediately. He's aged as I have, perhaps even more, but there's no doubt in my mind. My heart skips a beat just at the sight of him.

My temptation is to rush up and greet him, but I decide it would be better to wait until we can be alone. Inside, I'm flooded with joy. I'm *not* really crazy. Here he is, not just vague talk about him, but Wilhelm in the flesh, before me.

He comes in alone, but three men at the bar go over and shake his hand. They each tip their hats with their other hand as they shake hands. It's all very formal and not so hearty, not with the same kind of camaraderie that seems to be so much a part of the other groupings.

But they know what they want and sit at the reserved table, a U-shaped bench around a wooden table next to a large green tile stove. Because it's a cool evening, the fire is burning in the stove.

Wilhelm gave me a brief glance as he came in, seemed to linger a minute on my face as if perhaps he recognized me, but then settled down with the other men. I think it's my beard that threw him off; also, he wasn't expecting me.

I know, from the cards and from what Hilda told me, that they're going to play the game Wilhelm and I had often played at Franky's. Wilhelm is sitting so I can see his face in profile. I begin to wonder if I've taken one of the tables reserved for other players. There are still some men at the bar and there are no places left. But the woman who runs the place will have to ask me to move if she wants the table. After coming all this way, I'm going to speak to Wilhelm, somehow.

Wilhelm is still the same: about my height, but more lanky, with a little spring—more of a lope—in his step. He has a shock of white hair hanging across his forehead, almost into his eyes. He has no beard, but there are deep lines in his face, from his eyes down to his jaw, and from the sides of his nose deep beside his mouth. His lips are thinner than mine. He wears silver-rimmed glasses. He does not look like a happy man.

But still, despite these differences, there is something familiar about him, not just because I remember him from those wonderful days long ago, but because he resembles me in some strange way. If there could be a German version of myself, he's it. In making the mental exchange between us, Franky must have blended us physically as well. I can't keep my eyes off him as they order large steins of beer and start playing.

Some of the men at the bar begin drifting over to various games—*Schafskopf*, chess, backgammon, bridge, pinochle—to watch or kibitz. There's much thumping of cards on the tables, hard knuckles on hard wood, rough laughing, gloating, arguing. But loud as it is, there's a feeling of friendship.

I know I'm the only one not part of this place. I get up and drift with my glass over to where Wilhelm is playing. No one seems to notice me, but with decent haste, a group of four slip past and occupy the table I've vacated.

I'm happy to be watching the game as Wilhelm plays. I can

see his cards, although he holds them quite close to his chest. He's one of the least demonstrative of players but plays well. *Schafskopf*, when played with four players, is a game in which the partners change with each hand so each player is, in a sense, playing his hands alone, for his own benefit. I don't see any money on the table, but I'm fairly sure there's money involved because the score is kept so carefully. The method of keeping score is to mark the parts of a sheep's head on the table with points scored until the entire sheep's head is drawn. It's marked in chalk. This is how the game got its name. Wilhelm told me this was the old-fashioned way to do it, and taught me how.

At about ten, one of the men at the table stands up. He counts out thirty marks on the table.

"My wife will kill me if I don't come home early. This should cover what I owe and my beer."

He looks up at me.

"Maybe this one will take my place. Do you play *Schafskopf, mein Herr?*"

I nod yes and he slides out while the others make room for me to climb into his place.

The player on his right says, quietly:

"We play ten pfennigs a point, OK?"

I nod my head again. I look up at Wilhelm. Now he's looking at me more intently. He's the only one who seems not too pleased that I'm joining the group.

In watching Wilhelm play, much came back to me. We got so we could hardly play the game together because we knew each other so well, especially when it was only the two of us playing. Franky would rarely play. He said being telepathic made it very difficult to play without automatically cheating.

Up until now, Wilhelm has had the best of the others by far. I can see if he plays this well every Friday, even at ten pfennigs a point, he doesn't have to work very hard and still make a living.

But now, I use my advantage. It's as if I know two hands of cards—mine and Wilhelm's. I know just how he'll play each hand and why he's played each card. It isn't really fair, because if he'd have recognized me, he could have done the same. Within the hour, I'm clearly the winner. Other players, in other games, as they break up to go home, stop by to see who this is, this stranger who's playing so well. I think they begin to think I really am some kind of card shark. It's not very comfortable.

Finally, I've had enough. I really don't like card games or any other kinds of games. But it's difficult to quit when you're ahead; the others always want to get their money back.

"OK if this is the last hand?"

I look around the table. Only Wilhelm looks up.

"I stake all I've won on my having the winning hand this time. All right?"

The others look at me. Their silence is consent.

Wilhelm wins the bid and says he'll play with the *Grünen As*, that is the "green ace." It turns out I have the green ace in my hand so he's my partner for this game.

I see right away we have all the cards. We can win easily and it will only be worse. I'll walk away with the hard-earned money of these men. I look at Wilhelm. He's watching me closely. He stands to win considerably by this hand as well.

While he's looking at me, I take my chance. I speak in clear Fox; it takes only what sounds like a click and a grunt with a twist of the nose and mouth:

"Wilhelm, this is William. Let's not win. It wouldn't be right."

He stares at me. His face turns white to match his hair. He almost drops his cards. Then he looks down at them. It's his turn to play. There's an uncomfortable silence while we wait. He places his cards face down on the table. He looks up at me again and says in German:

"We cannot win. Do you agree?"

I put my cards on the table, face down.

"I agree."

The other players are stunned. Wilhelm reaches out for all the cards and shuffles them. He takes money from his leather pants, enough to cover the little he owes plus beer, and I pay for my beers. Then he slides out with the others and we all prepare to leave. We're the last in the room.

Wilhelm surprises me by rushing through the door, not waiting for me. I hurry after him. He's striding along the road toward his house, but I catch up. I speak to him in Fox.

"Wilhelm, this is William, your friend. What's the matter."

"Stay away from me. For God's sake, for your own sake, stay away."

I'm speaking in Fox but he answers in German. I can't understand why; he won't look at me. He continues his fast lope, almost running. I puff along beside him.

"Tell me, Wilhelm. Speak to me. What's wrong?"

"Everything's wrong. Please go away. I know things no one should know. I can tell only you, but I don't want to tell. Why should I ruin your life, too? There is only so much a human should have to live with."

We pass the old oak. Wilhelm looks at it as we go by, then he stops.

"There were times when I wanted to build myself a home in that tree, before lightning struck it twenty years ago. But that's all romantic nonsense."

He hurries on. I hurry after him. He stops again.

"Please, William. In the name of our friendship, leave me alone. Go home to America."

This he says in English. My heart leaps. His voice is mine. It's one more proof of what I believe.

"I left my bag at your house, Wilhelm. I came earlier and you weren't there."

"How did you know where I lived?"

"I went to *Haus Fürst*. Frau Doctor Demmel told me where you were."

He slows, looks at me. I can't see his eyes in the dark.

"It *is* true isn't it, all of it? You do know my mind as I know yours. It is so *impossible*.

"Wilhelm, help me, please. I'm beginning to think I'm crazy. My wife doesn't believe me, my children don't believe me. I live my life as Franky told us to live it and now I feel so alone. Please, listen to me, help me!"

We've reached his hut. He takes out a key and opens the door. He looks back at me. He speaks to me in Fox.

"All right, for old time's sake. Come on in. We can have a glass of schnapps together. But don't ask too much."

I follow him into the house. There is a low fire burning in a small fireplace at the back of the house. I didn't see any smoke when I came by myself, earlier. He must have come home before he went to the tavern.

He opens a closet beside the fireplace. There is a crude wooden table in the center of the room. There are two chairs. I sit in one of them. Wilhelm comes back with a bottle and two small glasses. He speaks again in Fox.

"It's so wonderful to hear Fox again, it's as if I've been partially deaf for over forty years."

He sits across from me heavily. He holds up the bottle.

"This is one thing Franky warned us against that I cannot resist. It is one of the ways I keep myself in one piece, in my mind. Is it as good for you to speak and hear in Fox as it is for me?"

"Yes, Wilhelm. I was only now having the same thought. It's like hearing music, music you know and haven't heard for a long time."

"Yes. We are spoiled for life."

He pours himself a drink of the clear schnapps and motions with the bottle to see if I want some. I nod. Already I've drunk three steins of beer, and I don't like alcohol, but I want to drink with Wilhelm.

He holds up his glass and I hold up mine. He looks me in the eyes.

"Prosit."

"Prosit, Wilhelm, to Franky Furbo and all he stands for."

There's silence.

"What do you want from me, William? You know if you've talked to Frau Doctor Demmel, Hilda, what happened to me, how my lovely Ulrika died, and the baby, too. You know how I live now."

"Yes, I know. I'm terribly sorry, Wilhelm. But you should try to live on, to show others the way Franky taught us. You shouldn't bury yourself alone in this forest. It is a waste."

"That is not why I am here. You don't know."

"Tell me, Wilhelm. Tell me why you are here."

"It is too terrible. You are my friend. If I tell you, I can never call myself your friend again."

"But if we are friends, then we should share all. I can tell you everything about my life, how I have lived, what I am doing, why I am here."

"Please do that, William. I want to hear it. Tell it to me in Fox. I'm sure no other language would do."

And so, there, by the light of the fire and a candle on the table, I tell Wilhelm everything, from the time Franky left me and told me to go to the American soldiers, right up until now, when I've lost confidence in Franky Furbo, all that happened, and have come searching for Wilhelm, to prove or disprove my life, all I've lived for. It takes a long time to tell. When I'm finished, Wilhelm is crying. He has lowered his head so it hangs over the table, and large tears fall onto the wooden planks and are soaked into it. I wait in the quiet.

"William, I'm so glad you did it. I'm so happy that one of us really lived as Franky told us. It makes all the rest almost worth the while."

"What do you mean, Wilhelm? What rest is there to make worthwhile?"

Again there's a long silence. Wilhelm has stopped crying and I hear only the sound of the fire.

"All right. Franky said I should tell no one, only you. But that I should not search for you, only let you find me if you would, if you could."

He looks up at me again.

"And so you are here. I hoped, prayed you would never find me, never come again into my life. I'm sorry but it is true."

I wait in the quiet. Wilhelm reaches behind him to a shelf under a window. He pulls over a box and a chessboard.

"Do you remember these, William? I have played many games alone by myself thinking of you and the games we played, the games we didn't play because we had so much to talk about. Those were marvelous times."

He puts the box and the board on the table, opens the box, places the pieces on the board. He's quiet. Then, in a low voice, he starts to speak. The pieces and the board are worn so they are almost unrecognizable.

"William, I cheated. On our walks with Franky, I made marks so I could find my way back if I ever wanted to. When he led me out of the forest, I noticed names of villages, crossroads, so I could find my way back to his tree, to his home.

"But I didn't. I came here and was happy with Ulrika. After some difficult times, I found work. I was happy. I told Ulrika about Franky Furbo and she believed me. I started building this house in the forest so we could live here and have our children, teach them ourselves, stay away from all the lunacy of the world. Ulrika became pregnant with our baby. I didn't think I could ever be more happy.

"Then, when the baby came, Ulrika died, and my little William died, too, the next day. Yes, I named him after you.

"Nothing seemed to matter anymore. I decided I'd go back to Franky and ask what I should do.

"I traveled to Italy and found his forest. I found his tree. I knocked on the door. It was all as it was before, except I was so large. Franky came to the door.

"He did not seem surprised. He made me small enough, and I went inside with him. He took me up to his thinking room.

"Franky looked me in the eyes the way he could do, as if looking through you. He said:

" 'I know you have been having a terrible time, Wilhelm. I've been expecting you. I would like to help you, but I can't. I shall be leaving here very soon, and I can't tell you where I am going.'

"I sat quietly, feeling despair, wondering what I would do if Franky couldn't help me. He went on:

" 'I know you are unhappy, and perhaps I should really tell this to William, but since you are here now, I shall tell you. Some human should know. It is only right, and I know I can trust you not to tell anyone else. The one person you may tell what I am going to tell you is William, but only if he comes looking for you, only if he needs your help. Do you understand?'

"I nodded. I didn't know what he was about to tell me but I trusted him as we always trusted Franky. For me, he was like a God. He still is in a strange way. But it is so hard. When you know what I know you will understand what I mean."

Wilhelm stops again. He pours some more of the schnapps in our glasses.

"Well, William, this is the story Franky told me. After I've told you, you can never again be the same, so drink up in your wonderful ignorance. If I didn't feel that telling you is what Franky wants, I wouldn't do this, I would show you to my door and permit you to live in your blissful happiness.

"This is what Franky told me."

From this point on, Wilhelm's voice changed. It was as if I were listening to Franky himself speaking to me in Fox. It is hard to explain, but somehow, through Wilhelm, I felt Franky was speaking to me.

CHAPTER 9

FRANKY'S STORY

"*F*ranky *talked to me in Fox. You know how it is—it's almost like telepathy in that everything is so clean and clear, so beautiful.*

"*I had only been in Franky's thinking room a few times while we lived with him. Remember, he'd invite us up there on special occasions or when he had something very important to tell us. It was almost empty except for a desk with a chair and a large chair in front of it. Light from a window fell on the desk between us. The walls were lined from floor to ceiling with books, and they were cataloged as in a library. The atmosphere was quiet—a place to really think. I've tried, here, to imitate that room, but it's impossible; only Franky Furbo could make things have a life of their own.*

"*Franky sat in his desk chair and indicated I should sit in the large, comfortable chair. The light came through the window so it lit his eyes with that amazing yellow amber glow, almost like fire, the way they'd glow when he was trying to impart some special thoughts to us. We sat quietly, Franky looking at me carefully. I still felt as if he were trying to decide whether to tell me something important or not. I knew it had to be very important for Franky to glow the way he was glowing, a reverse kind of telepathy that enhanced Fox even more when he spoke it. I waited. Then he started speaking":*

One day about two months ago, Wilhelm, there was a knock on my door, downstairs. I was all the way up here in my thinking room, working on a new children's story designed to help children know the joys of helping one another instead of constantly competing. You know how I feel about that.

I ran down the stairs. There in the doorway stood the most beautiful vixen I've ever seen, could ever even possibly conceive, and she said to me in perfect Fox:

"Are you Franky Furbo?"

You can imagine how shocked I was. I was so excited and pleased, I'm sure my pink tail was a shining red. I stepped back from the door and she followed me in. Finally I managed to get my voice back.

"Yes, I am. But, how is it that you, a mere fox, can speak Fox so beautifully? What is happening?"

"Then it's true! I've found you at last!"

Tears ran down her muzzle and she kept looking at me so closely, so intently, I was more embarrassed than I've ever been in my life.

And she was so beautiful. She had amber eyes with a touch of green and a lovely shining coat, reddish with slight tinges of gray on the outside tips of the hairs. Her tail was a pale color, between the color of her eyes and the pink of my own tail.

I'm listening to Wilhelm and I'm having the strangest sensations. At first, it's as if I'm becoming Wilhelm, that what's happening is a continuation of the long-ago past life I have of his in my mind.

Then, stranger yet, I feel myself being metamorphosed into actually *being* Franky Furbo, *experiencing* what he is telling Wilhelm and what he, in turn, is telling me. I realize Franky must have planned it so, that he intended I have a "real" experience of that which he is telling me across the years. It's frightening, but I find myself succumbing to this loss of identity as William Wiley, becoming Franky Furbo so I can understand. I listen, hear, feel, know, as Wilhelm continues with Franky's story:

I invite her to come upstairs. She follows me. I'm so happy, so agitated, my paws are shaking.

She keeps following me with her eyes. I have so many questions to ask, but I can't keep from staring. She speaks again, her voice so low, her Fox so beautiful; I feel my own Fox is nothing but gross sounds and awkward movements, like some farm animal.

"I can't believe I've actually found you. You are everything I've imagined. How difficult it must be for you, with all your talents, living back here in these primitive times.

"You see, Mr. Furbo, I've been looking for you through fifty thousand years of time and through all the space on this planet. We'd just about begun to believe that perhaps you were not of this planet at all, that you were not even an individual."

I'm listening but not understanding. I know I should say something.

"Would you like some tea?"

She cocks her head, smiles, looks at me intently.

"Do you have what is called 'herb tea,' made without any stimulants?"

I actually have fifty-two different varieties. I offer her my personal preference. I put on the teakettle and hope she will go on speaking Fox. I'm interested in what she has to say, but, more important, I want to hear this beautiful, lilting, dancing as she speaks. I sit down and wait, all of my body quivering.

"This will be difficult for you to comprehend, but I come from fifty thousand years in the future, where foxes are the dominant creatures on this planet. I am a scientist, what you would probably call an anthropologist or perhaps an archaeologist in these times. My specialty is the origin of our species. It's been a long search and at last it is rewarded. I have many questions to ask and many things to tell you. Would you be willing to answer some of my questions?"

I don't want her to stop. I nod my head. Also, what she is saying is beginning to sink into my brain. It's so strange, so exciting, I still can't understand, believe. I go over and take the tea water off the heat; I pour some in the teapot to steep.

"First, I know there are still primitive foxes in this time, as there are in ours. Do you have any relations with them?"

I pull myself together. After all, I *am* supposed to be an intelligent fox.

"No. I don't. They are merely simple hunters, have no language worth considering. They live in the ground and care only about eating and reproduction; they are not very intelligent. I moved away from them a long time ago."

"But were you born of a fox, a primitive fox?"

"Yes, my brother and sisters in the same litter with me were normal foxes. My mother was a red fox, but she was killed trying to catch

chickens from a human farmer. This loss was what decided me to move here and develop my own life."

She isn't writing anything down, but her eyes shift away from me as if she's registering what I say in some complex notation system inside her brain. Her eyes come back to me. Their beauty is such I can hardly look into them.

"How long in earth years has it been since you were born?"

"By the time I could calculate years, I'd probably been alive one year. Since then I've lived almost twenty-five years, I think. This is much too old for a fox, so I suppose in this area of existence also, I'm some special breed of fox. I suspect I'm some blend of a red and gray fox, but that doesn't explain anything much either."

"You are a radical mutation. That much we know. Your father was part of some experimental work being done by humans, and he escaped. He bred with your mother. I've seen that. He was killed by the same human who killed your mother, within a few weeks of that breeding. We do not think the experimental work being carried out on him is responsible for your mutation, however. We have another theory for that."

I begin to feel like an experimental animal myself. Her mind is so sharp and clear through the Fox, and it isn't only her language. I can see—read—her mind, and it's straight and logical. I can tell, also, that she can read my mind. I decide to say something about this.

"But you know what is in my mind, why do you ask me these questions? For me, this is the first time I have ever been with another telepath. I don't understand."

"Then you must know I know you enjoy hearing me speak in the Fox of our times. It is only right and correct that I speak in Fox,

now, if it gives you pleasure, especially since all of our language is based upon your creation. It gives me great pleasure to speak with you, too. Telepathy has its limitations; it is too removed from the physical."

She turns her eyes away from me and I can see how her tail, too, changes color slightly; also, her nose wiggles in a smile. I try to close off her mind, block my own.

"Thank you. You must understand this is all so new to me. Please tell me more; tell me all you know."

"That can wait. First, would you answer a few more questions before we leave?"

I wonder who's leaving. Is she with someone else? It's all so confusing.

"Of course. I'll answer any questions. It's true I am much moved to hear you speak such beautiful Fox."

"This is somewhat foxial. Are there any other foxes of your quality with whom you have met, or of whom you have heard? We are especially interested in any vixens with whom you might have had relations. Have you had sexual relations with any ordinary foxes?"

Now I definitely have "red tail." I'd thought along these lines many times. But never had there seemed to be any solution. I take a deep breath.

"No, I've never heard of any foxes like myself, and naturally I have been searching. I do not like living alone. I could not bring myself to have . . . relations . . . with an ordinary fox. I am not attracted to them in that way any more than to a rabbit or dog. I do not feel part of their species. So, I live alone."

She registers this. She looks me in the eyes again.

"Have you perhaps developed parthenogenesis? I know it's a characteristic of some very low life-forms, but it is one possibility."

"No. Nothing like that. I don't think any fox could ever manage anything like that."

"That is our finding, too. It is only one theory."

I wait. She is so beautiful, so cool and so warm at the same time. Everything up until now has been worth it.

"Have you experimented with cloning, making copies of yourself?"

"No. How would that be done?"

"I'm sorry. I forgot. Of course, this concept hasn't been developed in this time yet. It is a way to make biological replicas of yourself."

"But they would all be male, then, wouldn't they? And you are obviously a vixen, not a male."

She stares at me again, wiggles her nose.

"I expected you to be intelligent. We knew this must be the case, but I hadn't expected you would have developed your logical faculties to such a degree, or that you'd be so gallant."

She smiles, turns her head, looks out the window.

"Am I being too arrogant? I don't mean to be; it is all so marvelous that you are here, that I have found you. Our world will consider it the most important discovery in thousands of years. What, by the way, have you discovered of your many capacities beyond the human?"

"Well, I can talk Fox, a language I invented, not as well as you, but it is something. I can learn all other languages easily. I can

transmute matter so as to make myself large or small, invisible, or seem to take any form that I know, including human. I can move over great distances quickly, almost like flying, but not quite: I guess that would be called transmigration of the body.

"As you know, I'm a telepath. I can also transfer information from one human brain to another, and mentally communicate with almost any animal form I've encountered. I think that's about it."

"You have other skills you have not yet discovered. It will be a joy for me to introduce you to them. It seems so strange to be the one to show you—the source of all our civilization—some of the abilities we have only because of you. It is strange, isn't it."

Her warmth and gratitude are in her voice and in her mind. I feel it, and again I'm sure my tail is glowing.

"Now, would you please come with me? You have a skill you have not discovered —the ability to move through time. However, you can only move into the past. After all, the past, no matter how far back, is all we really know exists. I'm trying to tell you that there is a future from which I come, but for you it does not exist except in my mind.

"However, if you will enter into my mind, hold on tightly to my body, theoretically I should be able to take you—at least your mind—with me into the future. And hopefully, if we hold tightly enough, your body also. Will you come with me?"

She must have read my mind because her tail glows as brightly as mine.

"May I know your name?"

"I'm called, in Fox, Raethe. May I call you Franky, Mr. Furbo? I've known your name a long time and have always thought of you as such. I remember the thrill when I became convinced that you must be the source and that was your name. Do you mind?"

"No, please. Raethe, let us be on our way. I am anxious to see this world of the future where you live."

At Raethe's instruction, we wrap our arms, legs, and tails around each other, with our eyes as close as they can be. To get our eyes close it's necessary for us to open our mouths and overlap our upper and lower jaws. She'd told me I must try to blank out my mind, to let it become hers, before we can move together forward in time. But this is very hard. I'd never been so close to another creature, let alone such a beautiful vixen.

But, finally, with the strength of her mind, I feel myself melting and a warm, red darkness comes over me. It seems like only a short time before I come back to myself. Raethe has unlocked our jaws. She slowly unwraps our tails, then our arms and legs. She looks at me appraisingly.

"We did it. You're all here with me, mind and body. This in itself will be something to report to the research council. I'm so happy."

At that, she slowly brushes her beautiful tail across my muzzle. From my own flushed reaction, I know this must be the way foxes kiss fifty thousand years in the future. It seems so natural, as if I've always known this.

I look around and am disappointed. I had expected to see a myriad of sky roads, glass buildings in complicated forms, amazing transport systems, but we are in an open glade. There's nothing but trees and fields to be seen in any direction. Perhaps we have landed on an uninhabited part of the planet. Then I do start seeing small animals—squirrels, rabbits, birds, even a fox—scurrying at the edge of the forest.

"Are you sure we're there, Raethe? How far do we need to travel to arrive at your civilization? Shall we transmigrate ourselves?"

"We are there, Franky. This is the way the planet is now. We are only a few steps from the entry to the research unit where I work. You see, we foxes consider ourselves custodians of the planet. The entire earth's surface is exactly as it was before man ravaged it. Except for a few preserves, where we have some re-creations of the world during human ascendance, it is like this. Isn't it beautiful?"

I have to agree. I'd never seen, smelled, or known in any way the earth so beautiful, even in my forest. Raethe takes my paw in hers.

"Come, they're waiting for us. I sent a message to them before we left that I'd found you."

She positions me with her on a small square of grass. The edges can just be perceived. I don't know by what method she activates the mechanism, but suddenly we're descending into the earth at great speed. We come to an even, easy stop.

"We discourage body transmigration, except in emergencies. There have been too many accidents and too many unnecessary and uncalled-for invasions of privacy. By using ordinary methods of transport that don't violate the ecology, we find we get around quite as rapidly as we want and still maintain our integrity."

I'm following her down a large pathway that is not much different from the earth above. There is a glowing ceiling with sunlight and the appearance of clouds and blue sky. There is grass, and flowers bloom around us.

"We try, even down here, to keep the sense of a natural world. The advantage, of course, is that we need very little energy to

*maintain temperature. Most of the light you see is generated by
systems related to the photon energy of the sun. The fact that
humans didn't use this and insisted on the pollution of the atmosphere with fossil fuels is one of the great mysteries to our
historians and specialists in human behavior."*

She walks up to what looks like a rock wall; it opens and we are
in a large room. There are many foxes there, at least fifty. They
lounge on the floor, stand or sit in curved chairs with holes in
back for their tails. All stand when we come in. Raethe turns
toward me.

*"Colleagues, here he is, Franky Furbo, our source, our origin; in
human terms, the traditional Adam, progenitor of a new race."*

Noses twitch, waves of appreciation, curiosity, and joy surge
through my mind. I bow, not knowing what to say.

*"I found him on the thin peninsula jutting into the inland sea, the
peninsula that was called, at that long time ago, Italy. It is where
the ancient warlike civilization called Rome originated.*

*"He lived in a tree. The date, in old earth years, when I
found him, was April ninth, nineteen-forty-eight. He speaks Fox.
I shall allow him to speak through me to you as he answered my
first questions."*

I look at her and then hear myself speaking from her mouth. It
sounds so blatant, so stupid after listening to her speak her own
beautiful rhythms. All crowd around. I can tell from their eyes
they are recording all this in their own minds for future reference.
I feel alone. I'm listening to myself speaking from fifty thousand
years in the past through somebody else. It's very difficult to
accept.

When her report is finished, I am led to one of the reclining chairs at the head of a large table. The table is not round, square, oblong, or any form I've ever seen; it undulates to fit the forms and positions of those around it. There are many questions, mostly elaborations of the questions Raethe had asked me. I try answering them as best I can. There is discussion going on, both in Fox and by telepathy. It is very active in terms of mental activity in the room, but there is little sound. The prime concern still seems to be about my own remembrance of my origin and the possibility of my reproduction. I realize that, in a sense, they are looking for Adam's rib, the mate for the first in a new creation. After what seems several hours, Raethe speaks up.

"I think we should give Mr. Franky Furbo a rest. This is very much to absorb in such a short period of time. After all, he's been awake for over fifty thousand years."

There's a ripple of laughter, both in Fox and of the mind. Raethe leads me out of the room. Outside she turns to me.

"Would you prefer to stay in quarters by yourself, or to stay in mine?"

She looks into my eyes. Her nose isn't wiggling, but her tail has changed some color.

"Raethe, I don't know the customs here. Are the foxes monogamous? Do you have a mate? Would he mind having a strange primitive fox share accommodations with you?"

"Do you want to read my mind? I can make it open for you if you want."

"No, you know how I love to hear your voice, to hear you speak Fox. I should like to hear you tell me, whatever there is to tell."

"We are monogamous but not exclusively so. It is more the tendency and the tradition rather than any rigid rule. We have noth-

ing resembling human 'marriage.' Most of us make a commitment to each other for life, but it is not binding. We see it as the most logical of systems, and we are a very logical species."

She pauses and smiles.

"If you are concerned, I have not made a commitment. I have no mate. You may stay with me if you will, without any problem. There would not be a problem, even if I did have a mate. After all, we have developed some civilization. At the same time, I recognize that you have lived alone all your life, and living with someone else might prove uncomfortable. I can understand that. You have the choice."

"I choose to live in your quarters, Raethe. I hope you don't mind if I live somewhat crudely. You must remember, fifty thousand years have passed and ways of life must have changed tremendously. My ways might seem like those of an ordinary fox or a dog in my times would seem to me."

She takes my paw again.

"I'm not worried. I think I can live with a 'cavefox.' I'll enjoy introducing you to some of the advantages of these times. It will be a great pleasure for me."

We go up to the surface again. We walk through wooded vales, along ridge lines, in a balanced environment of animals and plants. The air is so incredibly clean and oxygenated I'm almost faint, or perhaps it is because I'm so close to Raethe. We don't talk much. She points out some of the more beautiful sections of the landscape. She says we are in what was once the cradle of human civilization, between the old rivers of the Tigris and Euphrates. Two ice ages have passed since my own time, and with the development of water reserves and land conservation, this is all the

Garden of Eden again. She smiles at me as she says this. She holds both my paws and lines me up on another small square in the ground, smaller this time.

"Now you shall see my home. We have our choice to live in communities or to live alone. I prefer to have my own space here, but more people live with others or in couples."

With that we descend deeply into the earth. When we glide to a stop, we are in a place exactly like that we've just left. I can't believe we're underground. I look around.

"You see, Franky, I like nature very much. I prefer things as unspoiled as possible. Come, see where I cook."

She has a small stone cook-place. I wonder how she can cook down here without the smoke filling what has to be an underground cave despite how it looks.

"It doesn't smoke. I burn wood that has been totally carbonized. It gives off heat but that is all. See, it looks just like wood."

She holds up a piece. It has bark and grain. There's no way to tell it isn't an ordinary small log.

"I know this is all very artificial to someone like you who has lived in the real world, in a real tree, burned real fires, had real rain, real storms, but it is the closest I can have. Come see where I sleep."

There is a tree, or something that looks like a tree, an oak. In the tree she has built a platform with a ladder to climb up into it. I climb behind her. She has a bed made from what looks like wood bark and hay. She stretches out on it. She looks so lovely.

She must read my mind because she sits up promptly.

"You should be very tired, Franky. You can sleep here if you want or I can make another bed for you. I have much to do in order to complete my report. I shall wake you for dinner, which I shall cook myself."

She slides past me out of the bed. I don't know if she plants the idea in my mind or she's only stimulated the thought that was already there. I'm suddenly so tired I barely manage to slide into the middle of the bed and stretch out. I don't even hear her go down the ladder. I don't have time to think about all that's happening to me. I thought I had a big brain that could understand almost anything, but it seems like an insignificant brain right then as I fall asleep.

When I wake, I'm surprised to find Raethe in bed beside me. She is awake watching me. I turn toward her.

"It was so nice watching you sleep, Franky. You seem to sleep so much more deeply than we do here, and your dreams are so different from ours."

"You could telepath my dreams?"

"You can do the same to me. I hope you don't mind. I wanted to share them with you and to find out more about you. In your dreams there is so much you might not know about yourself. The most important thing, something I really hadn't realized, is how alone, how separate, how alienated from your world you have been. It must have been a frightening experience.

"You also dreamed about someone called Lucia and another creature named Dominic. Are they your brother and sister, or someone else?"

I tell her about Lucia and Dominic, how they are human, about how I learned to read, to talk, about the trap, about how I learned to fear humans in their aggressiveness but how I can still relate to children, and how I make the money I need by writing books for them.

"Oh, yes, books. We have few books now. They were such a distraction from full communication. We share now through speech and telepathy; it is so much more complete, so much richer. It is one of the strange phenomena of your era we've never understood. Humans held on to the printed word as a way to transmit thought, long after the invention of other systems for distribution. The book, the printed word, forced natural language, with all its richness, into very limiting symbols. The almost exclusive use of these symbols for communication seriously impaired the development of the human mind. Books were a temporary necessity, but were continued too long after they were of use. Why did it take so long for humans to start a literature based on the voice, using tapes and discs?"

It's very pleasant lying out with Raethe on her bed in a tree. I feel refreshed and want to wash, to make myself clean. I really don't want to talk about books, or try to defend them. For me, they have been the way to knowledge. I'm addicted to them, although I know Raethe is right.

"Yes, Franky, let us bathe together. Have you discovered yet how to degravitate?"

"No. I've thought about it but have never quite figured what I need do. As I said, when I covered long distances quickly, I almost had the feeling of flying, but that's all."

"Oh, degravitation is different from that. Come, we'll bathe together and I'll show you how to do it."

159

We climb down the ladder. I smell something good cooking. I guess our foxness survived a radical mutation and fifty thousand years of evolution, when it comes to food and eating.

Normally, foxes aren't very big on washing or cleaning themselves, except for licking their paws or coat directly with their tongue. But I'd learned to love swimming in the pond near my tree house and had installed a small shower in the basement so I could wash up on cold days. I look forward to a chance to get clean and wonder just what foxes here in the future have arranged for this kind of thing.

Around the corner from where I'd been sleeping is a rock wall; over it flows a continuous fall of water. I'd heard it before but was too tired to really notice it. Perhaps the flow of this water is what put me to sleep. Raethe goes under first and I follow. The water is body-warm and slightly perfumed. The smell is clean and refreshing.

"Now let me show you how to degravitate. Combined with bathing or dancing it is marvelous."

With this, she closes her eyes, lifts her arms, and lets out a deep breath. Gently she pushes off from the basin below the waterfall and drifts slowly past me. It's so beautiful to see; she gracefully turns in the air, twisting her body. She laughs as I watch her go under the water, be driven slowly down by its force, then swing out and rise again.

"See, Franky, isn't it beautiful? Please come join me."

"What do I do? How can I fly like that?"

"First take a deep breath, then lift your arms to the sky and think of clouds and birds."

I do all these things.

"Now concentrate all your mind on weightlessness. Try to shed your weight as you would mud from your feet or sleep from your mind. But you should learn to do it yourself. Actually, it's easier than swimming."

I concentrate and at first feel nothing. Then, with a slight push of my foot, I'm off the ground. I look and my body is horizontal to the basin of the pool. I kick my feet and pull with my arms. It is like swimming. I wonder why I'd never been able to do this before. I turn in the air and look up at the artificial sky through the trees. I'm truly flying.

"I'm doing it, Raethe! Is the air different here on the planet now or down underground? Why is it I couldn't do this before?"

Raethe floats past me, she pulls her damp tail past my face again. It smells of her and of the perfume from the waterfall. I'm afraid I'll lose my concentration and drop.

"You just never thought of it, that's all, Franky. There are many things you can do that you just didn't think of. There are so many things I want to teach you. It must be very difficult for you to conceive of these things about which you know nothing."

We float and twist under the falls. It's miraculous. Afterward we drift over to another section where warm air is blowing in shifting currents, also lightly perfumed, and we are dried. We play in the currents of air. Raethe floats close to me. She looks deeply into my eyes.

"Oh, how I wish we had some music, Franky; we could dance. I'd like to dance with you. Do you know how to dance?"

"I've never tried it. I've had no one with whom to dance."

"See, it's the way I said: If you don't think of it, you never learn how. But we'll have fun together exploring all the wonderful

things you can do. Now, we'd better go over and eat our dinner. I'm sure eating is something you know about. Besides, I'm starving."

With that she settles to the ground and walks back into her primitive kitchen. I float along behind her.

"Raethe, how do I turn myself off? How do I come back onto the ground, gravitate myself again?"

"Oh, that's easy: turn your mind off it. Do this slowly while you are near the ground or you can hurt yourself."

It works just like that. I bump my knee slightly but stand up. The gravity seems very heavy to me at first but quickly I'm accustomed to it. Is it possible that gravity is only a thing of the mind? Mr. Newton would be surprised to hear that. It's amazing the kinds of things one can learn to accept.

Our dinner is delicious. I'm not quite sure what I'm eating. It resembles the taste of chicken or duck but doesn't look like it. All the food has quite different tastes, each goes perfectly with the others.

We both eat and, at the same time, talk quietly. It's so civilized; I realize how much I've disliked eating alone. Raethe tells me the names for some of the things when I ask. There are various sorts of seasonings she encourages me to try. She assures me there is no meat. Each dish is unique, seems to strengthen the taste of the other dishes. The seasoning, too, accents the individual taste of each food rather than covering or disguising it.

Finally we sit back, finished. We've each been sitting in the kind of chair that reclines and has a hole for our tails so they don't get crushed. Raethe leans forward.

"Now I have many things to tell you. It was decided at the meeting yesterday, while you were asleep, that I should be the one to

instruct you in what we have learned over the past fifty thousand years, about what we would like of you, of what we can give you.

"It was you who helped make the original great leap, but since then we've discovered and made use of many talents you brought to us."

I lean forward. It's such a strange position for me to be in, to be an inferior creature surrounded by superior beings in knowledge, skills, wisdom. I sit back and wait. Why didn't I ever think to make a chair like this? I was only imitating the chairs humans used.

"The main thing you should know is that you were probably not a completely accidental mutation. Our scientists here—astronomers, mathematicians, geologists, astrophysicists, and others in branches of science not known to you but dealing in general with the metaphysical and cosmological—are convinced there is a time cycle, somewhere in the neighborhood of fifty thousand earth years, which is critical to the development of our planet. This time cycle comes back upon itself in a two- or three-dimensional form or force, and it is at this time when major mutations occur.

"Our geneticists are convinced that normal selection, evolution, as it is sometimes called, is not enough to explain many of the drastic changes in life-form on our planet. Yes, it is a factor, a constant ongoing process, and probably, when we test you thoroughly, genetically, we shall find there have been subtle changes between when you occurred and us, now; but these will be minor."

I listen to her, her beautiful Fox. I try to keep my mind on what she's saying, but I can't keep myself from wanting to fall into her eyes, wanting her to brush my face with her tail or to take the

**chance myself and brush her face with mine. She smiles, a slight
wiggle of her nose. Her tail pinkens.**

*"Perhaps we were wrong. Perhaps I am not the one to explain
all this to you. You are not paying attention."*

**"I'm sorry, Raethe. Please go on. I'll try to keep my mind on
what you're saying."**

*"I'm having some similar problems myself, so don't feel sorry,
Franky."*

**She takes a deep breath, looks away from me, up through her
tree into her artificial sky. She has such a beautiful neck, thin and
edged with a ruff almost the color of her tail.**

*"As far as we can tell, time only seems to stretch off in a linear
fashion, without apparent beginning or ending. But the mathematicians assure us this is not true, that time curves just as all
space curves. It is because we have access only to such a small
segment that it seems straight, unending, unceasing.*

*"The theory is that there is some combined movement of the
planet, the sun, the solar system, the galaxy, in the vastness of
our universe, which brings about this fifty-thousand-year cycle,
so time, on this planet, in its enormous curve, passes in close
conjunction to earlier times every fifty thousand years.*

*"The rise and fall of dinosaurs, the reptilian age, which had
been discovered even in your early times, is an example. Our
scientists have gone back through millennia of millennia in time
and found that radical mutations causing great changes in the
life on the planet have been a regular feature. There is not always
an apparent change related to the cycle; sometimes there are
skips of a hundred thousand or a hundred and fifty thousand
years, but changes do occur within the rhythm of the cycle."*

She stops and looks to see if I'm comprehending what she's trying to tell me. I'm doing my best to concentrate, to understand, but my eyes, my mind, keep drifting away, toward Raethe, so beautiful, there in front of me.

"The two most recent examples have been the radical mutation of a mammalian primate—an ape—to man, and of simple fox to super- or mutation fox.

"The first new creature, man, appearing approximately one hundred thousand years before our time here, asserted his dominance within a few thousand years and reigned supreme up to and through a good part of your own era, long past the time of your life.

"By the way, Franky, our life-span, us, the mutation foxes, is between one hundred and thirty and one hundred and fifty earth years—about twice that of humans. I have thirty-five years, several years more than you; I hope you don't mind."

She looks me closely in the eye, in the mind. I know she'll find nothing there to which she can object. She turns her eyes and mind away. But she smiles.

"We are convinced from our time investigations that you are the mutation that was scheduled for your period. Somehow, your radical mutation was successful and led to the civilization we now enjoy. Do you understand?"

I understand what she's saying, but I still can't believe it. My mind isn't prepared for such a large-scale view of nature, of the planet, of time. I look at her.

"But what difference does it make? Why did you search me out, bring me here? I'm not complaining; in fact I'm very happy to be here with you, but it's obvious the mutation succeeded because

you *are here, that somehow I will,* did, *reproduce. It's like looking through the back side of a looking glass.*"

Her nose twitches and her eyes twinkle.

"Do you mind if I record some of your responses, Franky? I've been trying to tell my colleagues of your incredible logical leaps and they can't believe me. You see, they still see you as a very primitive specimen, much as scientists in your time would have felt if they could somehow have brought a sample of what they called Cro-Magnon or Neanderthal man up to their present. I imagine it's something of time pride. I don't think they want to admit that fifty thousand years of civilization and evolution have actually effected such little change."

"Sure, go ahead, Raethe. But I'm having exactly the opposite reaction. I'm amazed at how superior you are to everything I am. It's a great shock for me to suddenly find myself reduced to something of an ignorant moron."

"That isn't so, I can assure you. But let me tell you some more. You'll understand better why I have dragged you from your own time, why we are so concerned.

"We suspect that one way, besides the counting of years, whereby it becomes apparent that a radical mutation is about to occur is sort of a reverse tribal trace memory. It's almost as if vibrations, thought processes, regress from the new mutation back into earlier times and we experience it as a forward nostalgia, a series of desires without chance for realization.

"These, we feel, are the new skills that will be indigenous to the next mutant. We here, in this cycle of time, begin to think in those terms. For example, as I've told you, we cannot move forward in time, only backward. Now, our scientists are desperately trying to penetrate the barrier of time to 'see into the future,'

not just guess, but actually move forward as I moved backward looking for you.

"Also, the pressure is strong toward bodily or mental transmigration off this planet into space, to other planets, perhaps other galaxies.

"There are others who are experimenting with animal photosynthesis, sunlight providing enormous energy without the need to eat or defecate. The list is unending.

"We are also becoming more aware of our limitations as species. Our philosophers, psychologists, sociologists are delving into our natures, discovering kinds of regressions to our former identity as primitive fox—atavistic behavior of which we do not approve, cannot justify, and still cannot seem to transcend. We are more ruthless, prideful, narrow, willing to take advantage of situations or over other species than we should be. We value ourselves for our nonviolence, our desire to act as protectors to the planet and all alive on it, but if a persistent weakness in a species or a situation is presented to us, and it is to our advantage, we take that advantage."

I begin to feel my head swim. These ideas are so beyond anything I could ever imagine. At the same time, they are answers to the kinds of questions for which I'd been searching all my life. The trouble is I didn't know how to form the questions. So much was hidden from me. Raethe smiles.

"I *know you must be tired listening to all this, but these are things you must know, Franky. I'm almost finished now. Yes, you are finally getting the answers to the questions you have had all your life. It must have been very difficult for you knowing enough to question but not having enough information to discover any* *answers and no one around to help you. But now I'm almost finished; please hear me out.*

"A perfect example of our limitations is our relation to the human species here. They have been discouraged from their hostility, their competition, aggressiveness. We try also to discourage their tendency to imitate, ingratiate themselves with those they consider superior. This fawning is similar to that of the domesticated wolf, the dog, which was kept by humans in your times.

"It is against our laws to 'keep' a human, to take advantage of this regressive behavior, but some foxes do. Even those who don't often find it difficult to refuse the servile desire of humans to participate in our lives by minor domestic services, favors. It is a problem.

"There are other kinds of awareness to which we are recently becoming sensitive. It is a sign that a future mutation will not have these faults and by some regressive emanation is making us conscious of them in ourselves, trying to help us improve.

"The important thing is that the social psychologists are sure these desires for change, awareness of need for change, come to us from the new mutants who will have these skills and abilities and not have our faults. For these reasons, we are convinced a new mutation is about to happen.

"We have no physical way to measure what we call time, its placement or displacement. There is only the movements of celestial bodies in relation to the earth, and the seeming generational aspect of our own existence; but the psychological expression of it is here.

"Therefore, we feel our function now is as 'custodian to the planet,' the maintenance and protection of every species now existent. It is for this reason we have allowed the planet to become as it once was, unspoiled, with nature as the dominant source.

We've gone underground and we search continuously for the mutant we hope will come about so we can protect and nourish it, allow our earth to make another leap forward in progress.

"My studies were, in a sense, a research into the past to discover how the great mutation of foxes occurred and how it survived. Our interest is in our own beginnings, in the mutation— you, Franky, who are the basis for our civilization. It is an effort by us to understand and participate in your mutation so as to prepare us in our acceptance of our new role as lesser creatures on our earth. We pridefully hope that there will be less resentment, less hostility, a gentle passing of the mantle of authority to those who will lead the planet to greater achievement in the universal development. Do you understand?"

"Yes, but you already know you are here, that somehow it did happen, that the event is an actuality. Why are you so interested in the cause, the original impetus? Isn't it all ex post facto, a search after the fact? I guess I don't understand."

She stares at me, wiggles her nose.

"Again you've done it. Yes, this is one whole school of thought on the subject. It is a very practical and logical viewpoint, if how things happen is not as important as what happened.

"The trouble is, we are not as sure now as scientists in your time were, or even our own scientists here have been, until recently, that cause and effect are directly, lineally, related. We are beginning to suspect this is another illusion, that, theoretically, all of the past fifty thousand years could disappear or have an entirely different sequence if certain critical aspects of the total sequence had not occurred. It is another reason for our concern. We know we have the skills to go back into your time; we have been there for several centuries now. Is there something we did *or didn't do that makes all that seems to be real here, now, only a temporary reality, an illusion, a delusion, which could collapse around us at any moment?"*

I'm beginning to understand something of how all of it holds together, or might not hold together. It's so momentous, so beyond anything I could ever have conceived myself, I'm overwhelmed. She goes on.

"In your time, fifty thousand years ago, many of the skills you have, and we have now, had already been considered, by scientists, by writers of fiction, even by comic books.

"There were also physical advances in the nuclear-energy field with which humans were not ready to cope. Their emotional, mental development was not strong enough to deal with these forces. It was a dangerous time and it was necessary for some of us, the earliest, to realize what was happening, to enter into those times and by mental manipulation discourage the carnage that might have been released."

I look at her, astonished.

"You mean you've been monitoring my age concerning the use of nuclear weapons? When they dropped those bombs on Hiroshima and Nagasaki to end the war with Japan, I had fear for the human race, for any life to continue."

"Yes. It was a risk we took. We hoped that when humans saw the horrible power they were capable of unleashing, even at that primitive level, they would come to their senses and desist, but they didn't. The competitive, hostile, domineering aspects of their nature totally overwhelmed any rational understanding of what was involved. And the monitoring that had to take place over the next hundreds of years has been or, from your point of view in time, will be continual and has required much vigilance.

"You see, we knew it was our world that was at risk. We knew that somehow we had survived, but we wanted to avoid any serious damage to the planet or to the life on it. We also knew from our narrowing down of possibilities, that the mutation which was to be the founding of all our own existence was about to happen. You were about to be born!

"It was totally possible, perhaps still is, that a planetary catastrophe of immense proportions can occur and all of our existence, our history, will become a nonevent. It is a great responsibility to keep this from happening. And later, after your time, with the proliferation of even more deadly weaponry, the task becomes a thousand times more demanding."

"But, Raethe, you speak of the past and future as if they were independent of each other. Here we are, we're talking, discussing this, and still you insist that a catastrophic event in what seems the past to us, here, could make all this not happen. I don't understand."

"That is because you are still locked into linear time, cause-event thinking. It is a very difficult habit to break."

"But Raethe, how do you know you are not being monitored now by whatever will be the next dominant species? How do you know they have not been the stimulus for you to go back in time to search for me?"

"We don't. But it is a much-discussed possibility. There is an entire branch of our science dedicated to the discovery and communication with any monitors that might now be here. All of us, knowing our limitations, our failings, hope there is such a monitoring."

"So, you're saying that somehow it all ties together. That there is probably a kind of mental overlap between cycles, in forward

and backward projections. You also think that this monitoring aspect gives a physical binding."

"Yes, that is what we believe now. We think that only in the last few mutations has there been the capacity for this mental or physical overlap, but we have no way of knowing. The farther back into time we go, the more dim it becomes, the harder and more dangerous it is for us to understand or to move. When I was in your time, I was almost to the limits of what I, as a mere anthropologist, could manage. Specialists in this kind of time movement can go deeper, have gone through at least five distinct cycles a quarter of a million years into the past, but it is very difficult and dangerous; many good foxes have been lost to us."

She stops, stands up, comes around to my side of the table. She brushes my face back and forth lightly with her beautiful golden pink tail. Her eyes glitter.

"Perhaps we've had enough of this talk for one time. I sense you are a brilliant fox, probably, in some strange way, more intelligent than most of us, even with our years of experience and evolution. Most likely we'll find it is because of your enormous mental power and concentration, your persistence, that we have survived at all. I don't think I've ever had any experience with a fox like you."

I'm stunned. I must look like the most idiotic of foxes as I stare up at her. I stand and she comes close to me. I find my entire body quivering again. It's a sensation I never dreamed of and it's happening to me. I look into her eyes and feel all of me almost dragged, pulled toward her. She reaches out and takes my paws.

"Do you want me to teach you to dance, Franky? It is one of our most pleasant activities; foxes love to dance. I sometimes think *that humans, toward the end of their dominance, called their most popular of dances the 'fox-trot' as a sort of forward trace to our times. But we don't trot; quite the contrary."*

We leave the dishes on the table and Raethe snaps the fingers of her paw. This is something I do not think I can do; perhaps there *has* been some evolution. I try it secretly behind my back but make no sound, my paws are not that flexible.

Music, music such as I'd never heard, seems to fill the air; it comes from all sides and surrounds us, almost pushing us together. Raethe degravitates and I degravitate with her. She holds on to my paws and we begin slow gyrations in the air. We are led by her in a sinuous, twisting, interrelated set of movements. It is not gymnastic but choreographic, as if we are following some special patterns she can see or feel. She keeps her eyes on me through all our turning and soft passings. My eyes are fastened to hers, too.

There is continuous invention, at the same time repetition enough so I feel we are experiencing together. There is a wonderful feeling of variety within consistency. I try to stay with her as she abandons herself to the movement, the music, somehow willing me to follow her, to move with her in some invisible, convoluted counterpoint.

"You see, Franky, you do know how to dance. You dance beautifully, with much more strength and force than most foxes. Perhaps sometimes there is an awkwardness, but, still, you are quite graceful; if we dance more, I feel you will be a fantastic dancer.

"Come, I should like very much to follow you in your movements. Till now, I have been the leader; let us follow your dance. I want to know you better and dance is the most complete of fox communications, far better than Fox, or telepathy. You only need move as your body tells you. It's like degravitation was—some-

thing that is already there. All it takes is the confidence to make the beautiful dance movements inside you come through."

At first I'm reluctant, slow, not trusting my instincts, the natural soma of my body. But then, as Raethe takes my cues and elaborates on them, I begin to be more confident, move more surely, with greater vigor. I feel the warmth of her brain, the grace in her body, as she matches my movements, improves on them, makes them more.

We dance for a long time and I am not tired. I look into Raethe's eyes and we drift together. She weaves her tail around the back of my neck and across my face. I do the same to her and we stay a long time that way, the music playing, the two of us lost in each other, each of us, one to the other, all else floating around us unheeded. She looks deeply into my eyes and I into hers. We both know this is magic, something special, more than dance. She breaks slowly away from me.

"I think we should stop now or this little anthropologist is just going to float away into the pink mist of a dream, out of time-space, or forget to keep myself degravitated and fall."

We come back to the ground slowly. For the first time in my life I know the desire to mate. I feel her desire matching mine. We take each other's paws and go up the ladder to her bed, and there our dance continues, in gravity and with the greatest tenderness and passion I could ever imagine. I know nothing of what to do, as in our dance, but she guides me, teaches me, brings me with her to heights of joy and sensuality I've never known or imagined.

Afterward we sleep. I wake first. The lighting system of her home, tuned to the light on the earth surface, is still dimmed so it seems early morning. I look down and somehow the dishes from the meal last night are gone. All is in order. Are there servants in this future world? Did subservient humans come in and clean up after us? I can't believe it, but I don't care. I lie back. In her sleep, Raethe's tail passes gently over my entire body. I stay still and feel so close to her. My own tail, almost on its own, starts to explore, to caress Raethe. This is not the flying passion of the night before; this is a gentle coming together, a being one physically I did not think possible.

I'm so happy in my love for Raethe that everything else seems unimportant. But a small insistent worry from my primitive past seeps in like poison. Is this the way she is with *all* foxes? Does this only mean one more evening in the life of an unmated vixen in this world of the future? My superfox mind says it doesn't matter, there should be no possession, no exclusive desires in fox relationships, but I am still a part of my time. Is it possible for me to escape from this residual sickness?

I'm watching her sleeping, then she opens her eyes. She looks closely, deeply into my eyes.

"You really are, aren't you? I didn't dream it all. You really are Franky Furbo, the original to all of us. I feel as Eve must have felt with Adam as a human, but I am a fox and my feelings must be much stronger. I feel so alive. Thank you, Franky. Now all my life seems to make sense. I've never known I could love like this."

I can see and know she means this. I feel terrible for the thoughts I've had.

"I know, Franky, but you come from another time where duplicity was much more common. I understand."

I feel my own nose twitching.

"Raethe, one of the most difficult things is living where everyone is a telepath. There are no secrets."

"Not unless you want them to be; you can always close your mind. Another day I'll show you how. Now I have such pleasure reading you, feeling the intensity of your feelings. Please let me be selfish just a little while longer."

I take Raethe in my arms. She comes against me strongly yet gently. I feel the incredible sensation of being one with another.

"Raethe, I know I don't have to say this, you know it already, but I want to have the joy of saying it anyway. I love you. I don't ever want to be away from you again."

We hold tight to each other and I hear her heart beating against mine. I still can't believe all this is happening. Not even all the things Raethe has told me are as difficult to believe as this, what I'm feeling, what Raethe is feeling for me. We stay together like that a long time. Then Raethe breaks away, looks into my eyes.

"Come, Franky, dearest, we must go back to the research center. There is much to do. Please try to cooperate with them."

There's no need to answer. She knows. I want to help as much as I can.

On the way to the center we stroll through the woods, walk around a lake, holding paws, brushing each other occasionally with our tails, stopping now and then to hold tight to each other. We don't talk much except through our minds, and there is so much we can tell each other, so much each of us wants to know.

On the lake I see two humans fishing. They wave to us, then put their hands together as in prayer and bow their heads. Raethe makes the same movement toward them. I imitate her.

"I'm sorry, Franky, this is so difficult for me. I don't know how to react. I find myself avoiding contact with humans because it makes me so embarrassed when they do that. I know they do it from their hearts because they admire us, are grateful for this peaceful, calm, beautiful world. Sometimes, however, I wish they would show some resentment, hostility, as they did in the first years of fox dominance, almost fifty thousand years ago. I know their nature. I know this subservience is a strange displacement to their inner feelings of anger, resignation. Come, let us continue with our walk."

We arrive at the research center as we did before. The large conference room is virtually empty. The center table has collapsed to a smaller one, and a young vixen is waiting for us.

"Pleased to meet you, Franky Furbo. My name is Gallia. Dr. Pleisert is waiting for you."

I follow Raethe. We go into a small room with huge equipment mounted over a simple fox chair. Dr. Pleisert is a large fox with a heavy dark side growth beside his muzzle, almost like a human beard.

"Please, Franky Furbo, would you sit in that chair?"

I sit. I watch Raethe. She is preparing to leave the room. I don't want her to go.

"I'll be back soon, Franky. It will be better if I am not here, as my emanations of emotion could spoil the readings."

She leaves. Dr. Pleisert begins to attach various measuring instruments to me. He lowers a large dome over my head. He's constantly checking a bank of recording devices.

"Now what I want to do is make a record of every thought you've had since the time you were born until this moment. Is that all right with you?"

I nod yes. I wonder why telepaths would need such a complicated instrument for this, but perhaps they want an official record for analysis. I'm interested in what he'll think of my thoughts in the past twenty-four hours.

There is no sensation, only a slight humming and a brief dimming of my sight, as when there is a surge of electricity in the world from which I come.

Dr. Pleisert detaches all his instruments, checks that his measurements are satisfactory. He comes back to me smiling. I don't wonder. I've sensed by my own experience that foxes are very discreet but also have a fine-tuned sense of humor.

"That was just fine. I'll send this on up to Doctor Aymeis; she'll review it and be with you in a few minutes. She is our foremost psychosociologist. You may go outside in the waiting room."

Outside Raethe is waiting for me. Our minds let us each know how glad we are to be together again.

"So now you'll be seeing Doctor Aymeis. Well, it's been nice knowing you, Franky. I'll tell you now, Doctor Aymeis is one of the most beautiful foxes of our times, also one of the most talented."

She reads me.

"Oh, no. You don't know Doctor Aymeis yet. But I'll wait for you anyway."

A few minutes later I am called again by Gallia, the receptionist. I follow her into another room. Seated behind a large free-form desk with moving colors somehow flowing through it is a truly, incredibly beautiful vixen. I stare.

"Well, I can read you really are a fox. Your reactions to me are not much different than any male fox of this era."

Her very fine and slightly pale nose quivers in amusement.

"I've just experienced your life. But you are a most unusual fox. I had not expected such strength and wisdom in an unevolved creature. I'm almost convinced that we might have lost almost as much as we've gained in the selection process of our evolution over the past fifty thousand years. Or perhaps you are truly exceptional, even within the species."

I only watch her. Raethe is partly right. This vixen is almost like some kind of witch. Her mind is prancing through mine, almost making my mind dance as I danced with Raethe. She looks down.

"Could you answer some questions for me?"

What can I possibly answer that she doesn't already know?

"Of course, that's why I'm here."

"You have never had sexual relations before last night."

It's a statement not a question. I say nothing.

"Do you have any guesses, any ideas, as to how you have been reproduced?"

I close my eyes to think. I've begun to try thinking about the problem. It is obviously the prime concern of these foxes, when it comes to me and my past.

"I don't think I cloned. I don't know enough about it, but from what I know, I don't think that in my time—remember I'm twenty-six, give or take a few years—in nineteen hundred and forty-eight, that there would have been sufficient development in those directions for me to have even considered it.

"Also, I suspect that with higher mammals the cloning would only produce same-sex creatures. It would be difficult to breed these. If you cloned me here, then sent the clones back, I think there would be the same problem.

"I'm quite sure I would never be able to have sexual relations

179

"Perhaps this is so. But perhaps this violation is exactly what has enabled us to be where we are today in this room.

"In elapsed time, this act would actually predate the rule that we have made and therefore not be a violation."

She sits down again. There is more muttering. Over the next two hours or more there is much discussion both pro and con. There is a silence. Raethe stands up.

"I understand all you say, recognize your objections. As an anthropologist who has devoted my life to finding Franky Furbo, I think I should have some say about this decision."

Everyone is quiet, both mentally and verbally, listening.

"I am willing, in fact I would be honored, to go back with Franky Furbo, the most intelligent, understanding fox I have ever known or ever hope to know. I believe I can endure the rigors of living in the primitive past. As you know, I have an atavistic interest in this ancient style of life, which I have tried to approximate, even here. Perhaps this has been some kind of preparation for what my future life is in the past.

"It is common knowledge with all of us that there are psychic overlaps in time and space. This could be a sign of what my role is meant to be."

She stops, takes my paw, and pulls me to stand beside her.

"It is probably no secret to any of you, but I love this fox, Franky Furbo, and he loves me. I think we could be very happy together under any circumstances and would have fine kits to advance our culture, allow our civilization. Please, in the interest of all of us, let this happen."

We sit and there is a long silence. Then, without verbalization, only mental exchange, the decision is made. There are no other choices.

When we realize, Raethe and I wrap each other in our tails. Dr. Aymeis hovers her tail over the two of us. There is the mental, the verbal, and then the physical fox expression of applause; fox tails wave, fox noses wiggle, while Raethe and I stand embracing, embarrassed.

One of the elders mentally signals for order. All quiets down. He looks around, then at us, his nose is not wiggling, his brow is furrowed.

"This is all very fine and I'm quite sure it is the proper thing to do, but we must remember the nature of humans. It is hard for us to realize now, but there were over four billion humans on this earth at that time. Before these two young foxes would be finished with their mission, there would be five billion. These young ones will be going back to a time of the humans. It is not a pleasant thought.

"We know something about humans. Competition, physical combat, warfare, hatred, violence—all were common among them. There was a constant striving for dominance, for superiority. They killed one another by the millions in a ritual called war."

He pauses. There's silence. He lowers his voice almost to a whisper.

"Can you imagine how this species would react if they even suspected there was another species on the planet superior to them in every way, a species that would, in time, become their masters—no doubt, kind masters, masters with their welfare in mind, but nevertheless, from their competitive viewpoint, masters?"

He pauses again. The silence deepens.

"They would make every effort to destroy this species! They would probably even use their diabolical weaponry in an attempt to defend themselves from us. Think of that. We must devise a way to protect our own!

"From here, we think that somehow a way was devised, but what, how? We must consult our ancient archives to be sure that every tenet, every detail is carried out to the last point. There can be no violations.

"We know there must be at least a million of us on the planet before we can announce our ascendance without violence.

"As you know, we must infiltrate, integrate with humans, as humans, using our superior talents to gain control of their politics, their media of com-

munication, their legends, their beliefs, so that, when the time comes, they will have been seduced to the acceptance of the inevitable, the era of foxes.

"In the meantime, we must remain hidden, preserving and developing our talents, instructing our young, preparing them for their roles."

Again he stops. He is obviously emotionally moved. He breathes deeply.

"As we all know, the maximum healthful reproduction rate for a couple in our race is four. A generation for us is forty years. With the inbreeding and line breeding necessary, it will take time for this critical number to be reached. We know we have no significant genetic faults that would impair such close breeding.

"Is there someone here to do that calculation of how many years it will take for two foxes to become a million, with the limitations just described?"

A hand goes up.

"Allowing for normal depredations and failure to produce the usual four, approximately a thousand years. That figure corresponds with the beginnings of our historical period. After that, the ideal number of five million foxes on the planet was easily reached and maintained.

"All right then, I just wanted to have this understood."

He sits down and the decision is made. Raethe and I will go back to the old calendar earth year nineteen hundred and forty-eight, to live out our lives together.

William, at this point, Franky looked at me. His eyes glow but show sadness for what he reads in my mind, my heart. Franky went on:

"We've been back a month, Wilhelm. We are preparing to leave for the place where we shall live. I'm sorry I cannot tell you where it is; too much is involved. It is not my decision."

"But where is Raethe? Where is your wife? I would very much like to meet her."

I'm stunned. Where am I? Who is this across the table from me? Then slowly I come back. I come back from the Council of Research, back from fifty thousand years in the future, back from Raethe, back from being a fox, back from briefly being Wilhelm, and I find myself here, shocked, in this simple hut with Wilhelm, with a candle, a chessboard, and two glasses of schnapps between us.

All I've experienced in the past few days comes rushing into my mind. I feel I really *am* going crazy. Wilhelm's voice comes through to me at last.

*"**A**re you all right, William? I know how you feel. Here, take another drink."*

He pours some of the schnapps into my glass. I try to drink it.

"I tell you, William, my mind was reeling after Franky told me his story. I felt as if I'd lived through the whole thing myself, as if I'd been there. I wanted to go with him, to help him in his new life.

"I know, now, he had more than told me, he had implanted these memories into my brain, the same way he implanted your memories into mine and mine into yours. I was to be the messenger from Franky Furbo to you.

"Believe me, I was so much Franky Furbo at that moment he finished talking, all I wanted to do was meet Raethe. For me, it would almost be like seeing my Ulrika once again, alive and loving me. I asked Franky again if I could please see his wife."

"Wilhelm, she was downstairs when you came in but she made herself invisible to protect herself and me. She wasn't sure just what I was going to tell you. Also, she has a fear of humans.

185

Come down with me now and we can have tea together. I've already sent a message to her that we will be down and she can be visible."

"We go down and it's true. She's sitting there—as beautiful a vixen as I've ever seen. She absolutely glows, and she does speak the most lovely Fox I've ever heard. William, I tell you, it's music, music like crystal glass tinkling, and her movements are so graceful, integrated, it's hard to believe. I easily understand why Franky loves her so. I felt very alone.

"After tea, Franky tells me I must go, that they have much to do. He repeats how I am to tell no one except you, and you, only if you come to me for help. I beg once more to come with him, but he says it is impossible. It is not his decision to make.

"So now you've come and now you know. As the years went by, I thought more and more about it. All that happened has remained clear in my mind, but it became soured by what this meant to the human race.

"Think of it, William. All our civilization—our music: Mozart, Beethoven, Chopin, Vivaldi; our painters: Rembrandt, Van Gogh, Dürer, Chardin; our writers: Goethe, Camus, Shakespeare; our scientists: Einstein, Helmholtz, Steinmetz, Oppenheimer; all nothing, mere cats scratching in a sand box, domesticated animals rolling in the sun, amusing themselves. It is all nothing.

"All our politics, our religion—only delusions, play for a few fanatics. There is nothing worth doing. We are at the end of our time and we have disproven ourselves with our foolishness, our wars, our greed, our lack of love for one another. We have failed. Do you understand?

"I have a difficult time even being with my fellow men. Except for you, I can talk seriously with no one. Just knowing true Fox as it has become, as it is spoken by Raethe, and comparing it with my own, with yours, is discouraging. Comparatively, beautiful as it is, our Fox sounds like the grunting of pigs."

He stops. He is crying again. I begin to understand why he didn't want to speak with me. I begin to wish I had not come, had not found Wilhelm. My children's stories seem so foolish. The only things worth my life are Caroline and our children. I want to get back to them. It doesn't matter about Franky Furbo, what can it possibly matter. We're quiet some more. Then Wilhelm speaks again.

"There's more. Franky told me how they're planning to survive. I see it as the real 'thousand-year Reich,' and this is no joke, no political propaganda. It is diabolic."

I listen and am even more impressed with the basic superiority of Franky, he and his fellow foxes. I've tried to live the life he wanted me to live, but it could never be adequate; I'm not a dedicated enough person. All I've believed, all I've lived seems as nothing. I begin to understand how Wilhelm feels.

Finally, Wilhelm and I say good-bye. I invite him to come visit with us, but he says no, it would be too hard. He'll live his life out here in this forest and enjoy his little beer and game of *Schafskopf* when he has the chance. I understand him. I know I'll never come back again, either. It's all over.

CHAPTER 10

GOING HOME

I pick up my bag from behind Wilhelm's house in the lean-to with the wood. I slide my book back into it. It's dark. I look at my watch; it's two in the morning. I didn't want to stay overnight with Wilhelm. He didn't invite me; there was only the one small cot where he slept, anyway.

I trudge down the long road through the forest. I stop at the *Alte Eiche*. It doesn't seem so old now. When one has listened, experienced life as it will be fifty thousand years from now, a tree that might, at the maximum, have lived two or three hundred years is not very impressive. I try to beat away these thoughts from my mind. I don't want to become like Wilhelm—sad, hard, disillusioned.

Also, I don't want to believe what Wilhelm has told me. But why would he lie to me? Except for when he was dying or in great physical pain, I'd never seen Wilhelm cry or even come near to it in the months we lived together. No, he believes what he told me, and it doesn't seem likely he could have made it all up.

Also, I know that when he was telling me, it was Franky Furbo talking, making me know, feel, all he'd felt as if I had been there myself, fifty thousand years in the future. It truly happened, really is. But, now alone, walking in the forest, it's hard to accept. My mind keeps trying to deny what it knows is true.

So, what if Wilhelm *did* talk to Franky Furbo and this is what Franky told him? Maybe Franky lied. I don't believe it. Why would Franky lie to Wilhelm and through him to me? As far as I know, everything he told us, things that at the time seemed impossible to us, have proven to be true. No, Franky wouldn't lie.

But would the vixen have lied to Franky? Could she be part of some vast conspiracy, involving drugs or hypnosis or some combination, to convince Franky he went into the future and is the progenitor of a new race of superbeings? But why would anybody or any group want to do a thing like that? Or is it possible that Franky Furbo is victim of some complicated delusion, as I'd begun to feel I was?

No, none of those things make sense. It all has to be true.

Wilhelm talked about the "thousand-year Reich," the time it would take to have enough foxes to assert themselves, peacefully, without resistance, but that's not what occurs to me. It's more like the medieval idea of the millennium, the belief that a thousand years after Christ's death, the world as humans knew it would come to an end, the good rewarded, the evil punished, with Christ's kingdom reigning on this earth.

For a long time there, nobody did much of anything but pray, fast, wait for this millennium to arrive. It was one of the main reasons for what we call the Dark Ages. Only after the millennium had passed and nothing happened was it possible for the Renaissance, the true rebirth, to begin. There was a great outpouring of confidence and energy.

In a certain way, the coming of a reign by foxes is similar to believing in the coming of the reign of Christ. All human activity will seem as nothing, judged by outsiders, by outside criteria; a superior kind of being would become ascendant.

It could be paralyzing to human activity. Wilhelm is an example of what could happen—a general pessimism, inertia, a loss of belief in the value of effort.

Something like this has happened in the Hindu world with their belief in dharma and karma, reincarnation, caste, all the rest of it. The value of effort to improve oneself is removed. One's duty becomes the mere carrying through of expectations—dharma—in a particular life, to ensure, improve karma in another.

No wonder Wilhelm didn't want to tell me. I can't help but wonder why Franky wanted me to know. There must be some reason. He was so careful to teach us how to live, to instruct us on all the failings of humans, trying to encourage us to live better lives, giving us simple instructions by which we could improve. In a certain way, we were his disciples, his effort to send forth emissaries to help others find the way.

But that was all before he knew his *own* identity, his *real* role in this life. We were but a premature, hopeful effort on his part. Now the reality has been made known to him and perhaps he has abandoned this effort as hopeless.

I feel betrayed. I understand Wilhelm's dejection, his anger, his discouragement. I actually find myself falling into the primitive, primate approach to threat—competition, destruction, violence.

I consider going back and asking Wilhelm where the tree in which Franky lived might be, to take it on myself to search out Franky and his mate, to find them and their progeny, to kill them. It's almost the same kind of reaction I had when Billy said he didn't believe in Franky Furbo and wanted the ending to the story changed. I changed it and destroyed all that I'd created for him and the other children. It's so easy to give way to these primitive impulses. I'd never do it, but this gives some idea of how depressed, alone, betrayed I feel.

But I know none of this makes any sense. There can be no

holding back progress—change—and if Franky's story to Wilhelm is true, and I'm convinced it is, the entire development of the fox superiority has occurred in the future.

Whatever action I might try to take is probably already denied by what I now know will be. That is, unless all the talk about there not necessarily being relationship between cause and effect, that what seems to have happened or will happen is not immutable, is true. This idea is hard for me to understand, accept.

Also, I know that such behavior is stupid and completely contrary to every feeling for life, for the way creatures should behave, all that Franky taught us, the ideas that have altered and ordered all my life and the life of my family through the past forty years.

I walk along and into the town of Seeshaupt. There is still a light on at the Post Hotel. The night porter is surprised to see me at such an hour, but there is a room. He shows it to me. He's wearing an old-fashioned long flannel nightgown complete with cap and tassel. With his glasses and long mustache he looks like something from one of my old Franky Furbo stories.

The room smells of mold and is musty. I throw open the windows. Out my window I see the moon shining on the *See*. I switch off the overhead light and turn on a small lamp beside my bed. At the head of the bed, the mattress is tilted up. I know I can never sleep like that; it would be like being in a hospital or being in traction at Franky's. There's a wedge-shaped chunk of mattress under the real mattress, so I pull it out and stand it against the wall. Then the bed is flat.

I'm dead tired. I undress and climb in under the eiderdown quilt. Everything in the room is white or wood. I turn off the light and settle in. I try not to think too much, but my head is still spinning.

I'm trying to adapt myself to the idea of this new "millennium." It seems sad somehow. The good thought on which I finally sleep is that I can relax about us humans blowing ourselves off the earth. It means my children, grandchildren, great-grandchildren through about forty generations can live in safety and peace. It sounds like a good trade-off to me. If I weren't so tired, I'd go and tell Wilhelm this good news, but he already knows. His problem is mostly one of pride. I go to sleep happily, swallowing pride, enjoying the taste of it.

In the morning I take the train into Munich, where I make good connections, with only one stopover, in Turin, to Perugia. I eat my breakfast in the *Bahnhof*. I'm so accustomed to being in Germany, speaking German, hearing it, I have a hard time realizing I'm going back to my old life in Italy. It's difficult to believe it's only been a few days since I left home.

I look at the hustle and bustle around me. It all seems much less important. I feel detached, as if I'm watching an ant colony or animals in a zoo. Somehow, knowing the temporariness of it all gives me an inner peace I haven't known in my life. It gives me confidence to know the world is going to go on, improve, that the foxes really are going to live as Franky tried to help us, Wilhelm and me, as mere humans, live. It makes so many things that didn't make sense before seem reasonable.

Actually we all know we have only one life, or at least that's what I've always thought, so there's no great difference knowing that in a thousand years humans will be pets to superbeings.

To be honest, from another point of view, it won't be much different from most people's idea of heaven. After all, in that scenario, one leaves this mundane world and goes to one far superior where there are no worries, no cares; where you are taken care of by a loving God; where you are loved. It isn't all that much different from the fox world of the future. It's just that we, personally, as individuals, don't achieve this world; it will be our descendants. The only Hell would be not having children, not being able to participate in any way in this heavenly state. I look forward to being home with Caroline and Billy.

I board my train. I throw my luggage up on the rack and have just settled in when the train lurches to a start. I'm still surprised at my calm. Perhaps I'm in some state of shock, but I don't think so. My resentment toward Franky has completely disappeared in the night. He was trying his best to help us within the limitations of what he knew at that time. It's obviously necessary that he carry out what has to be done to ensure the safety and advancement of his species for our earth.

I wonder if there are similiar kinds of evolutions and mutations, slippages in time, going on with other planets all through our galaxy, all through the universe. It deepens my calm to think about it. I begin to feel privileged knowing something about what's happening, or seems to be happening at least, on our planet.

I arrive in Perugia late in the day. My bicycle is exactly where I left it. Caroline must not have come to pick it up. It's a good thing I locked it. I'll bet she'll be surprised to see me home so soon. I had no idea everything would happen so quickly. My mind is still awash in time, the magnitude of it and, at the same time, its ephemeral quality. The concept of time moving in a giant circle or globe through space is almost more than I can imagine. But it does help explain Franky Furbo.

One thing I'm sure of now: after all that's happened, I'll never again doubt in my own mind the existence of Franky Furbo, my time spent with him, the comradeship I had with Wilhelm, the nearness to death I experienced. It is a jewel I shall cherish inside me, but I don't want to try making Caroline or the children believe with me. That doesn't make sense.

It's wonderful to see our little house again as I pump my way up the hill. I feel I'm coming back home, that I'm inside myself once more. I'm not depressed as I was that first night I knew. I feel elated, excited to be one of the few to know what's going to happen, what the world is going to be like.

Most of us are cut off from the immensity, the eternity of time, locked into our little lifetime span, but I've been privileged to have a view of time out of my own life. It's something to be happy about. What does it matter if our role, the human role, is not as leader, but as part of the *whole* earth, maybe the entire ecology of the universe? In the smallness I feel about myself is also lodged a sense of a greater existence, a fuller identity.

When I open the door, Caroline is right there. I think she'd been watching me pedal the bike up that steep hill to our little terrace. It's not like her to come rushing out to meet me. I know that.

But she is so welcoming. We hold and kiss, looking into each other's eyes. There's the question in hers, and I wonder what she sees in mine. Little Billy comes over and gives us both a big hug while we're holding on to each other. I run my hand through his hair. All our children have the same dark reddish hair as Caroline.

They've just finished dinner but bring out what was left over. Caroline has made her special spinach lasagne, and it's even better warmed over. She pours me a glass of our delicious grape juice. I think of the beer and the schnapps I drank with Wilhelm; I drank more alcohol that long evening than in the rest of my life. I think of him alone in his dark hut surrounded by his fears, his sadness, and I'm a happy man looking at my beautiful wife and wonderful child. It seems cruel to be so selfish, but that's the way it is. I know I'm smiling like an idiot.

I know too that Caroline is waiting for me to tell what happened, what I've found out. I'm sure she's said nothing to Billy of the true reason why I've left. There would be no reason to disturb his peace.

For some reason, I'm still not ready to talk. I wonder also if Franky intends I not tell what Wilhelm told me or if he wants me to share this with my family. I know Wilhelm was allowed only to tell me; perhaps this is the same constriction for me, but I don't think so.

I need some time to think about all this. If Caroline brings it up I'll try to tell the truth, but I'm not ready. I also doubt she'll ever bring it up. This is my problem, my search, and she will respect it. It's the way she is.

We put Billy down to bed. He takes his place on the farthest end of the bed away from us, as is his right, so Caroline and I have some privacy. As I said, I've rigged a curtain that pulls between ours, the space nearest the window, and the rest of the bed. Franky insisted, when we were with him, that children should not think of sex as something to be hidden or ashamed about, but as a natural and beautiful thing through which people share each other and bring others into this world.

Our children have usually been there when Caroline and I have made love. Our ecstasy was a shared experience.

Caroline has never had any trouble with this, but sometimes I would be the one to pull the curtain because of my own past. In the orphanage I think I was polluted with bad feelings about sex and my own sexuality. I guess not even Franky Furbo could completely purge me of those dark feelings.

So, I'm surprised when Caroline pulls the curtain. I think it's the first time in all the years we've been married.

A profound part of me is still feeling very alone and separated, much in need of the comfort and sense of continuity, love, and care that can be so well expressed in the intimacy of lovemaking. I'm happy Caroline comes to me, and we become one. Much of the black thoughts, still lingering inside me, are erased in our mutuality of feeling.

Afterward, Caroline is stretched calm beside me, our hands intertwined, each of us on our back; only the tiny night-light is lit over the mantel. I always leave it burning in case someone must go to the toilet or want a drink of water. Also, I think it is so if one wakens in the night, the house, our home, is visible to give comfort, to seem alive as a loving friend not just a building. Caroline turns toward me.

"Did you find Wilhelm?"

I pause. I'm still not ready, but I can't lie about it.
    "Yes, I did."

"And what do you think now? Do you still believe in Franky Furbo?"

I pause. Caroline is waiting in the dark.
    "I found out you were right, Caroline."

"What do you mean, William?"

I hesitate again. I want to say it correctly, without hurting her but still giving me some time.
    "I found out it just doesn't matter. I found out, also, it doesn't matter that it doesn't matter. Whether I believe in Franky Furbo or not, it doesn't matter, because you were right: we love each other and that's all there is that really counts."
    I leave it there. I haven't lied, except by omission. I hope she'll be satisfied with this limited explanation. She lies back again and I

know she won't ask me to elaborate. Perhaps she'll never ask about it again. It would be like her.

I wait till I hear her regular breathing and then go to sleep happily. I know in my heart that all is well and everything will work itself out.

The next morning I find Billy has already climbed across the bed to be with me. I must really have been dead to the world, because Caroline is up and out of bed, fixing breakfast in the kitchen. I stretch over and give Billy a hug. I'm feeling so inside myself, so inside our little world. It all comes back, everything Wilhelm told me, and it's not frightening at all. It's good to know I'm not going to be one of the ones who cower, waiting for the millennium.

Billy cuddles against me. He's awake. He might even have been awake before me. He lifts himself on his elbows so he looks into my eyes.

"Daddy, would you tell me a Franky Furbo story?"

It's natural; I guess it had to come, but I hadn't thought much about it. I look back into his eyes, his yellow-flecked brown eyes.

"I thought you said you didn't believe in Franky anymore, Billy."

"Aw, geez, Dad. Does that mean I can't have any more stories? I'm not really sure whether I believe in Franky or not. The more I think about it, the more I'm not sure. Besides, I know you wouldn't have told me Franky Furbo is really true if he isn't; you wouldn't lie to me like that. Also, I know I like Franky stories more than any stories I've ever heard or read.

"Besides that, I know you're right, there's got to be a *true* ending to every story. You can't make up any old ending from nothing just to please me or anybody else. I know that now. I didn't know it before."

I give him another hug. God, in some ways he's so like me. All the others were more like Caroline, what people in Germany would call *einmalig*, sort of individually unique. I've always been the ordinary garden-variety type around our house, except for all the Franky Furbo business, and now I know even that wasn't my fault, it was only an accident.

"All right, Billy. I'm going to tell you the most important Franky Furbo you've ever heard or will ever hear. It might be so important it could be the *last* Franky story you'll hear. Do you understand? Are you ready?"

I know he doesn't actually comprehend. So often I've started stories with similiar introductions to build up suspense; it's all part of the fun. And, to be honest, I'm not quite sure just what I do mean. But I start:

"One day, quite a while ago, only a few years after I knew Franky and lived with him, Franky Furbo heard a knock on his door. He was up in his thinking room writing a story and thinking, so he ran down his three ladders to open his door."

I pause. I can still go back.

"There, standing on his doorstep, was the most beautiful vixen he'd ever seen, and she asked him, in perfect Fox, 'Are you Franky Furbo?' "

I go on and tell the entire story just as Wilhelm told it to me. I realize as I'm telling it, that Franky, through Wilhelm, has planted every detail into my mind, so that, as I tell the story, it's almost as if I'm remembering it, as if it all happened to *me*.

Never, through all the years with my children, have I ever told a story so well.

Then I finish with the last part Wilhelm told me: the method by which Franky and Raethe would live, to protect themselves from being killed by humans, to give their children a chance, so that after about twenty-five fox generations of forty years each, there would be a million superfoxes like Franky Furbo.

As I'm telling this last part, Billy is pushing himself up from the bed, sliding onto my chest, staring into my eyes. Also, I can sense that Caroline has moved from the kitchen and is standing beside our bed.

I wonder if I'm doing the right thing. She could be even *more* angry with me now. This is perhaps *too* much to ask such a young child to understand, to believe, to live with. In a way, I've made the entire Franky Furbo saga into a deeper mental trap. I stop. Will Billy go through the same pangs of rejection, of failure, of discouragement, as Wilhelm is suffering; as I suffered myself, briefly? I begin to wish I'd kept this most important story to myself.

Billy continues to stare into my eyes. His face is excited. He has a hard time speaking.

"You . . . you mean Franky Furbo is alive right now and is married to Raethe and—they're changed so they look like human beings?"

"That's right."

"And they live apart from other humans and don't send their children to school—they teach them themselves?"

"Yep. That's what they're doing."

"And does Franky Furbo still write stories for children—so he can have money and—to help teach children how to live?"

"I guess so."

"Why, Daddy, that's just like *us*. We're living just like Franky Furbo!"

I look up and Caroline is smiling down at me. She leans forward and kisses me.

"So, now you know!"

CHAPTER 11

GOING TO GROUND

"**W**hat do you mean, 'Now I know'? I don't know anything. I'm not even sure who or what I am anymore. Hey, did you just talk in Fox?"

"That's good, dear, that's the way it's supposed to be. I'm so glad it's all finally over. I've loved you so very much, as only foxes such as we can love, but I couldn't tell you; you had to find out yourself."

"What're you talking about, Caroline? I haven't found out anything, only what Wilhelm told me. And it all seems so crazy, impossible, I have a hard time believing any of this stuff. What's going on?"

Caroline leans down and kisses me again. I keep my eyes open, something I don't usually do, and as I look into her open eyes they change color until they give off the golden yellow glow, like an amber fire from inside, the way Franky's eyes always did. It scares me.

"Dearest, try to let go, and I'll do my best to loosen you from the bindings on your mind within which you've had to live all these years.

"You'll never know how many nights I haven't slept, knowing you for all your wonderful gifts, your insights, your skills, your sensitivity, your massive intelligence, watching you struggle along in this limited human identity we felt you had to adopt so all of us could be preserved. It didn't seem fair.

"Sometimes it was like watching a much-loved, favored child who had been stricken blind and deaf, crippled but knowing that inside itself this child remembers all it was before, only can't really express anything. I'd walk through the farms and hills crying so hard I could scarcely breathe. It was a part of coming back with you I hadn't thought about, could never have realized.

"But first let me continue with the story Wilhelm told you. I'll tell you the parts he couldn't tell."

I watch her. She's slowly becoming something else, someone different from the wife with whom I've lived all these years, and at the same time, *more*—deeper, stronger. I'm loving this person she's becoming, more powerfully, passionately, than I've loved Caroline, and I *never* thought I could ever love anyone more than I loved my wife.

"Back there, or perhaps it's up there, fifty thousand years in the future, when we realized who Franky Furbo really was, we were in a quandary. We knew from our own experience that somehow Franky Furbo had reproduced. I agreed to come back to this time as your mate and live with you, because we loved each other."

I realize she's speaking in fluent Fox, beautiful Fox. I can't move. I still can't comprehend what she's saying.

Then Caroline slides onto the bed beside me. She beckons Billy to cuddle up against me and listen. Is she saying what I think she's saying? I really don't believe it. But I listen.

"Our greatest problem after we'd made the decision that I should go back with you was how to ensure the survival of the two of us and our progeny. As you know, from what Wilhelm told you, it was decided we would live as humans. If humans knew there was a species superior to theirs, their first response would be the competitive one: they would destroy us as they try to destroy each other. We had to plan against that.

"There was also the problem of you. I couldn't convince the rest of the council that you were not just a primitive, but a very advanced, intelligent being. Not even the testimony of Doctor Aymeis, the psychosociologist who had lived in your mind, could impress them. All her powers of persuasion, her expertise, were not enough.

"They couldn't believe that a fifty-thousand-year-old primitive who spoke in what seemed like guttural grunts to them and who was, in their eyes, awkward, backward, could possibly be trusted with the future of the fox species.

"I should say here that one of the failures of our race, probably another atavistic throwback to the original foxes, our forebears, is our righteousness, our false pride. It's the same kind of rigidity, difficulty in accepting change or new knowledge, that led to the death of your mother. This is only one of our failings; you will come to know others.

"You have already experienced another failing—our ruthlessness. Just as we were once primitive, ruthless killers of lesser animals in our aboriginal form, we are ruthless in our minds even now. You are, too, or you wouldn't have survived alone as well as you did."

She smiles. I'm between getting lost just listening to the sound of her voice, the beauty of her language, and getting even more lost as she tries to explain whatever it is she's telling me.

"I can sense telepathically, and also see from your face, that this isn't going to work this way. You've had so many blocks planted in your mind not to believe what I'm telling you about your true self that, with the limited human-level mind to which we've reduced you (even though we left the ability for you to speak and understand Fox), you can never understand. I shall need to take more drastic measures, bring you back, first.

"This is going to be a terrible shock, more than you would believe, but I think it's the best way. I've often discussed with our monitor how I should handle this part of the revelation, but I could never be sure. Now I see how it must be."

She smiles. She's so lovely. Billy, beside me, senses that something important is about to happen. He holds on to me even more tightly. I feel as if I'm catatonic. I can't move. Caroline has me in some kind of mental hold and all I can do is stare at her, listen, wait. My old idea that I might be crazy seems even more logical, acceptable, than what's really happening. Is this *my* Caroline talking, speaking Fox, trying to tell me that *I'm* Franky Furbo? It's all *insane!* I look down at poor Billy and try to smile. I'm sure he's even more in shock than I am. Could Caroline be putting all this on to shake me out of my belief in Franky Furbo? No, she wouldn't do that. I really *am* going bananas.

"Now, all you need do is relax, my darlings, listen to my voice, let your mind wander, each of you. I'm going to bring you to yourselves at the same time. It will be easier for Billy because I've been working with him since he was born. But you, William, have a whole life, a whole world, many blocks inserted between you and yourself, which I must remove. It will take time and much mental effort. Try not to fight me. Whatever you feel, let it happen. I promise I won't hurt you and what you will know and feel afterward will be worth all you've suffered."

Then, while Billy and I hold each other as if we're afraid of falling from the bed, from the world, from life itself, we watch as Caroline goes around the room and closes all the shutters, locks them, locks the door, lights a candle and puts it on a table at the foot of the bed. It's all so spooky, like somebody about to tell a ghost story. I smile down at Billy again.

Then she comes back and straddles the two of us with her knees. She leans close, hovering over us. My heart is beating in something between fear and passion. I wonder what Billy is feeling. She stares into our eyes; hers are glowing brighter than the candle. The intensity of her stare makes me feel as if I'm shrinking and expanding simultaneously. My head begins to spin and then float separate from my body. There's the sensation of layers and layers of fat or paint being carefully peeled from my brain, from my heart, from all of me. I feel a tightening inside, a loosening, a hardening, surrounded by a softening, of my whole body and mind. I lose all sense of time; it feels as if days and nights are passing, but none of us move. Again, there's that smell of almonds I smelled when Franky put Wilhelm's thoughts into my mind. I can't even be sure if I'm breathing, if any of us are. The passage of whatever passes for lifetime seems suspended.

I can hear Caroline in her beautiful Fox speaking to us. It's in our own mouths, in our own brains. I'm beyond wondering. I can only follow, wander with Caroline's voice, her mind, through seemingly endless red and orange tunnels.

But with each twist, each sloughing off of another layer, I feel closer to my inner self, to a self that always seemed to exist only in dreams.

I begin to hear Caroline's voice clearly again, first almost a whisper from far away, then closer, and finally I hear it with a clarity I've never known. I also know it isn't Caroline, my wife, I'm hearing; it's Raethe, my wife of so long ago, long ago in the future. She stops. I feel myself released from the weight of her presence.

"So now you're ready to know. Perhaps you know already. I'm not sure if I've been able, William, I mean Franky, to remove all the blocks between William and yourself. You were given a complete identity by the most masterful mind manipulators in all the world, up there, fifty thousand years from now."

I'm listening, but at the same time I'm looking. I look at Caroline and she is the most beautiful vixen in all the world, the fox I love. I look down at myself and I'm fox again, myself. I'm truly Franky Furbo. Franky Furbo really does exist, and I'm he! No wonder William had to believe in Franky: if there were no Franky then he didn't exist.

Thinking this, I find a cloud of doubt, of unreality, pass through my brain. It's almost like the sensation when you know you know something but can't remember it.

I turn, and there beside me is Billy. He's a fox, too. I again think of little Matthew in the story I told. Billy looks exactly like him. There are certain visual memories still in my brain, as William, which apparently can show up at strange times. Billy is enjoying looking down at himself. He turns and speaks to me in perfect Fox, better Fox than I could ever teach him.

"Boy, look at me! I'm really a fox! I'm like Franky Furbo myself. And you know, I can read minds. I know what you're thinking, Dad, and what Mom's thinking, too."

"All right, now you two settle down. Move over and give me a little space to stretch out and rest. I'm very tired and both of you should be, too, especially you, Franky. Let's all take a nice little nap as foxes together, then I'll tell you the rest of our story."

With that she climbs in between us, and before I know what's happening, I'm asleep. In my sleep I have mixed dreams, some dreams of William as they fade, and the rest, dreams of my life as a fox, my life living in my tree, and my life in the time of

Raethe, so long in the future, but a place and time where I've been. I think some of my dreams are coming to me from Raethe as she's stretched out beside me. But my mind can enter hers too and perhaps these dreams are hers as much as mine.

It's going to take some time getting accustomed to the free flow of telepathy. Maybe Franky Furbo got used to it, but poor William Wiley, the person I've been for over sixty years, is still uncomfortable with other people's thoughts flowing through his mind.

When I wake, Raethe and Billy are already awake and mentally speaking to each other, trying not to wake me. I listen for a few seconds, but they know immediately I'm awake by the emanations from my brain to theirs. I look down at my fox body. I look over at Billy and Raethe. It's all so strange and familiar at the same time. I'm having a hard time adapting to this new identity, to myself, and what really is.

"Don't worry, dearest one. It will all come. I've been talking with Billy and he's doing just fine. By the way, his real name isn't Billy. When our monitor baptized him, he gave me the name he is supposed to have; this is part of our archives. His name is actually Sarva. I hope you don't mind; I think you'll get used to it. Billy is a hard-sounding name in Fox, as you probably already know. By the way, as you most likely noticed, Sarva speaks perfect Fox. Surreptitiously, in the night while he slept, I've taught him, without his knowing it, over the years. Our other children also speak this beautiful language you invented."

I realize I do know. Also, I know Sarva is the perfect name for him. He smiles and I smile back.

"You said monitor, Raethe. Do you mean the priest who came and baptized each of the children was monitoring us? I don't understand."

"Actually, he was more of a contact for me. When I needed help or wanted to pass information back to the research center, I could use him. He is a specialist in space-time travel and also a psychosociologist. It was very kind of him to stay here in the past with us for the twenty years he did. I don't know how he managed to have a post as priest in Perugia, but he has tremendous powers of telepathy and hypnosis. He most likely used those to mask himself. He's the one who knew enough about the mentality of the Italian human peasant to realize baptizing the children would be an aid for our integration and acceptance here, especially mine."

"And do the other children have different Fox names as well? I've got an awful lot to get used to."

"Yes. I know it's all very hard for you now, Franky, but you'll find it much easier as time passes. Our oldest, Kathy, is called Trais, Matthew is Hinva, and Camilla is Panta. All these names have become, in time, common names in Fox. One of the things that interests me is that they are the first, but they are named according to what for them is the future. You see, Franky, even I have trouble sometimes with the time overlap."

"And how about 'Franky Furbo'? How does that fit in with Fox? I just chose it without any help, even before I invented the language. It's a name that's half American English and half Italian. I only knew I wanted a name, so I made it up, or is there some kind of time twist here, too?"

"It is a name unique to you. It was only when we'd developed our skills in going back to the past that we knew of you and your name. *No one in our time is named Franky Furbo; it would be considered sacrilege. It is not a name a fox of our race would choose, anyway. I love your name, Franky, as I loved you when you were William. I would love you by any name. I hope you know that.*

"But now it is time I tell you about yourself, about what is true and what is not.

"This is very complicated, and I've gone over it many times, both to remind myself of all the complications and also to prepare myself for this moment. Most of it concerns you, Franky, but Sarva may listen if he wants.

"Whenever you have questions, interrupt me and I'll try to answer them. I could tell you all this by telepathy but I want you to hear with your ears as well as your mind. Try not to read my mind but let it unfold as I tell it to you in Fox. If you try to take in too much too fast you could lose your way and it would only take us longer. Are you ready? I know this is all going to be a terrible shock, especially for you, Franky, but you must know these things. Some of them seem terribly arrogant and ruthless for us to have done to you, but we could see no other way, so much was at risk. It was the only way the council would agree to let me come back here and live with you as your wife. It meant much to me and, I believe, to you too."

She looks at the two of us, smiles, then closes her eyes briefly as if putting all in order. I shut down my own mind to hers and wait till she's ready to begin. I have a feeling that after this, much I have valued and loved will be lost. I look around at the comfortable small house we've lived in so long, so happily. It is built for human-sized creatures, I can see now from my smaller stature as fox. It all looks strange, huge, different already. Something in me wants to hold on, not to go into this world where Caroline-Raethe is inviting me. I wait.

"Back there, when we decided the best solution within our history, related to what we knew, was for me to come back with you, there were many decisions to be made.

"As I've said, the research council did not feel you were capable of dissimulating effectively because of your close contact—from their point of view, your contamination—by the world in which you'd been born, the world in which you'd lived.

"It was decided you had to be given a complete human identity, one that you would accept as your true nature. It had to be an identity within the geography of where I had found you and close, to within a few years, to the time I arrived at your tree house in the forest.

"When it was explained to you back there, you understood and agreed to what was being suggested. You were so brave, Franky; I was so proud of you. I still am.

"As you remember, there had been a human war, one of many, which had raged a few years earlier, not far from where you were living in your tree house. We had sent invisible, telepathic-hypnotic technicians to search for someone from the battlefields who, because of the upheavals, injuries, and deaths, we might use for your identity when we found you.

"Finally, they found William Wiley. He was dying. He was in a hole near a bridge not far from where you lived, close enough for our purposes. He was of the right age, and, best of all, he was an orphan and had no family. With him was a German soldier also at the point of death.

"Before William Wiley died, and there was no way to save him, three telepaths, independently, absorbed every memory left in the dying brain of this young human. They also absorbed every physical feature, including the terrible wounds of the body."

"You mean I'm dead? William Wiley is dead? I can't believe it."

I feel faint. There is almost the sensation of dying, as if a breath

of me is being extinguished. William Wiley is still inside me, but now he's dead. I really can't accept it.

"But it's true, Franky dearest. The human you became, William Wiley, has been dead for more than forty years. He was listed as missing in action with the human military of that time. In a sense he was. Our technicians reduced his body to the minimum, about the size of a spider, and buried it on the hillside near to where he died.

"Before he expired, they also siphoned off the greater part of the identity of the German soldier. They buried him there as well, beside you. That was the real Wilhelm Klug.

"If you want to, sometime I shall take you there. I have been there myself. Strangely, perhaps because I love you so and have lived with you so long, I wanted to see where the last remains of the body on which you were modeled was lying.

"In any case, the technicians came back to us, fifty thousand years into what we here call the future, with their psychic, psychological, and physical data. They shared it telepathically with the members of the research center, and it was with this information they designed the human you would become."

"You mean, without telling me, you somehow changed me into a dead man named William Wiley and I've been living that way, not knowing it, all these years? I've lost a good part of my life, have gotten old, not even being myself! Does that seem right to you, Raethe? I feel as if I've had a huge part of my real life stolen from me. At the same time, the person I thought I was all this time is gone, in reality, practically never really was."

"As I said, William, we are ruthless. But we are not all bad. We told you everything that was going to happen, everything we wanted you to do. We asked your permission and you agreed.

You also agreed it was best if during the time you were William Wiley you not know you were also Franky Furbo.

"Still, there was concern that if you lived too long without knowledge of your real self, something of your nature, your strong personality, might be lost. It caused considerable concern for those involved. We sat in on many long meetings while the details of how to bring about the desired results and still not abuse your psyche were discussed. We all really did care for you, Franky. You are sacred to us as our original progenitor, without which none of us could be. Also, there were selfish concerns that if we didn't prepare this properly, we could make mistakes or even a mistake that would affect or even reverse the progress of our species retroactively.

"Our knowledge of time sequence is similar to the knowledge humans had of electricity when it was first discovered. We can see the results, use time to our advantage as a convenience, but we don't know much about its many properties, so we had to be cautious."

"OK, so what happened next? Now you've got William buried and you have all the essential information about him up there in your time and you're going to turn me into William Wiley and send me back. Is that right?"

"Yes, but it was more complicated than that. There were many stories, events, seeming memories, that had to be implanted in your brain as real. There had to be blocks placed so no accidental event in your life—unconsciousness, a fever—could trigger you to lose a part of your William Wiley identity, or discover the reality of yourself.

"In order to keep the concept, that is, the persona, of Franky Furbo alive, an entire history had to be invented, which you were to believe . . . more than that—to become. This is the history you probably still believe about you and Wilhelm being in the hole

together, dying, and having Franky Furbo, as fox, come to rescue you, take you to his tree, save your life, talk to you about human lives, about how he wanted you to live. It was necessary to implant in you the desire to live apart from humans, thus to protect you and your children.

"Franky Furbo, as a separate, fictional character totally created from your fox identity, told you much about yourself, what we knew about your real life as a fox, but you were not to know these stories were truly about you; they were to be about a fox, Franky Furbo, independent from you, with whom you stayed briefly at the end of the war along with the German, Wilhelm Klug. That way, you believed in yourself, as Franky Furbo, but didn't recognize that it was actually you, yourself. Also, for reasons of safety, we implanted the memories and language of Wilhelm in your brain. It helped verify to you, as William Wiley, that you really had lived with Franky and Wilhelm in the tree. Do you understand?"

To be honest, I'm not sure I do anymore. I'm finding myself resentful of being so manipulated, even if I did agree to it forty years ago, or fifty thousand years from now.

I try getting it all arranged in my mind. Those stories I told the children—that I wrote about, that I believed myself, about the fox in the foxhole, about living in the tree, about Franky, about Wilhelm—never actually happened! They were created out of nothing by a bunch of fox scientists in the future. No wonder I used to feel I was crazy sometimes: I was. I had all these different identities, events, true and false, warring together in my mind. I'm feeling weak now, depressed. I didn't know Franky Furbo could feel that way. This gives some idea of how difficult it is for me to adjust: I'm still thinking of Franky as someone independent of myself. I take a deep breath.

"So I became William Wiley and you brought me back to my own time, here. Is that it?"

"No, it couldn't be done that easily. It would have been impossible for me to transport you, as human, across so much time. It was necessary that you come back as fox, holding close to me while you, as William Wiley, existed only in my brain.

"Then, when we were here, back in Italy, while resting, recuperating in your tree house, I searched until I found this small house, not far from where I had found you in the first place. We were back in time to only two years after you, that is, William Wiley, died. We worked for a month until everything that had been so carefully stored in my brain was safely lodged in yours, including all the blocks and posthypnotic suggestions. It was so strange watching you change under my own eyes, my hands, my brain into someone else. You became someone who had been in my brain, someone I loved but who was entirely different from the fox I love so deeply."

So, there doesn't seem to be anything left that I really did on my own, not even search for and find this house. I'm beginning to feel like a living robot, someone programmed for someone else's convenience. Would there be anything left to be proud of when Raethe's finished telling me the whole story? Did I ever actually do anything except be an accidental mutation? I know Raethe knows all that I'm thinking. I look her in the eye. Is this the woman I've loved all these years, in two different times?

"Franky, my love, it was difficult for you then, as it was for me, as it is difficult for you right now. But let me go on, it isn't much more. Please bear with me.

"The big advantage for you was that when I was finished, you remembered nothing. I reentered you into the life of William

Wiley, as you'd been given to remember it, just at the point in your artificial history where you went up to the American military and told them your story about where you thought you had been during the past many months, that is, living with a fox and a German soldier in a tree in a forest.

"It had been decided that it would be good if you had the experience of insisting on the identity of Franky Furbo, resisting all attempts to break down your implanted memories, blocks, posthypnotic suggestion, artificial life history. It would at the same time reinforce and test the effectiveness of our transplantation.

"From that moment on, till now, you lived as a human. We had given strong posthypnotic suggestion for you to go to the West Coast, to Los Angeles, as soon as you received your medical discharge. We didn't want you to return to the place where William Wiley had been born and where he grew up in Philadelphia; we didn't want to take that chance. Also, we wanted you to meet me at the University of California at Los Angeles.

"I was so glad to see you, to flirt with you, to feel us falling in love again. It wasn't necessary for them to implant the love you had for me, because it was always there, as mine was for you. I know you felt it immediately when we first met. You see, I could still telepath.

"I had chosen to look the way I look as a human. I didn't want the very pale skin of a pink American human, but we didn't want to call attention to our uniqueness unnecessarily, as would happen if I chose any other color; many humans are peculiar about color. I insisted, however, on having hair something close to the color of my tail and a medium-dark skin, just somewhat lighter than my hair. We foxes are very vain. I was so vain I haven't allowed myself to age as you were allowed to. This has been a subject of much discussion and disagreement with our monitor. So I let myself age somewhat and stayed out of the way *of humans in general, mostly staying in this house. I think I might have been afraid you would be like a human and not love me when I had wrinkles and gray hair.*

"Don't worry, Franky, I know you're vain as I am; after all, you are a fox, but you are still young by fox standards. You only look old as a human. Remember, we of our race live twice as long as humans. You, at human age sixty-three, are actually only, by fox development, in your early thirties."

Raethe smiles. She's so much like the beautiful fox I knew in the future—coquettish, laughing eyes, in the best ways a young vixen, at the same time a full-grown fox. But what she's telling me is so horrible, so destructive to my own image of myself, both as William Wiley and as Franky Furbo, that she frightens me. I look again at Billy to see how he's taking all this. He's staring at me, and I can see it is with awe and wonder. I give him another squeeze. I look at Caroline-Raethe.

"And so I studied literature and art while you studied economics, and I told you all about Franky Furbo and you convinced me you believed, when you knew so much more than I did. You must have thought I was the most foolish creature in the world. How could you have loved me?"

"That was no problem, dear one. Hearing you tell me about yourself, as someone else, so conscientiously, so seriously, so anxious that I believe, was such a wonderful proof of your love for me both as Caroline, human, and as Raethe, fox, that I loved you even more. I knew you were doing all you could to help our race of foxes survive. You were my hero. You still are.

"A part of the posthypnotic suggestion was that when we left the university we would move here to Prepo, to the very house where I'd turned you from a fox to a human. The specialists in

mental manipulation were convinced this was important, that this metamorphosis that had taken place be near to where we live and also near to where you had lived as fox."

"OK, Caroline-Raethe, let's talk about the past few days. Why did you decide suddenly to allow Sarva-Billy to deny Franky Furbo? Why did you pretend not to believe in him yourself? Was it all part of the plan? What happened? By the way, what about the other children; what do they know?"

"When each of them was ready to leave home, to go off and make their own nest in another part of the world, I told them. I not only told them, I broke the blocks I'd put into their minds as I was teaching them, so that now they could truly know themselves for what they are. Each of them experienced briefly being fox, speaking Fox, before they left. Each of them knows they are not to take back their visible fox identity again without my permission, or yours. It is the sacrifice they must make until they are finished breeding. Then they can choose.

"We, you and I, Franky, are finished breeding now. Our race of foxes has a long life, but our breeding period is relatively short. Foxes will rather consistently have four kits, one at a time, at least five years apart. Our gestation period is exactly one year, 365 1/4 earth days, so we are born almost precisely at the same time of year as we are conceived. No one knows exactly why this should be.

"You and I have a long, happy life ahead of us to live as we want. It will be pleasant to enjoy our children and grandchildren when they can come visit with us.

"I felt it was time for you to know. I challenged you to prove your belief in Franky Furbo and sent you off to see Wilhelm. It had been decided that it would be far better for your reemergence

as fox if you participated in the process, if you weren't completely passive. Does that answer your question?"

"Yes, I think so. But what about Wilhelm? Does he exist? If not, with whom did I speak in Bavaria? Or was that all some kind of posthypnotic experience? I don't feel I know anything anymore. Did I really go see him? Did he actually go visit with Franky Furbo, hear the entire story of Franky fifty thousand years in the future, or did he think he did, or dream he did, or what? He seemed so real to me. I can't believe I dreamed it or that it didn't happen. Tell me about that."

"Of course, you did go to see Wilhelm, or the fox who was playing Wilhelm, and you found him. Actually, as I said, we took a record of his entire life when he was in the hole with William Wiley. He was created in your mind, as an extra identity. He was to serve as a comrade in your delusion of life with Franky Furbo, living in the tree. He was also a key, whereby, when the time came, you could gain access to the complex that had become your life. Wilhelm was a catalyst to your comprehension in finding yourself.

"As I said, while taking information from your brain and about your body, one of the technicians was doing the same with Wilhelm as he died. It was not known then how this information could be used, but in case William Wiley proved inadequate or not of use for our purposes, we might have used him.

"Almost by accident, this information on Wilhelm Klug proved valuable in this other instance, for the process of introducing you to something of your reality.

"One of our social research scientists with a special interest in hostility and aggression in humans was there in Bavaria, in that hut in the forest. He wanted to live for a while with Germans, so as to carry out his investigations."

Caroline-Raethe stops and looks at me carefully, both with her eyes and telepathically. I know I'm manifesting my confusion, resentment, consternation. She goes on more slowly.

"This investigator assumed the identity of Wilhelm and lived where you found him. His isolation made it possible for him to return to his own time or stay there, as he desired. He has been of great value, not only in helping us understand the nature of aggression in humans but also in our own analysis of some of our more critical faults. His work is highly praised by all.

"So, it was a lucky chance he was there for you to visit. It made everything much easier. We gave him the story he told you, and I removed the block that had kept you from going to search him out over all these years. The wife Wilhelm had in your version of his identity was a reality in the original Wilhelm's own life. We hypnotically encouraged her to stay with her family near Nuremburg after Wilhelm's death. It was then easy to create an illusion of her there in Seeshaupt, to seem to die in childbirth and thus give reason for Wilhelm's seclusion and disillusionment. Wilhelm's feigned disillusionment, in turn, forced you to come to terms with much of your own resentment and fear about what you were hearing then and, I hope, with what I'm telling you now."

"So, then, William Wiley is dead, really dead. I'm going to miss him, as I miss Wilhelm. Wilhelm, next to you and our children, was my closest friend. I guess I can't count Franky Furbo, since I seem to be he, myself. It's hard to be someone, or to think you're someone for over forty years, when it seems to me like sixty-three.

"Oh, and now I understand why I didn't have any memory of my life before the orphanage: you didn't take it."

"William Wiley died before they could complete the reading of his brain. We could have made up some more artificial history, or memory, for you, but most of us felt there was too much danger in doing that; perhaps it could defile your adult personality with unnecessary or unintegrated information. So we left it vaguely blank. You were only to know you had lost your parents when you were eight years old. We gave you no memory of William Wiley's parents because we had no information on them. Did you miss not having childhood memories?"

"Not particularly. But maybe it explains my love for children, my desire to write children's stories, both as Franky Furbo and as William Wiley. Franky never had what could be considered a real fox childhood—his mother died when he was so young—and William had no memory of childhood at all. Perhaps, in both identities, I was making up a childhood for myself when I wrote those stories. It could be.

"So is that all of it, all I should know? And what do we do now? I'm feeling as if I'm simultaneously at a birth and a funeral. Part of me, William, is sad to find he isn't real, but the main core of me, Franky, is happy to be back, to continue with his life. And what about you, Raethe? How much of what I've known as Caroline, as Raethe, is real? Do you really love this primitive, awkward, recessive fox, or this stupid, naive human? I'm not sure of anything anymore."

"Oh Franky-William! This is what I've been afraid of all these years, that when it came time for you to know all, you wouldn't have confidence in the things that truly are real. I know how horrible it must be for you to see, hear everything, everyone you've come to believe in, to love, as real—destroyed, taken away, or changed drastically. To see yourself bared—a victim of manipulation, psychic violence, invasion of your most profound inner nature. I was afraid you'd lose your ability to believe anything, *even the most true things, such as our love.*

"All I can say is, look into me, hear me, feel me. I open now my heart and my mind to you. Sometimes only saying things means nothing, even in Fox."

With this, I feel her passively making herself a part of me, entering into me. I know the depth of love, of concern, of admiration, of respect, of passion she has for me. I feel a love in myself for her, with every part of my being, with an intensity of which I didn't know I was capable. The last fetters between me and myself, Franky Furbo, are finally removed. I'm vibrant with a sense of aliveness.

Words, even Fox words, would never be enough to tell Raethe all I feel. I radiate from my inner being the love I'm feeling and we wrap into each other. Her fur, her paws are so soft. She swirls her tail around me, and I mine around her, so we are as one. Sarva comes and holds on to the two of us.

"Isn't it great we can be foxes together, Mom, Dad? I wish Trais, Hinva, and Panta could be here with us to share all this. I know they already know, but I guess I'm still human enough that I wish they could really be here."

"But they are, Sarva. Didn't you know? Do you think we'd welcome your dad back, after all these years, without their being here? Look!"

I look, and there, spread out on the bed, each in his or her respective position in their old places, are our three other children. Trais, farthest from us, is very pregnant. Her husband and brother, Hinva, has his arm around her. Panta has come close to Sarva and they wrap their tails around each other. It's only then that my mind realizes I'm seeing them all for the first time as foxes, as they really are, not as the human forms someone else gave them. Raethe turns to me, then to the others.

"This is a moment I only managed to convince the research coun-cil was fitting because of all we've been through together, but it can't last more than a few minutes. It is too dangerous. Take a good look, each of you, at all of us together, because we should either go invisible or back to our human form very quickly. Even now we are putting in danger the entire continuation of our race. That is why, as we propagate, our young must scatter themselves over the entire planet. Panta, you must go back to your lovely island in the north of Japan this evening. I suggest you transmi-grate yourself, the same way you came here. Obviously, Trais and Hinva will be leaving, too, for their home in the Chilean mountains.

"I hate to be so insistent about this, but it was made clear to me that this is the way it must be. As you all know, we foxes can be ruthless, must be sometimes. But for now, let's be human and have a big meal together for old times' sake. I have cooked up special dishes for all of you; each will have his favorite."

We look around at one another. I'm so proud of our kits. They're each different but obviously of the same family. We all hug in a circle, wrapping one another in our tails. It's a wonderful moment for me. Then Raethe speaks again.

"All right, now let us each transmute into our human bodies again. Is everyone ready?"

Our minds simultaneously confirm, and without any effort on my part, I'm William Wiley and the children are human again. It's fun because now it all fits. We're just ordinary human beings, living a not-too-ordinary life in a small house on the side of a hill.

The house is our home again. Caroline and Camilla open the shutters. It's daytime. It seems like years since Caroline closed the shutters. It turns out to have been two days. It's good to be resurrected as humans even though we'll never be the same.

I'm in the process of realizing that I have three separate identities. Starting at the bottom, I have the memories, the language, the childhood of Wilhelm, that is, his life until he was killed at twenty. I also have the seemingly real memories of him I gained as William when we lived together with Franky, then also the pseudomemories of my visit to him just a few days ago in Hohenberg.

After this, I have the entire lifetime, except for some childhood memories, of William Wiley. I have all that was taken from the human, long dead now, with that name, plus what was created for me, my whole "seeming experience" with Franky Furbo as fox, actually with *myself* in another artificial existence. Then, there's the time from when Franky, actually Raethe and the research council, took me to the American soldiers and I began what could be called my "real" life as William Wiley in "real" time. It's very confusing, even for me with all my supposed fox intelligence.

And above all that, most recent in my current memory but the oldest of my identities, my true nature as mutant fox, is Franky Furbo. Born in the first part of the twentieth century, transmigrated bodily to the future, fifty thousand years from now by Raethe, then brought back and put into a hypnotic reserve for forty years, living only in the fantasy of William Wiley, a dead young soldier—a transplanted fantasy at that.

And now what am I? I should be most comfortable in terms of identity as a mutant fox, Franky Furbo, mate to Raethe, father of Trais, Hinva, Panta, and Sarva. But that isn't everything. I have a strong personal as well as foxial history; the most important part of my life—being in love, being married, being father to my children, writing stories for other children—all these things are important, too. They constitute the greater part of what I know of as my life.

Everyone's waiting for me to sit down at table. It has been our custom as humans to join hands before sharing food, looking into each other's eyes and saying simultaneously, "Hmmmmmmmmmm-mmm Gooooood!" I recognize, now, how this is a very foxy way to start a meal.

Caroline reaches for my hand and I hold Kathleen's. We close the circle. Billy's eyes are clear, sparkling with excitement. I have a hard time seeing him as fox; I'm not used to it. All I can see is the little boy before me who came to my bed about a week ago and asked for a Franky Furbo story.

We look at one another and I start "Hmmmmmmmmmmmm," everybody joining in until we're out of breath, then a deep inhale and a strong "Goooooooooooooooooooooood!" We all clap and start eating. Caroline has outdone herself. This is food fit for the "foxes."

We eat and talk. We talk about ourselves and human things, as if we all didn't know. I sense, feel, this is a part of the way it's to be. As humans, we can know our fox identity now, but we shouldn't talk about it unless it's necessary. Even our telepathic skills are blurred like static. I try to communicate directly with Caroline's mind and she looks at me, shakes her head. OK, I understand.

After dinner, we all help with the dishes, then spread out on the bed. It's the way it's always been. Outside, the sun is just going down. Caroline is the one who brings up the subject, the question that's been bothering me. I think she's the only one of us who still has telepathic powers intact and can communicate about our fox-hood.

"Well, dearest one, how do you want to live your life now? We should stay here a few more years until Billy is ready to join Camilla, but after that we have a long life to live, and since we're together now, here, I think it's a good time to discuss this. We might not have the chance being all together again in one place for a long time; it's too dangerous.

"William, I think you should be the one to make the decision. You're the one who has sacrificed the most. I feel terrible about what you had to go through, and I hope to spend the rest of my life making up for it. You're the father in a certain way to all of us, even me. How do you want to spend the last three-quarters of your life?"

She stops, smiles her magic smile at me, waits. I know she'd been reading my mind while I was acting so human, being angry, resentful, childish; I forgot she could telepath me. I smile back.

"Well, I think you have a pretty good idea of the things I've been thinking. I don't feel this is just my decision, though; it concerns all of us. Especially you, Caroline. You're the one who has left the life you've known, grown up in, loved.

"I was there with you; I know all you've given up. If you want, and it's possible for me to join you, obviously we should go fifty thousand years ahead again and stay there. Is it possible?"

Her love comes rolling into me so my mind seems to stumble, tumble. I try to stand before the force of her power.

"I think it would be possible, but it is not what happens. I know Franky Furbo never lives in our time."

"How do you know? You told me that even foxes of our race cannot know or move into the future, only the past, the past from the time in which they live. You can't know if Franky Furbo will live in your time."

"Yes, but I know."

She pauses, reaches over and turns into me, whispers in my ear.

"I'm sorry, it isn't fair, but I've been listening to your mind in its thinking. I think I know what you *want* to do, and I know what I want to do, also. Remember, in my time, I was considered peculiar because I had such an attachment to things of the primitive past. I tried to create artificially what I thought was the environment in which you lived. I believe now there was a spiritual transmigration into me from your time, probably *from* you. It's the only thing that explains my fixation, the passion that made me a specialist in your era, searching *you* out. I have been *very* happy here, living the way we've lived. I should like to live that way, only with no more secrets between us.

"The great pain for me has been knowing we were fooling you, taking advantage, and that there were so many things I couldn't share. I'd like to stay here and live with you as we've lived but both of us knowing what we're doing and why.

"That's how I know. Tell the children."

She leans away from me and looks into my eyes. I'm stumped for a minute but then know she's right. I sit up in the bed.

"Well, your mother and I have just had a consultation, and I think that the decision we've made is the best for all of us. First, I'll review the alternatives in case you haven't considered them.

"Your mother and I could possibly go into the future from where your mother has come. It is a life of high psychological and technological development, where the foxes are the custodians to the world, constantly curious, investigating all phenomena, trying to create a life that is beautiful and sane. There are comforts you have never known, titillating experiences that stretch the imagination, but since you are born in this time and we foxes cannot move into the future, none of you can go there. If your mother could take me with her again, and that is doubtful, we would have to live alone without you.

"The second thing we could do is go back and live the original life of Franky Furbo as he designed it for himself. We could go forty years or more into the past and live in the tree house I built, where your mother found me. I could continue writing children's books and your mother could continue with her anthropological, archaeological explorations. For safety, we could make ourselves invisible to all except ourselves, or we could live as foxes. You could each come to visit us there with your children, or alone, as you desired. It is an attractive alternative and one that we will probably adopt at some time in the future.

"*Our* function as progenitors is almost over; we are not ourselves as critical to Fox species survival as we once were. All of you are born and the new generations of foxes are started."

I look at Matthew, Kathleen, and smile.

"The third alternative is to continue living here for a while, just as we have the past forty years. It seems strange, considering all the powers we have as foxes, but I know I've become quite content living as William Wiley with my wife, Caroline. We would probably need to allow ourselves to seem to age and then leave here before our longevity brought too much attention onto us, but that's in the future.

"It would be easy for you to visit with us here. There would be nothing out of the ordinary if you did. The villagers here know and accept us. So, that is probably the course we shall follow. OK?"

I look over at Caroline. She nods her head solemnly.

The children all break out in applause and shouts of approval. Billy stands on the bed. He jumps up and down.

"It'll be great knowing, secretly, we're superfoxes with all kinds of extra powers and at the same time living the wonderful ordinary lives we've always lived. We'd have like a private club of just our family. I think that's neat. I was sort of afraid of what was going to happen. Now it's nice to know we're going to be the same, but different. And won't it be great to go visit in Franky's, I mean Dad's, tree house? I've dreamed about it so many times. Now I can actually go there someday."

I'm very happy the decision is made. I feel like someone who's gotten involved in a monumental decision situation and because the possibilities are enormous, unending, feels overchallenged. The pressure is off for the time being. I sense all of us are sharing similiar feelings. I turn to the children and smile.

Right then, like light coming through a crack in a shutter, comes a compacted thought into my mind from Caroline-Raethe.

"William, one more thing you should know. I meant to tell you before but forgot. It probably isn't too important to you, but you should know. We have, as a part of the plan in preparing humans for dominance, invaded the mind of a human born on the same day and year you were, with the same first name you've lived with—William. It isn't really his name any more than William is yours, but it is a name he chose, as you chose Franky when you were a fox.

"We've implanted in him the desire and ability to tell stories to the four children he has, four children, just like a fox. These stories have been about a creature called Franky Furbo, a mutant fox, which he thinks he has invented. He was born in the same city where William Wiley was born in America and went to the same university you went to in California. He studied painting and lived as an artist away from his homeland in Europe, but not in Italy.

"Ten years ago we gave him the ability to write novels, and now he has written six of them, all after he was fifty years old, and they have had some success. Right now he is writing the seventh novel. It is about you, the life you've lived, and the arrival of the mutant foxes. This book will be widely read, and some humans might even suspect that it is true. We think it will be just enough of an introduction for humans without frightening them too much.

"Now, come, tell us a Franky Furbo, please."

As Caroline said, all that didn't particularly interest me, but I was really ready to tell a Franky Furbo story. I had a real one to help celebrate Christmas, which had been bubbling in my mind ever since I started on my trip to find Wilhelm.

"OK, so who's interested in hearing a Franky Furbo story? Christmas is just around the corner and I feel a Christmas story, with Franky Furbo, elves, dwarfs, the North Pole, Santa Claus, the workshops, the whole thing, coming into my mind."

I pause. Everybody snuggles closer. Caroline puts her arms around me and kisses me. I close my eyes.

Franky Furbo and the Year Christmas Almost Didn't Happen!

One cold night, just a few weeks before Christmas, Franky Furbo was wakened from his bed by a quiet knocking on his door. At first he thought it was only branches blowing, but then he decided to go down to see.

He opened the door and there were two tiny creatures standing on his doorstep. They leaped in the air and flew right past Franky, standing there in his pajamas, and onto his table. They had wings of gossamer and wore tiny green pointed hats. . . .